C000185223

Purely Academic

a satire

David Stephens was born in Woking in 1950 and for the past three decades has worked in a number of universities in the UK, Norway and sub-Saharan Africa. He has drawn upon this experience, and the prevailing winds of neo-liberalism that are blowing through Higher Education in Britain, in the writing of *Purely Academic*. He currently spends about three months of the year as Professor of International Education at the University of Brighton and the rest of the time in Peru where he writes, cooks and researches his next novel which will be set in Barranco, the Bohemian suburb of Lima where he lives.

Dear Linda,
Fellow writer and
friend,

David Stephens

Purely Academic

a satire

_____

David Stephens

Arena Books

Copyright © David Stephens 2017

The right of David Stephens to be identified as author of this book
has been asserted in accordance with the Copyright, Designs and
Patents Act 1988. Names & characters in this work are purely fictional.
First published in 2017 by Arena Books
Arena Books
6 Southgate Green
Bury St. Edmunds
IP33 2BL
www.arenabooks.co.uk

Distributed in America by Ingram International, One Ingram Blvd.,
PO Box3006, La Vergne, TN 37086-1985, USA.

All rights reserved. Except for the quotation of short passages for the
purposes of criticism and review, no part of this publication may be
reproduced, stored in a retrieval system, or transmitted, in any form or
by any means, electronic, mechanical, photocopying, recording or
otherwise, without the prior permission of the publisher.

David Stephens
Purely Academic *a satire*

British Library cataloguing in Publication Data. A Catalogue record

of this book is available from the British Library.
ISBN-13   978-1-911593-11-9

BIC classifications:- DS, AN, AP, APF, DSA, DSB, GT, DD, DN, DNJ.
Printed and bound by Lightning Source UK
Cover design
by Jason Anscomb
Typeset in
Times New Roman

For my father

George William Gurney Stephens

1924 - 2005

'A purely academic question: having no practical or useful significance'

Merriam-Webster Dictionary

Chapter One

Meeting, a coming face to face for friendly or hostile ends
Chambers Twentieth Century Dictionary

Doctor Gurney Sleep, lecturer in contrastive linguistics wanted three things in life: recognition, promotion and sex. Not necessarily in that order. His mentor, Nigel Williams, the Professor of Applied Linguistics, regularly achieved all three. And there was no denying it; he also had a way with words, which was appropriate for such a senior academic at the top of his game.

'It's the bloody 'L' word, Gurney, the bloody 'L' word.'

'Love?'

'No, you twat.'

'Life?'

'Lucy, Gurney, Lucy. Second Year English. Blonde, blue eyes and very …'

'Lovely? Sorry that's six letters.'

Whenever he ran into the professor, he found himself both defensive and at a loss for a few words – apart from *sorry* – which, for a linguist, albeit a lowly one, troubled him.

'Lust, Gurney, lust – that 'inordinate craving for sexual intercourse to the point of assuming a self-indulgent and sometimes violent character.' Shorter Oxford English Dictionary. One of its best.'

The Professor paused, only for effect, for he, unlike his mentee, was never at a loss for words.

'The immediate desire for the flesh of another, considered a sin, dear boy, by all the three Abrahamic religions.'

'You fancy Lucy?' A young, slightly diffident, quiet type he recalled meeting towards the end of last year who chewed gum and who seemed like most of her peers, to be more interested in her changed ring tone than anything he might have to say. The bearded Welshman leaned closer.

'In Amharic, the name Lucy is synonymous with *you are wonderful.'*

Gurney smiled and wondered whether in Welsh the name Nigel might be synonymous with *clever dick* or perhaps *cocksure* - and more to the point - how on earth did a son of the valleys get to be called Nigel?

Not expecting or requiring any further response from him, Williams thrust his pelvis forward and pushed past him into the committee room. September, in the academic calendar, was the month of meetings: pre-meetings, planning meetings, ad hoc meetings, referral examination board meetings, and of course, meetings about meetings. This one went under the impressive name of the Faculty Research Strategy Committee. FRiSC, as it was known, met three times a year and consisted of eight senior academics, and for the purposes of democracy one junior member of staff, a position occupied by Doctor Gurney Sleep, a position he was assured by seven of the senior academics that would stand him in good stead when his application was once again considered for promotion. The eighth, his mentor, took a different view.

'Faculty Research' - oxymoron, boy, oxymoron, that's what this is,' Professor Williams had enlightened him following one legendary lengthy meeting the previous year.

'It derives from the Greek term meaning *sharply dull*…as I tell my oxymoronic first years is an expression, usually an adjective and noun that contains an inherent contradiction. *Military intelligence, compassionate conservative, bad sex,* are just three that spring to mind. This committee contains not one but two inherent contradictions, namely *faculty* and *research* and *strategy* and *committee* for as you and I both know, dear boy, this Faculty knows sod all about research, and when it comes to strategy, well I can't for the life of me remember a time – but I am relative newcomer here – when it ever did anything but look backwards.'

Gurney entered the room and sought the chair furthest away from the Chair and one nearest the door. September. A new year. A fresh page. He tried to reduce his tendency to slouch - who was Alexander and what was the technique? - and considered his three immediate desires: recognition, promotion, and sex – probably in that order - though he would happily have given up all hope of promotion and a life time of recognition for just one night of oxymoronic, breathless sex. He ran through the litany of failure that seemed to him – and the Appointments & Promotions Committee – to characterise his paltry efforts to get a leg up and a leg over. How had it come to this?

Since his arrival at the 'South of England's most applied to university' at the beginning of last year he had done everything – everything - that had been demanded of him. He had taught unpopular courses, he had sat on the library privatisation sub-committee, the enterprise and business initiatives sub-committee, even the car park fines appeals sub-committee but to no avail. As far as Appointments & Promotions were concerned he did not exist.

Like many of his age and gender he thought about sex. A lot. Research reliably informed him that men of his demographic considered some sort of carnal act every three minutes which presumably included periods of sleep and attendance at Faculty Research Strategy committee meetings? He blushed at the thought and then he blushed at the thought of the thought. And then he blushed at the thought that one of his colleagues might be able to read the thought and in turn think him a gauche, retarded young man in need of firm instruction in the ways of the fair, and particularly well-endowed, weaker sex, not something to be included in the curriculum vitae of a thrusting academic worthy of promotion. He groaned aloud interrupting nobody as the committee awaited tea, coffee and sandwiches which had been booked for the start but had yet to arrive. Like him, he thought, booked to arrive and yet to come.

He shifted his thoughts to the more appropriate matter of promotion. It was clearly not a reward for good teaching. He loved teaching and considered himself a more than passable instructor. Not he the egocentric academic sounding off about the 'book in the pipeline' or the lecture series on the East Coast. And he had learnt about an important correlation early on in his probationary year, that there was a direct relationship between student enjoyment of his teaching and the lack of knowledge he possessed of the topic under discussion. The less he knew about something the more they seemed to enjoy it. He was a living contradiction of the bumper sticker, 'if you think education is expensive, try ignorance'. It was as if his reckless willingness to instruct a subject beyond the limits of his field or specialism struck a welcome chord with his youthful charges. It was as if they sensed that he was like them, pigmies pootling around the foothills of learned academia. Conversely, on the rare occasions when he had been asked to teach something about which he knew something – in this case the subject of his doctoral thesis - which dwelt for some three hundred pages on comparative forms of verb conjugation in selected Indo-European languages – his students seemed to shrink visibly away from him as if his erudition was in some way infectious.

His and their eagerness to embrace ignorance had initially worried the course leader until it became apparent that encouraging this junior academic to teach courses about which he knew absolutely nothing solved a multitude of logistical and staffing problems. With feigned sickness, sabbatical leave and research 'away days' now firmly established in the newer universities – of which this was one – course managers recognised the value of having amongst the staff an amiable - if un-promotable - colleague such as Gurney Sleep. He was, of course, unlikely to advance but as the chair of the Advancements & Promotions committee was fond of saying, 'Blue Skies thinking and not teaching, though important of course, had to be the preserve of the few and the denial of the many.'

Being unaware of this Gurney had spent his first few months of his probationary year mastering the art of lecturing. He was after all a *lecturer* but soon realised that when academics say *lecture* they mean lecture; when they say *workshop,* they mean a series of lectures and when they say *round-table* they mean a lecture with a table arranged in a circle. When they say *tutorial,* they mean a one-to-one lecture delivered in a lecturer's office and when they say *office* they mean a room where little official occurs; and finally, when they say *hot desk* they mean just that, a shared table located somewhere between the radiator and the window - which for health and safety reasons - cannot be opened or closed by the inhabitants of the said shared room.

So, a university is made up of senior and junior staff whose rank and ability to teach can be judged from the size, location, and number of occupants in a particular office. The other more important members of the university community are the administrators and managers. They are to be found on the fifth floor of mostly purpose-built buildings far removed from lecture halls, libraries and of course, the Student's Union.

The fifth floor is home to the legion of university employees who make the institution tick: the accountants, market researchers, alumni liaison teams, the Social Engagement and Corporate Strategy Taskforce, worker bees, driver ants, all controlled and directed by the head of the university who holds the curious title of Vice-Chancellor. Gurney had only once encountered the VC – in Lidl of all places - and wondered for a minute what he did for most of the day. Meetings and more meetings, probably…

This meeting was beginning to come to order. He thought a little more about his somewhat surprising pedagogic success with his students. His course the previous year on Applied Feminist Linguistics had been particularly praised. The Dean, who was the course leader, had asked him to stand in for a Guinevere Lightbody, a staunch member of the recently formed Women's Collective who had made the ideological error in getting pregnant, somewhat to the dismay of her lesbian partner. Any anxieties he might have had concerning his knowledge of feminist linguistics, let alone their application, was soon assuaged by strong student feedback which rated his course *excellent* and *worthy of a repeat*. This feedback had particularly singled out his double session on 'deconstructing the men's mag: a content analysis of the language of erotica' the final part of which he had attempted to explore the cultural linguistics of *hard* and *soft* in relation to *core* and *on-line*.

A chairperson's cough. He sat up. False alarm. Nothing was happening. Point three, *matters arising*. Another oxymoron. Gurney looked around the room at what might be called a *representative sample* of academia. There was Rob – no one remembered his surname – who had once nursed hopes to be a rock star and, so he had said, had auditioned unsuccessfully as lead guitar for a one-hit-wonder band called *True Shit*. Rob was forever in the world of the 'gig' and was currently involved in a languid affair with a third-year journalism student who wrote the occasional piece for the lesser known music press.

Then there was Doctor Clive Wilson, a world leading authority on the sub-clause, whose latest book *What if?* was selling well. Next to him sat an Australian visitor who was not called Craig or Bruce but looked as if he might be, and who had clearly been out in the sun too long. He was dressed in a white roll neck sweater and had announced on his arrival that he had come to the university, 'to get away from the bastards back home', forgetting that the Dean had spent 'many fine years' at his 'back-home' institution.

To his left was Ambrose D'Arcy, a rare visitor to the university that employed him who considered that his best work - which was unreadable - had only been achieved because of the warmer climes of a Tuscan villa. For any, who might have thought that such a lifestyle had disappeared in the age of research assessment exercises, rigorous teaching loads, and work should think again. Mister D'Arcy, prolific writer, and producer of monographs, had realised early on in his career that it was less about being 'present' and more about getting results. And of course, his villa was put freely at the disposal of any of his colleagues when he was not in residence. Which was not very often.

The remaining two chairs were occupied by underlings from the Registry, one whose function involved taking notes - she would once again ask Gurney for his name at the end of the meeting - the other a tall thin man who announced at the start of the meeting that he was part of an on-going rolling action team monitoring university committee performance. Which was presumably shortened to something along the lines of RATMUC.

And then there was the Dean and his right-hand man, Professor Nigel Williams.

The word 'important' had been uttered. Gurney sat up straighter and looked alert. His mother had liked to utter the word 'important' when his father was about to return home, though Gurney could never remember anything of importance his father had ever done or let alone said.

The Chair tapped his Parker fountain pen on the Formica table, waited an important millisecond and addressed his colleagues in a manner that suggested he was about to share a secret.

'At the last Dean's committee, it was decided that all faculties, schools, centres and units would be afforded an opportunity to discuss and reconsider their academic identity, their raison d'être, their unique selling point.' 'He smiled at his use of 'unique selling point.' Important to keep up.

He paused to survey the faces of his eight colleagues arranged before him. Most deeply resented him, not for his well-known lack of ability to teach, or to carry out research or even to administer his faculty reasonably well, but for his competence in defusing mutiny, side-lining dissent and making any who dared to question his authority know that when it all went tits up it was all their fault.

'Team. Are we not all linguists? He paused. 'And so, are we not all professionally interested in the naming of things?'. Another pause.

Apparently, it had cost the University twelve thousand pounds to be told by Bryce, Peterloo and Tring that the Centre of Applied Linguistics or CAL as it was known, was vague, 'dated' and more damning, 'unlikely to appeal to the young'. After six months deliberating the University management had done what it always did in circumstances that required decisive leadership: it delegated the decision to a raft of committees that toiled at the base camp on the lower slopes of the blue-sky climes of the fifth floor. It was called 'cascading' or more oxymoronically 'distributive leadership.'

'And so, we are charged...' - the Dean had a penchant for military metaphors – '...with not only reflecting upon what we do and who we are - but on providing a distinctive, and may I add durable moniker of such activity and identity'. He rubbed his hands and glanced around at his charges.

'Doctor Sleep'?

He was about to agree that this indeed was his name when he realised he was being asked a question.

'Are we not singing from the same song sheet? Ducks in a row?' Gurney nodded and pretended to write down the words 'ducks' and 'sheet' alongside a doodle of a gallows and a hanged man.

He turned his thoughts to the purpose of the committee. Universities are adept at devoting or expending energy and enthusiasm to the organisation, management and recording of the wasting of time. A central plank of this noble endeavour is the 'committee', a word unrelated to the idea of 'commitment' unless you are of the view that to spend large amounts of time when clearly qualified to do something more worthwhile makes one worthy of being committed. He looked up and pondered the discourse of what he was currently unengaged in.

There was the *chairperson*, an important male academic - unless you were in soft disciplines such as Education or Nursing - who had a chair, is a chair and enjoyed chairing. Then there were the *minutes* - a record of events that took hours to write and were never read. A *point of order* - rarely made - usually involving an important male academic eager to remind those present that he - and not just the chairman - could point and order. The *action point*, a useful procedural device for instructing a more junior colleague – often not present - is to do something the committee had decided upon or had run out of reasons to postpone. And finally, there was *tea and biscuits*, the essential prerequisite for a successful meeting particularly when delivered by two of the catering staff pushing a loud and directionless trolley about half way through the meeting, and so creating an intermission of divine length.

Somebody to his left, Rob perhaps, started to speak. 'Was it not time to address the substantive item on the agenda, namely the renaming of the Centre?' At this several suggestions were made by the more vociferous members of the committee. These ranged from a return to the 'saner, simpler world' in which a thing's name actually attempted to represent what it actually was, to those leaning towards the 'vital and ambiguous' or possibly postmodern – that veered away from *centres* - nothing is central, all is peripheral - towards the sexier and more fluid descriptors that attempted to brand less by what was and more by what wasn't – after all aren't we more what we weren't that what we were?

After about thirty minutes of this the committee realised – or perhaps *felt* - that some sort of decision had been *arrived at*: a small working party would *sound out* the opinion of junior faculty, the *'student body'* and anyone else it could think of, and then in about three months it would report back and present a list of the three suggested names for the committee further to deliberate upon and with any luck choose one of them. And finally – silence around the room, - who would be willing to be *tasked* with such an onerous responsibility? For the second time that afternoon Gurney groaned and then smiled weakly. For reasons, he recognised but could not name – another failing for a linguist – he felt tired and depressed.

Chapter Two

I own buildings. I'm a builder; I know how to build. Nobody can build like I can build. Nobody. And the builders in New York will tell you that. I build the best product. And my name helps a lot – Donald Trump

The highest honour that can be granted an individual is to have a building named after him. Whereas in the past it had been Mary Magdalene or Corpus Christi, in today's corporate world it was the benefactor whilst still living who got to cut the ribbon at the grand opening of the institution named in his honour. And it was usually a him. For reasons known only to himself, the Vice-Chancellor announced, without consultation, at the start of one of his *playpen* – discover-the-inner-child-in-yourself workshops – that the new School of Arts block would henceforth be named after the University's Chancellor and chief benefactor, one Antony Charles Lynton Blair.

This succeeded in uniting every employee in opposition not just to the name but to the seemingly arbitrary way in which the decision had been arrived at. The Professor of Russian Studies, Sergei Tupolov, had slyly suggested an alternative, *Soviet Block* which would reflect he argued a redesigned lecture hall, 'divided down the middle with a high wall, searchlights, and barbed wire.'

But it was to the Blair building that Gurney returned to at the end of the meeting. He entered his room and looked out the window. Whoever had designed the building however had clearly been influenced by a form of Soviet brutalism or perhaps by Foucault's Panopticon in which every corner could be viewed by those in control. The building consisted of five fingers sticking out like sore thumbs upon a hillside, the rolling Sussex countryside providing a refreshing bucolic backdrop.

Although the meeting had finished early it was already getting dark. An innovative feature of the building, and appropriate for a university, was its *intelligent lighting*. Move and the lighting remained on, think and be still, and you'd soon find yourself plunged into gloom, something that Gurney had experienced even with the lights on. He looked out at sequence of rooms in the first finger. Each of the occupants had developed their own particular response to the gathering darkness. Professor Williams was waving both hands wildly above his head and mouthing what appeared to be the words 'fucking' and 'hell'. Gurney waved back. It was sufficient to brighten his own room and to motivate Williams to mouth what appeared to be the same phrase but extended to include all architects and the head of Estates, who rumour had it had had the final say over the chosen design.

Gurney sat down and looked at the blank computer screen. He knew he *could* and *should* – his two-favourite modal auxiliary verbs - open up his inbox and get deleting, a not unpleasant task from which he gained little enjoyment but more regained a sense that it was he and not them who were in control of his life. Particularly if the mail said 'urgent' and remained unread.

He looked around his room. It was tidy. Perhaps obsessively so. One of the departmental secretaries, Amber had brought him back from holiday a card which said, 'a tidy desk is the sign of an absent mind'. She had said she had found it very funny and that it had reminded her of him. He said he didn't mind, although in fact he did. When he'd mentioned it to Williams he'd been treated to a five-minute lecture on anal retentiveness, and a reminder that it was constipated mathematicians and not linguists who worked it out with a pencil.

There were times when Gurney wished he wasn't in this room but another.

The Double Locks Inn just up the canal from Countess Wear has two rooms above a snug bar with roaring open fires and a welcoming mine host. Gurney and Lucy - no let's call her Hayley - rush in through the bar and up to their room, giggling like schoolgirls on a day out. She's wearing a short tartan skirt; a pink cashmere roll neck that accentuates her perfect figure. He's in country squire mode with brown corduroys, check shirt and brogues. Should? he certainly will. She throws her arms around him and he loops his hands around her waist. They kiss. Gurney looks long and hard.

But not into the cornfield blue eyes of Hayley Masterton but rather the wildly gesticulating arms of Williams who seemed to be holding what appeared to be a large industrial hammer in his right hand.

He switched on the computer and somewhat wearily opened his in-box. Delete, delete, delete - he decided to delete an invitation from the VC for drinks and yet another invitation from a lonely Russian girl who just wants to 'meet a nice Englishman and do a nice fucking in dark'. He's immediately put off by her absence of the definitive article. There is also a further email from Alana, who is now the Vice Chancellor's secretary inviting him to the year's first *open-circle time*, as the mail says, 'an opportunity to return to a care-free time when we can show and tell.' Reluctantly he agreed to attend and considers the possibility of borrowing Williams' heavy industrial hammer.

And then he saw the mail. By nature, not easily surprised, he looked at the sender's name. Amy. It's from a Hotmail account and so he has no idea where she lives or how she got hold of his address.

It's a short message of one line, two if you count the salutation, 'I've been thinking of you. Love, Amy.' His initial reaction is to reply immediately, to pour out his heart to the girl who has broken it. There wasn't a day or an hour when he hadn't thought of her, hadn't wondered what had become of her his childhood sweetheart. Lovelier than Lucy, bluer eyes than Hayley, she had remained for him a symbol of all he had gained and all he had lost. A *could* instead of a *might-have-been* in other words.

He stood up and moved his arms sufficiently to brighten the room. Williams had obviously given up. All the rooms in the first finger were dark. He was alone. He had to reply. What is it Julie Christie who says to Alan Bates in

Far from the Madding Crowd, 'don't be so urgent?'. But he feels urgent – he *can,* he *should,* he *must,* he *will.*

How to start? His hand hovers over the keyboard. 'Dearest Amy.' Not cool. He tries 'Hi, just passing and thought I'd respond whilst the iron is hot'. Hopeless. He wants to say, 'dearest and loveliest of all corn blue-eyed women I have ever known please come with me to a small bedroom above a cosy bar with a welcoming mine host and do a nice fucking in dark', but he can't and anyway he doesn't do rude well. It reminds him of his mother and another room, a dark one, where he was sent once when he had said the word 'bottom' in front of the vicar.

He looks at the message again. What had she been thinking when she said she was thinking of him? And not about him? He considered the role of prepositions which made a pleasant change from modal auxiliaries.

Perhaps he should start by telling her how difficult it was to start a reply, a sort of post-modern reflexivity much in favour at the moment? He could present a kind of 'faux' dearest italicising the word to show it was all rather a joke. But it wasn't. And what if she believed him and thought she wasn't *dearest* to him but was just some sort of friend who's got in touch and not the long-lost lover now found? And that he thought about her every millisecond of every minute in a hopeless way? The room and his mood started to get darker. He stood up and gave a sign of the cross with his right hand to the god of intelligent lighting and unrequited love.

'My dear Amy.' Cool, sense and sensibility.

'Amy'. Yes, that was it. Simple, cool, modernist. Neither formal nor too urgent and lovey-dovey. But how could he sneak a 'dearest' in so that she would know?

'Hi dearest Amy.' Canon Collins meets cool. He looked at the words 'have been thinking of you' and wrote, funny, you should have been thinking of me'. He deleted 'of' and 'about me'. He thought for a minute: 'by coincidence I have been thinking of you and our weekend at the 'Double Locks and that old Russian saying about fucking in dark'. He deleted all the words except 'dearest' and 'fucking'. Then he deleted 'fucking'. Stood up and said 'bottom' as loud as he could.

'Amy, great to be back in touch after what must be twenty years. I too often think of you and wonder what you're up to. I'm intrigued to find out more. And what you were thinking of when you were thinking of me. Do get in touch wherever you are. Love, Gurney.'

It would be tomorrow when he received a reply and again he would be surprised.

*

Gurney parked his car – why could he never find a space outside his own house? – a good half a mile from where he lived, so that by the time he inserted his key and entered his lobby he felt tired and not as excited as he had been on the start of his journey home. But Amy! Who would have thought!

The lobby was not a place for anyone on the cusp of obesity. Fortunately, Gurney had the physique of Peter Crouch but without the athleticism. Three feet by two it had once been part of the hall now divided by a glass door emblazoned with a large Greenpeace sticker that said something about saving the dolphins. He often wondered what they were being saved for? In one corner of the lobby was an old walking stick with a knobbly African head carved into the handle. It was resting against a damp wall, the flaking crusty emulsion patterning the floor like dandruff.

Before he could move any further his mobile telephone vibrated with sexual innuendo. Amy! But she wouldn't know his number. He withdrew the device from the wrong pocket and raised it to his ear. As she spoke he crouched down and drew a small guillotine in the flakes of white plaster. He realised it was time to utter a phatic utterance of agreement, lest his mother ask him for the umpteenth time if he was all right.

His mother's voice seemed far away and a little crusty. With the other hand, he reached out and took hold of the walking stick and then silently mimed smashing it down upon the mobile. He valued phrasal verbs at times such as these.

'Are you all right dear? I thought I heard you say Arrrgh! Are you crying dear? You're not laughing, are you?'

He assured her he wasn't doing anything other than talking to her. His mother brought out the pedant in him. And the-balance-of-his-mind-was-unstable-killer characteristic. He was now getting cold and cramped in a room not designed for lengthy conversations, not that discussions with his mother could in any way be called conversation, more exercises in interrupted listening.

She seemed to have stopped. He put the phone back in the correct pocket and entered the hall of his small ground floor maisonette.

He had turned half of his front bedroom into a small study. The wardrobe contained his one suit, two pairs of shoes and an old coat once owned but never worn by his father. It also contained two cardboard shoe boxes. In each of these were numbered piles of letters, each bundle held in place by a yellow rubber band. He took out the first bundle in the second shoe box and at random selected a letter. He had read them so many times he hardly needed to hold the violet paper in his hands. But it was necessary to do so now if only to once again savour the emotional charge the letter had given him when he had first received it some twenty years ago.

His sleep when it came was a troubled one and so he woke grumpy and tired, almost worn out by the effort in waking up.

Outside it was bright and he started to feel better as he walked to the car. It was if the gods who decided these things knew that this day would be the one that would change forever the life of Doctor Gurney Sleep.

*

It was awhile before he could switch on the computer to scan his inbox. Williams had been waiting outside his room when he arrived with a petition he was sending to the Estates Office about the 'fucking ignorant lighting.'

When he finally got rid of him he saw immediately that she had replied. 'Wow that was a quick reply! Great we're back in touch. I've so much to tell you! Where are you? I'm writing this from my blackberry on my porch in sunny Phoenix – and when I say sunny I mean sweltering haha! Let me know where you are as I'm heading England way + it would be great to hook up. Love as always, Amy.'

Resisting the temptation to frown at her banal use of lexis (repetition of 'great', imprecise employment of 'hook up' etcetera) he sat looking at, or more precisely, peering into the screen. He had an hour before his second-year option lecture on standard and non-standard forms of English – was 'hook up' non-standard or just colloquial? But no time now to look up hook up.

Knowledge, that is what he needed. Not self-knowledge, that would come later. For now, his quest was to gather, harvest, down-load as much data as he could of her, her life the past twenty years, her world, so that when they did meet – and they would - he would be prepared this time, wouldn't be caught unawares – his knowledge (little as it was) undermined by her knowing (far greater).

No, this time he wouldn't be caught unawares, he had the skills! It's what they paid him for after all! The combination of his cerebral emotional intelligence and the machine's computational wizardry!

As he liked to remind those whom he was charged to teach, research is a two-way street, the *writing down* and then the *writing up*. The first involved the unearthing of all the digital produce rooted out by his harvest mouse, the second the delivering up of a crafted celebration of love and thanksgiving. He flexed his fingers over the keyboard, wished he could flourish a crack of his knuckles, and began the *search*.

*

He ended his class early with a cheery West African non-formal pidgin 'we dun finished' and rushed back to his room. He had left his machine on but had been careful to ensure his mail box was closed. This was his affair, or so it would be when he had 'dun finished'. He laughed good naturedly at his change of fortune and change of mood.

The internet is a wonderful thing. Or so Gurney was reliably informed by his colleagues who spent an inordinate amount of time and energy cutting and pasting turning one forgotten unread academic paper into a newer snazzier version that would wow the editors this time.

But where to start?

Gurney was perhaps the only person within the Blair building socially disconnected. He was of the Facebook-less generation, unaware of the joys of being linked-in, reunited or even *liked*. For a moment, he wondered whether his worrying lack of promotion and recognition was perhaps not entirely disconnected to his aversion to networking professionally or come to that, socially. As Williams liked to say,

'it's not who you know but who knows you – and your additional problem Gurney is that no-one, apart from dear deluded me, knows or particularly wants to know you.'

He picked up the pencil his mother had given him last Christmas. She was convinced that the best she could do for her son was to supply him with a steady stream of writing utensils, most of which came from the charity shop she helped out with each Friday morning. Next to the pencil was a yellow legal pad. He'd read somewhere – Japan perhaps - that this colour was associated with creativity.

He jotted down four words: 'facts, knowledge, interpretation' and finally 'non-verbal' – the images and pictures of her he was sure he would find. These were the foundations upon which he would rebuild a relationship he should never have let go. He sighed and then checked himself. Now was no time for self-pity.

First the easy bit – facts.

His morning *Guardian* lay open next to his legal pad. Apparently, the latest research into men's happiness – or lack of it – had found the following:

'40% more men don't want sex with partners than 10 years ago'. Generally, Gurney was less choosy, though specifically he wanted more sex – any sex – and with one ex-partner of 20 years ago.

'2.7 million men in England have a mental health problem'. Presumably this excluded the 60% above?

'5% of men have experienced suicidal thoughts compared to 2% of women'. Ergo more men than women must attend faculty research sub-committees.

'1 in 5 men aged between 18 and 25 has a low sperm count.' What about men aged between 40 and 41?

'40% of men say they are depressed about job, work, and money.' If recognition and promotion equate with job and work, did sex and money? Or was that work?

'81% of men are seeking treatment for hair loss'. Clearly a bald fact that did not apply to him, for one blessing his father had bequeathed upon him was a good *barnet* (non-standard).

'60% of Englishmen are overweight. And took refuge in continuing sex with their partners over the past 10 years?' As far as he was concerned he'd consider the cusp of obesity for any amount of continuing sex.

Facts about her would be reliable, though triangulated, by other sources: knowledge of a more qualitative kind gleaned from friends and family, *interpretations* of what he knew to be true – and his letters and his imagination told him a great deal – and the internet images he felt he was sure to discover if he looked hard enough. What facts did he know already? She was called Amy, was a year younger than himself, and was working in sunny Phoenix which he remembered was in Arizona. Can't be too many Amys sitting upon sweltering porches with blackberries? He had no idea of her surname. She had surely married, probably more than once since they had known each other.

He typed in 'Amy, blackberry, porch', and 'Phoenix.' Two proper and two common nouns. The results were disappointing. He added 'sex.'

A number of things happened including two pop ups that had been clearly designed to evade the University's sophisticated filter system. The first referred to a winsome healthy-looking young woman called *Anne Angel* who wriggled and gyrated and told him that she wanted sex with him that night. She had clearly no knowledge of him, or of international time zones, or of the fact that he wasn't particularly keen on women who gyrated.

The second was more alarming, informing him that problems of the prostate were not insurmountable. A short course of an amazing new drug and 'Yes sir! The mountable life of the happy gent could be resumed.'

He deleted 'sex, blackberry', and 'porch' and with a stroke of genius added 'English'.

There was just one result, the headline from the financial pages of an Arizona newspaper announcing the recent promotion of one Amy Wilkinson, an Englishwoman, to the post of Vice president (Sales) for the successful luxury goods company *Grand Canyon.*

It had to be her! He marvelled at the computational wizard with its little mouse that had foraged and delved, rooted, and found. He had a lead and something more precious; a connection to his past but more importantly to his future. Cornflour blue.

Chapter Three

Critical Mass: an amount of material (such as plutonium) that is large enough to cause a particular result - Merriam-Webster Dictionary

Tonight, was his weekly couple of pints with his only friend on campus, Linden Slackly. Linden had once been a promising linguist whose dreams of an illustrious academic career had been cut short by the offer of a sideways move to a post in university administration that paid more, was from 9 to 5, and required no imagination. His job mainly involved servicing committee meetings a little like the one he had just sat on but despite this he had lost none of his interest in words. At their first encounter, an ad hoc planning committee to look to ways of planning more efficiently, Gurney had been quietly impressed at Linden's determination to render his service to the committee in a solid yet agreeable fashion. Linden's playful reminder to the committee that it would help if they too could be more efficient in their use of time – 'minutes take hours' – for example had confirmed in Gurney's mind that here in deed was a friend indeed. Linden had had one great love in his life, a fellow administrator called Lucy Dance, who sadly had only performed a brief pirouette for him before flitting off to a Northern university where she had risen to the rank of Deputy Registrar with responsibility for university privatisation.

For Gurney, he was the friend he could trust and, into the second pint, could confide a little. They drank at the *Open House*, which they had chosen largely because it served cheap beer, was rarely frequented by students or staff, and was often closed, something they found an amusing example of contrary nominative determinism.

On this occasion, the *Open House* was actually open though half-deserted as Gurney stepped through the door and into the saloon.

A solitary drinker sat hunched over his pint of mild, a drink popular with the regulars. Williams looked up from his mild. His greeting was anything but. 'Trust you to choose the worst pub possible in this august city, Gurney but that aside, what are you having?' Williams wasn't a man known for his largesse. It worried him. Perhaps he was the harbinger of bad news, and anyway how did he know he'd be here?

'Same as you, my favourite tipple,' he lied. He'd have preferred what he and Linden usually drank which was a blonde, slightly fragrant pale beer popular with the gay community, or so he was reliably informed by the mine host of the *Open House*. Eventually they were served and Gurney carried his beer plus two packets of crisps to the table which was close to a laid but unlit fire.

'First the bad news Gurney.' He paused and impressively downed about a third of his glass.

'I've got almost everyone to sign the fucking petition, including Margaret in the office who reminded me she only signs books of remembrance – I told her this was remembering a time when you could fucking switch a fucking light on and off – but when I took it round to Hickey, that fucking communist head of Estates, he told me they were quite willing to strip out all the intelligent lighting and replace it with something 'wiser' such as gas lamps and intimate candle light. If we so wished. Bastard.'

Gurney sipped his pint of mild and replied that perhaps working by candlelight would enhance their life experience, particularly if accompanied by a selection of bath and body products. He added, unhelpfully, that he was sure it would be possible to fine a range of candles of the highest quality. Williams looked at him and downed the remaining beer in his glass.

'Are you fucking listening to me?'

The crisps - and Williams' total disregard of anything resembling social graces – and possibly the empty room – resulted in a loud passing of wind from the professor of Applied Linguistics. Like many who had been educated at one of the country's top public schools, albeit in Wales, Williams felt it perfectly permissible to fart whenever the body or mood took him. It did however rouse the barman who enquired if they'd like something more. 'Or perhaps you gents have had enough?'

'And the good news?' He nodded towards the bar, raising two fingers to the barman. Gurney wondered where Linden was and whether Williams might have frightened him off.

'The good news boyo, is that I have a proposal to make to you that - nudge nudge, wink wink, say no more – that might well revive your annual application to the Appointments and Promotions Committee for the long overdue elevation to senior lecturer.'

Gurney drank deeply, some of the ale forcing itself up and down his nose and then onto his black leather jacket, which he liked to wear when he was feeling relaxed.

'You may have forgotten but this is the hundredth year of the teaching of our blessed linguistics at this fine university – OK so we were then an affiliated college of the University of Wanksville at the start – but the VC and lords on high have decided that we must organise a centenary - showcase what we have achieved - rebrand with the name change and in turn highlight the economic and social engagement of our discipline blah blah blah. And we're to brand the whole thing,' *in the beginning was the word,* God preserve us.'

It was Gurney's turn to stare at his mentor.

'And so, dear Gurney we would like you to lead on this, to bring your hidden charms and undoubted youth to the task in hand which will not only cement your place in the history of our august department but provide irrefutable evidence for your promotion to senior lecturer.'

Gurney thought fast but decided that, 'Why me for Christ's sake, why me?' was better thought than said. Williams had glanced over Gurney's shoulder and had seen Linden Slackly walking anxiously towards them.

'We'll talk more tomorrow, Gurney but I take it you're willing to step up?'

Gurney nodded, resisted the temptation to say, 'thank you', as Williams shoved the table back and pushed past Linden who had just entered the bar'.

Linden Arthur Slackley shook hands with Gurney, something they had done on first meeting which may have said something about their childhood and the importance their respective mothers had placed upon manners.

Both had a glint in their eyes – Linden wanted to share his recent news of Lucy and the possibility that she had tired of avoiding gun crime on her journey to work, and Gurney of his candlelit search for a lost love. He also wanted to sound him out on what Williams had just proposed and try to assess the administration's take on the proposed centenary. Like most university administrators Linden took the view that academics, particularly the most senior, possessed equal measures of altruistic endeavour - longs hours toiling in the lab to find a cure for brain cancer - with an egotistical childishness that most displayed when they did not get their own way. Think, throwing toys out of the pram. And more.

But Linden liked Gurney. He was not like the others, more like him. His insecurity masked by a little bravado – the black leather jacket for example – suggested that they were more brothers-in-arms than opponents working across the great divide, fellow linguists united in their desires to make something more of their lives, and retrieve lost loves, for Linden knew a little of Amy and how she resembled his Lucy.

Linden Arthur Slackley's life had followed a similar narrative arc to Gurneys. An only child to older parents, his mother had resigned herself to living in a home uncluttered by childish things. She was more than a little surprised when her kindly GP had told her that she was indeed twelve weeks pregnant with Linden - she was certain she would bear a boy, surprising to her own family and small circle of friends who considered her kind but diffident. She was also convinced that he would be named Linden after the wood of the old English lime tree that had stood beneath her childhood bedroom window and possessed of heart-shaped leaves and soft yellow blossom.

She vowed she would produce a son rooted in the English landscape of her own childhood; a growing up spent upon the ancient Somerset levels in a small village called Mark, where her family had made cheese which was sold and consumed within the bounds of the community. Her boyfriend, then husband, George had protected her from the rougher boys during their primary school years together and then with a shyness his son would inherit had made his intentions clear one cold November evening when they were both just sixteen.

He, like her, had borne their childless years with grace, expressing a heartfelt joy at his wife's news though harbouring a little anxiety that the boy –

he shared her certainty that they would produce a son – when he arrived might come between them.

Linden, like other solitary children, had learnt quickly to position himself securely alongside rather than between his parents. Like the wood from the tree from which he drew his name he was strong yet mellow, grounded in a love for his mother and father which stood him in good stead as he progressed successfully through secondary school and onto university. Yet he found his bond with them made it difficult for him to find attachment elsewhere, until at a moment, not chosen by him, he had fallen in love - or to be more precise - love had fallen upon him.

Four years, almost to the day, in the first week of his transition from junior academic in one university to a more senior administrator in another, and appropriately in the Fall, he had quite literally fallen onto Lucy Dance. As he descended upon her – he was carrying a pile of undergraduate dissertations to the desk of Derrick the departmental quality assurance officer – her squeal, which he first thought was perhaps a small animal trapped beneath his legs, remained with him long after he had apologised, had attempted to wipe splashed coffee off her blouse, had apologised for inappropriate touching, and had apologised once more for being apologetic.

'The least I can do is buy you another coffee.'

'I don't actually like coffee, thank you, Linden, I was getting one for Derrick.'

'What about a beer after work then?'

'I don't actually drink beer but thank you Linden, you're very sweet.'

'May I ask you what you *do* like?'

'What I do like actually is to be left alone, as I've work to do, but thank you for your kind invitation.'

At this she had smiled, as a social worker might smile towards a youngster with special educational needs. Which as it turned out was an accurate description of the relationship that was to develop.

Open plan offices, such as the one in which Linden, Lucy and Derrick worked had been designed to maximise space and light whilst affording those who worked there no opportunity to hide or enjoy a moment doing nothing. In this office, the boredom of incessant working or maintaining the appearance of working – which was in fact more tiring – was enlivened by the various sweepstakes organised by Derrick whose quality assurance portfolio apparently included the establishment and promotion of staff well-being. The previous week the challenge had been to accurately predict the total number of times a student enquired at the linguistics office window, 'is this the linguistics office?' something remarkable given the importance the department attached to reading and the large sign above the window which read 'linguistics office'. True they had omitted the word 'window.'

This week Derrick had decided that there would be two simultaneous sweepstakes, the first open to all, but kept secret from Linden, which was to predict the number of nights that would elapse before Dance waltzed off with another partner; and the second to estimate the number of times an academic member of staff poked their head through the office window and enquired, 'is this the Linguistics office?'

As it turned out Derrick himself won the first (being the only one to suggest one night) with Lucy winning the second - in fact no fewer than five of staff members had enquired about the location of the office, one of whom even arguing vociferously that if it *was* the office then it might be a good idea to display a sign saying so.

Linden's one night with Lucy had started well however. They had taken the university bus into town, had had a pleasant drink at the *Welcome Inn*, a favourite office drinking hole, and had then moved on to the city's independent cinema which was showing a series of films celebrating French prison dramas, one of which, *The Prophet* seemed to Lucy to be exaggeratingly grim and to Linden perhaps not the most appropriate film for a first date. Afterwards they had argued, not about the cinematic merits of the movie, but the reasons why a landlord might change his establishment's name from *The Shoemaker's Thumb* to the *Welcome Inn*. Lucy had many strengths and a number of qualities, the latter including blonde, wavy hair and a penchant for expensive perfume. Her few failings included an almost total lack of interest in how the English Language worked, and in particular the commercial usage of a simile, metaphor or pun.

Rather than view this as in any way a weakness it emboldened Linden patiently to enlighten her on the marvels of linguistic ambiguity something his date unambiguously rejected with a curt, 'I think I'll go home now if you don't mind or have you anything else you want to tell me?'

This brief but intense experience had burnished and furnished itself indelibly upon the psyche of Linden Arthur Slackley, so much so that it behove Gurney to remind him that what had happened had happened and that he now needed to get over what had happened and look to what might happen. In other words, to start employing the future subjunctive tense. When that happened, he could 'move on'. Before his friend could insist upon another pint Gurney asked him for the inside knowledge of the Centenary celebration. Linden serviced several higher order committees that passed deliberations down to the meetings Gurney attended.

But Linden had other plans. He wanted to talk about Leeds and the annual university administrators bash he had just returned from. Gurney had never been to Leeds but liked the idea of anything that included the words 'administrators' and 'bash'. More drinks and more pork scratchings.

Academics are fond of the term 'critical mass'. Slightly threatening it resonated potential energy and explosive force to the scientists, safety in numbers and revolutionary movements to those in the Arts. But suggest a 'critical mass' of university administrators and you were in danger of a serious point of order. But 'mass' there had been with keynotes from senior registrars within the Russell Group on 'herding cats-managing and academics' to lively breakout sessions exploring a range of topics related to the Conference theme, 'From public to private – higher education's unique selling point'. It sounded fun. Lucy Dance from nearby Manchester Cosmopolitan University, and a prominent rising star, had agreed a lunchtime drink with him on the second day. She seemed to have forgotten the misery of French prison dramas.

'How did you start?'

'She was getting coffee for Derrick...'

'No, how did the lunchtime conversation begin?'

Gurney had long had an interest in the under-researched area of the relationship between initiation of conversation and expected or unexpected outcomes.

'I went to kiss her on both cheeks but she just stepped back and offered me her hand'

'Sorry Linden'. Like many Englishmen of his upbringing he possessed more than enough apology for others.

'She looked good?'

'Yes, she looked good, really good. Made me feel shabby, wearing one of her control outfits, crisp, clean, and cool'. Before he had moved sideways into administration Linden had considered writing his doctorate on the use of alliteration.

'And calm and collected? And, pray, what did you say to this cool and charming, Lucy?'

Linden laughed. As much as he needed to talk about Lucy (it was more than a want) he enjoyed their bantering linguistic *Wortspiel.*

'She's doing really well in Registry but if the right offer came up she'd be happy to return down south. And well we all know that Gus Bywater is about to retire, a post she could easily fill and if she does well...'. He leant forward over the open bag *Mister Pork's* pork scratchings and rubbed his salty hands together.

'Back here Gurney! Back with us!'

'I then asked her if she was happy.'

'Happy?'

'Yes, I reckoned that if she started talking about happiness she might then start talking about us, when we were happy.'

'Did she? Sorry. Were you?'

'No, not really, she told me about her plans to one day be a registrar and how she'd start by clearing out all the dead wood, and then she mentioned somebody called Kim who she said was from Myanmar, Burma I think it was once called, who was working with her on university-business partnerships, that he had some brilliant ideas, and they often explored industrial archaeological sites at the weekends. One day she said when the Junta was overthrown he would take her to see the ancient ruins of his country. That would make her happy.'

Gurney was intrigued. Cool, calm and collected meeting hot, humid and in a hurry. He kept this thought to himself.

'And the Centenary – any matters arising? What's the word on the street?'

Like many men of their age they had both enjoyed the Godfather films and any opportunity to talk gangster rap. It also added a touch of linguistic bravado to the proceedings.

'Well it was the pro-VC at his last brown bag Monday lunches who had the idea of combining the rebranding of the department with the Centenary. It was the VC though who dreamt up the 'in the beginning was the word' thing.'

'And me? Why me? Was that Williams' idea?'

'In a way, it was. Once the decision had been taken – and I was taking minutes remember – they suggested Williams delegate it to, and I quote, 'someone able and willing,' and here Linden chose his words carefully, 'and currently under-utilised.'

'Under-utilised? What does that mean?'

Linden leaned forward and spoke conspiratorially.

'Well it seems that over the weekend Admissions have come up with a survey including projections of marketability of current university provision. Consumer choices, competitor analysis, that kind of thing. It seems, and I quote, that 'linguistics doesn't feature much on the radar of sixth formers.'

'What? All linguistics?'

'Not all. Not unsurprisingly modules that included stuff on tweeting, the sociological importance of sexting, googling and face-timing, that kind of thing were rated very favourably but the three courses that received the lowest scores were Joan's 'introduction to the phoneme', her 'advanced course on the development of the phoneme', and your own I'm sorry to say contrastive linguistics modules. All of them it seems do not meet the sixth form consumers' high standards of relevance and recognition, and we all know how important recognition is these days.'

'So, I'm doing this centenary thing to save my job?'

'Another way of looking at it Gurney is what Williams said, if you do it well you'll be translating from 'under-utilised' to promised promotion.'

Gurney found it hard to raise a smile. He'd been shafted but at the same time offered a lifeline.

'But what about my tenure? Surely, they can' just get rid of me because a bunch of stupid eighteen-year-old twats prefer tweets?'

'Yes, the pro-VC raised this and said that if you look at the small print of all contracts, including those when you were appointed, you'll see that 'uneconomic performance' is grounds for dismissal. But they also said that you'd need help, 'no way he can do this by himself' so they decided they'd advertise for a short-term centenary research assistant to run around and get the job done with you proving the steering, oversight, that kind of thing.'

At the end, Williams said, 'Promotion, that's the way forward' which we all took to me whoever steered would get as some kind of reward.

Would, could, should, no reason not to.

They supped up and agreed, as they always did, next time, same place, same time.

Chapter Four

During job interviews, when they ask: 'What is your worst quality?', I always say: 'Flatulence'. That way I get my own office - Dan Thompson

HR had provided a shortlist of three candidates for the post of centenary research assistant cum run-a-rounder to-get-the-job-done. Gurney was a little surprised that anyone other than the deluded or down-and-out in search of a warm office, would find anything remotely attractive in what was advertised, particularly given the level of remuneration – a temporary part-time contract of twelve months – shared, intelligently heated office (ah the down-and out-constituency), and a salary a little higher than that of a 'customer parking supervisor' at the local Asda. But then, he remembered, we do live in difficult times.

As they entered the room, Williams reminded him that the three candidates for interview had been whittled down from a long list of four - which had been culled from a total applicant field of six- with one of those being ruled out on the grounds that he already worked for the university full time. In the four years that Gurney had worked at the university, personnel had worked assiduously to implement the University's vision of a 'just and fair employer'. In terms of recruitment this involved rejecting the simplistic interview between a panel of three academics and the candidate during which they would ask searching questions about knowledge of the subject and possibly how to teach it, and replacing it with a whole day event during which the candidate would be invited to experience a range of activities which might include a campus tour, a presentation of 15 minutes to an assembled group of faculty, one-to -one discussions with whoever was available on the day, and finally an opportunity to meet with the disability, dyslexia and dyspraxia team. Gurney had been one of the first applicants to experience the whole-day interview 'event'. The campus tour had occurred during a violent rain storm which meant that his appreciation of the dyslexia team-meet had been dampened somewhat by him asking if they might lend him a towel.

Gurney looked at the couple of pages provided by personnel which summarised the application forms of the short-listed applicants.

First there was Stephanie Michaelides, a national of Northern Cyprus who was qualified in linguistics (good), had taught English at a Turkish primary school in London and was particularly attracted to the Master degree fee-waiver offered to all new staff (possible).

Then there was Michael Earl du Mas originally from Dallas who had gained employment in the United Kingdom ten years earlier, and had since spent most of his time teaching sanitation studies at the local City's technical college. He was especially interested in the 'hegemonic role in the suppression of indigenous dialects and pidgins' (good?), and looked forward to the Centenary 'showcasing the University's support for the culture of silence'(possible).

The final applicant was a Ms. Alice Hildebrand. She had a first degree in English from Girton – (very good) -, had previously worked as an assistant buyer for Boden and was inspired to apply to 'broaden her knowledge and experience of an under-developed part of the country' - (more than possible). She was clearly the only candidate he could imagine working with. On the one sheet of paper kindly provided by personnel he wrote four words: *might, could, ought,* and *would.* For good measure and balance he added a question mark after the final word.

*

On the morning of the interview, the first candidate Michaelides rang in to say she was withdrawing her application, which provided Gurney with a welcome hour to check his inbox for any further news of Amy. Nothing and no time to trawl the web for more of her virtual life.

The interviews of the remaining two candidates were to be conducted in the new building's most impressive location, the boardroom.

On the third floor if you approached the building from the front or the fourth if you entered from the back by way of the car park - a committee had been established to determine the final numbering of each floor - it offered grand views over the bucolic Downs.

When he arrived, Gurney could see both candidates talking animatedly to each other through the glass panel of the tiny waiting room. They both clearly enjoyed language and the sound of each other's voices which was cheering.

Williams, who was chair, arrived with the other panel member, Joyce Bedoe from HR. She quickly told them that they would each ask the candidate an identical question, the chair would establish their knowledge of linguistics, Gurney their relevant skills and experiences of running anything, and she herself the question, 'what makes you happy?'

Mr. Michael Earl du Mas turned out to be quite unlike his curriculum vitae, as was Ms. Alice Hildebrand. Du Mas was indeed a senior lecturer in plumbing studies (he taught the sanitation modules) but by his own admission gained no satisfaction whatsoever in training cohorts of the City's youth in knowledge and skills already in ready supply within the city's expanding Polish community. What he wanted was to deliver something more 'meaningful.'

'And would you consider working with Doctor Sleep here as *meaningful?* ' A limited number of follow up questions were permitted.

Du Mas not only suggested it would be 'meaningful' but added that he was sure the relationship they would forge would also be 'empowering to them both.'

'And running something?'

'I don't actually have any experience in running a large event as you are proposing but I do currently manage our College staff social committee.'

Gurney found himself noticing the precise way in which the American spoke as if his stilted delivery might impress his trans-Atlantic audience unfamiliar with his Texan drawl. Du Mas was clearly a principled man, though in Gurney's experience it was not always wise to be frank about personal preferences and peccadilloes, particularly during an interview.

'It is true I have not found the chairing of the social committee easy. My lifestyle choices of vegetarianism and personal dislike of alcohol, though in no way influencing the desired recreational habits of my colleagues, does however generate some disquiet amongst my colleagues.'

'And what makes you happy?' Joyce considered this question best reflected the spirit of the University's mission statement which was to create a working environment that was conducive to teaching, research and administration. Memorable replies included 'a privileged university parking space for my Mazda MX5' - immediately granted to the now Registrar – 'any track by David Bowie' - by a recruited catering assistant who looked remarkably like him - and the simple, yet not granted desire of 'employment' by a sallow and un-engaging young woman applying to join the University as a part-time hourly-paid crèche assistant.

Du Mas decided to take issue with the question, something Gurney half admired and half considered reckless.

'Asking me about my personal opinion of happiness, with respect, reflects an epistemological stance that privileges the Western discourse's fixation of the individual over the communal. What makes me happy in other words makes not a jot of difference to the common good.'

Joyce jotted down the word 'plumber' and next to it 'wet'. Gurney wrote 'couldn't' and 'mustn't' next to a doodle of a gushing tap.

Alice Hildebrand had sensibly decided on this occasion to take her mother's advice and dress up. Sensible yet expensive brown shoes matched a corduroy skirt and jacket set off by a crisp white blouse and pearl earrings. The chair was clearly impressed and impressive in equal measure. His one question not only managed to appear easy for Alice to answer but provided her with an opportunity to show she had read his latest monograph *Swot.*

When she opened her mouth, however she not only showed of a perfect set of white teeth but also revealed an accent that was anything but *swottish,* more a strangulated Estuary *mockney* much favoured by celebrity chefs and violinists. She was clearly well read in linguistics, and was suitably modest about her work at Boden - 'just running around making coffee really' -and she seemed genuinely eager to help Gurney deliver the Centenary 'on time and without embarrassment.'

'And happiness Alice?'

Gurney glanced over at Williams's notepad and saw beside the name 'Alice' he'd written; 'Christopher Robin went down with?'

'I'm happy when other people are happy, you know, getting a smile out of folk when things get rough'. Her voice had more of a cut glass tinkle this time, reminding him of an Indonesian wind chime he'd inherited from his aunt.

'And you'd be happy running around making coffee for folk like us? Under pressure, egotistical academics, never satisfied?' Gurney wasn't sure whether to affect a small laugh at this not being sure whether it was in fact an example of the chair's powers of description or attempt at humour.

As she rose to leave Gurney nodded at Joyce.

Could, Would, Should. Throw caution to the winds. *Must*

*

Joyce sent him an email later informing him that Ms. Hildebrand had accepted the offer and could start in a month's time. This both pleased and worried him. It would mean he'd have to work out some sort of work plan for her, and for himself. And some idea of what he was supposed to do. Why had he agreed to take on the bloody thing? Was it because Williams had asked him and he didn't have the guts to say no? And just as things were looking up on the Amy front he'd been landing him with *one more thing.* But the Hildebrand woman seemed genuine and willing to do whatever he imagined needing doing. Her job description was both extensive and vague on specifics. Just as long as it didn't result in him speaking like her. Perhaps it was just a hobby, *mockney* this week, *strine* the next. Maybe they could write something together on it *init?*

It was like a tree falling in the forest. If no one saw it fall did it in fact exist? If a paper was written by Hildebrand and Gurney and no-one read it likewise did it not exist? Did he exist? He sighed existentially.

Gurney was tidy but disorganised, a combination best illustrated by his reluctance to use his computer's outlook diary and his preference for a series of yellow post-it notes he arranged chronologically in his desk diary. A typical day's list might include: listen to Thursday's *In our time* - he admired Melvyn Bragg - return book to the library, write the first draft of article for peer-reviewed journal, hold a tutorial with an Amanda Heathcliff, go home. At the end of the day he would then strike out all tasks achieved, save the drafting of the research paper which would be carried forward to the following day.

At a deeper, more meaningful level, he knew how hopeless it all was and how hopeless he felt. Nothing he had achieved at this current rate was going to contribute to achieving his twin goals of recognition and promotion. He didn't even like to think of his elusive third aim.

He reviewed the day's list: interview, *done;* Heathcliff tutorial *to come*; Phoenix internet search *done*, go home *to come*. More cultural capital that's what he needed – the ideas of Pierre Bourdieu were currently in vogue – he recognised he had inherited a restlessness from his mother but he hadn't managed – yet – to translate that restlessness into any meaningful result *to come*. For the few who knew the Sleep family - and it was few as his mother had liked to keep themselves to themselves - it came as no surprise that their first and only child should be both diffident and diligent. Leaving aside the knobbly-stick moments of severe irritation, Gurney generally loved his parents, as much as he loved living quite a long way from them. But wasn't that part of the larger order of things, particularly in the developing relations between parents and solitary offspring? But at least Gurney had managed to make a break for it.

It wasn't that Gurney considered his childhood to have been in any sense deprived; if he was honest he found it quite difficult to recall much of it. It was almost as if it had passed by in a blur, unlike Linden, who could remember not only which cousin had given him what gift on a particular birthday, but what the weather was like at the time. If he lacked little remembrance of the minutiae of childhood incidents, he did possess a well-developed narrative of an interior landscape furnished by events and characters fuelled by his prodigious appetite for fiction. There were real people living on the outside, and more meaningful people who resided within. And he knew which he preferred to spend time with.

These fictional figures became closer to him than the small circle of school mates his mother invited to his annual birthday picnic – he was a summer-born child – an event that was remarkable only for his mother's forced jollity and his father's silent presence. Gradually he came to the conclusion that his interior people were more attractive than the real people his mother kept hoping he would meet.

It was his mother's ceaseless caring of him that perpetuated his reliance upon the knobbly stick and his sense that whatever he did or achieved would – and could - not be enough. Hence, to him at least, the reason for the regular one-way telephone calls, enquiring about his diet and his friendships; his mother's fervent hope that success in the former would lead to an improvement in the latter.

'You're not eating well enough dear' which was always followed by, 'whatever happened to that Scots girl, you know the one who came to Christmas one time? She seemed awfully fond of you.'

Moira had indeed been 'awfully fond' of him until that Christmas visit whereupon a diet of his mother's mince pies, a lengthy post-sherry argument about the existence or otherwise of Robert the Bruce - Moira liked to consider herself a nationalist - with his father, and an even more heated discussion with Gurney over the relative merits of the relative clause, had brought a speedier end to a dying relationship. Not that Gurney had changed his mind over the relative clause. As if.

As he changed from gangly child to beanpole youth, Gurney gradually came to the conclusion that other people were not like him. Certainly, his mother and his father were not and he knew enough about nature and nurture to be not a little surprised at this. On reflection, it was not his father's reading choices – 1950's classic science fiction- or his favourite record he enjoyed playing on his radiogram - James Last - that he found disagreeable; it was his father and more so his mother's conduct of an argument that he found most objectionable.

It was as if rationality played no part in any effort to persuade, as if evidence mattered little in the pressing of a point, as if language itself had no role to play in the securing of an argument.

He also took issue with the sources of his mother's opinions and general views of the world, culled he once reminded her from the *Readers Digest* and out-of-date copies of the *Daily Mail* she browsed whilst waiting for her hair appointment. It was this rationality that propelled him into academia where an opportunity existed to contribute to the critical mass of what we know about contrastive linguistics, and more specifically the modal auxiliary verb.

During his undergraduate years at a Norfolk university that had been designed to resemble a concrete ship, he had found a merry band of fellow passengers as interested in the finite verb as he was. First there had been Robert-the-Bruce Moira, with her shrill Glaswegian brogue, and then the hyper-critical crypto-feminist Rosemary, and then confusingly another Moira, who had succumbed in the end more to a need for friendship, so she told Gurney than to his greater need for something more sexual.

He sighed again and looked out across the Downs. But to work. Tutee Amanda was due in a moment and he needed to remind himself of who she was and what she might want. With any luck, she'd be quick and he'd have some time for Phoenix.

Most of the undergraduates he taught were unremarkable. Globalisation, he suspected had accelerated similarity and had reduced sharply the number of students who looked, or even more so, thought like him. She arrived punctually on the hour and seemed genuinely pleased to meet him.

Amanda was one of his tutor group who appeared to benefit in some undefined way from his readily admitted limited knowledge of the focus of her final year dissertation. She was interested in the role of the reduplicative in modern discourse.

'So, how's it going Mandy?'

'Going?'

Perhaps it was him but he noticed of late a tendency for his tutees to echo the final words of any question he posed, as if he were conducting some sort of person-centred Rogerian therapy session.

'In the search for literature?'

'Literature…?'

'Yes, aren't you looking at the role of 'the reduplicative in modern media?'

To be fair he had encouraged her towards an area of language he found interesting if a little mysterious, connoting for him visions of his mother whispering *'night-night'* or Moira once telling him that sex rather than friendship was definitely a *no-no*.

'Anyway, where are we?'

Before she had an opportunity to reply, 'his office in the corner of the new and intelligently lit Blair building', Gurney bid her farewell with a parting shot that she 'go go' to the library and look up at least one article that was on the list he'd given her last time. Then, 'same time same place.'

She reminded him of the Amy he had known back then, the same dark hair parted demurely down the middle, the same trusting manner that had led to *bye-bye* without so much of a *bang-bang*. His fault no doubt.

'So, try the library. Good place to sleep, too.'

'Too?'

He logged on.   No further messages from her but one from Alice suggesting they meet for coffee soon to discuss the 'exciting' job. Top of tomorrow's list.

Phoenix and *the search...*

He typed in *Grand Canyon Candles* and refreshed his knowledge of votive candles and wick dippers, cultural capital useful for when they'd meet. But it was hopeless unless he could actual meet her. Surely it wasn't too much to ask?

For a moment, he considered ringing up Grand Canyon Candles and asking to speak to their new Vice-President (Sales). Naff, and anyway, it was probably two a.m. in the morning. If only he could speak to her at 2 a.m. in the morning at the same time as his 2 a.m. in the morning. He groaned at his inability to be decisive. But to decide what?   To keep searching among the votive candle fraternity - Arizona branch - in the hope that further information of her life, leisure and love would emerge? And then what? What if he discovered she was happily married to Kevin, Vice-President (Partnerships) and they possessed three wonderful children with names such as Spencer, Corey, and Kyle? Wasn't it better to remain ignorant of what he had lost, rather than what another had gained?

He waved his arms slowly above his head to relieve the gloom and the cramp in his right hand. But all was not lost. Wasn't it her and not him who had made the first contact - and wasn't it her who had said it was 'great to be in touch' and wasn't it her who had said she had so much to tell him?

He stopped whatever it was he'd been doing, turned off the machine and left the room.

As he walked towards his car he saw Linden staggering under a weight of a pile of grey manila files. So much for that committee looking at a paper-less university. If he was free Linden suggested a drink that evening, outside of their routine, but he had something interesting to tell him. And yes, it was about Lucy but for Gurney it was also an opportunity to talk about Arizona, second chances, and to enjoy two pints and a couple of packets of pork scratchings.

Chapter Five

The student body; all the students that belong to a university or college -
Macmillan Dictionary

He was about half way home when he realised he would have to return, if he was to sleep secure in the knowledge that he had tried to contact her one final time. As he wove his way against the steady flow of traffic from the campus he spoke aloud the various postscripts he'd send when he arrived at his office.

'P.S. Thinking about you thinking about me.' Too desperate

'P.S. Are you by any chance the light behind Gold Canyon Candles?' Clever, but clearly from a stalker.

'P.S. Meant to ask you when you're coming my way? We might hook up and you could tell me all your news. In haste.' Perfect. Casual, cool, and clearly from a busy man. She'd like that being equally busy being an executive.

He typed the ps. quickly and hesitated before he pressed *send*. It was gone! He looked out in the direction of the darkened windows beyond. A ping informed him a message had landed in his inbox. It was from Williams suggesting they meet.

'I'm thinking of setting up a Centenary Steering Committee of the great and the good. We will need what they call an external critical friend. Any ideas?'

He hadn't but he replied suggesting they meet at 9.30 the following day which would give him an hour before he met with Alice. At least he'd have a task to give her which might create the impression that he wasn't as useless as he felt. A critical friend? In theory, a good idea so long as the emphasis was on the noun rather than the adjective. He couldn't think of anybody but no doubt the professor would have sounded out at least three individuals from his network of anybody who was remotely great or particularly good.

As he liked to remind Gurney, 'the reason why I'm at the top of the tree and you're still climbing is that you know no-one apart from me, and I know everyone, apart from you.'

He had a point.

'Not that you'd want to know some of the twats I have the pleasure of knowing but you never know when one of them might become useful, invaluable even.'

'A twat?'

'Not a twat you twit, but someone who can provide some sort of legitimacy and authority to what you and Alice are going to dream up.'

He dismissed the idea of shaking his fist at the opposite darkened window and left the building for the second time, nosing his car towards the city where he liked to think he lived, and the *Open house*. She'd reply immediately, wouldn't she?

'Darling, you remember the *Shippe,* or was it the *Olde Shippe,* just off Cathedral Close next to that place selling those chess sets we promised we'd buy when we set up home?' He'd dash off a ha ha and it would all be sealed. Lips not cheeks would be offered upon meeting, the watery November sun breaking through the seasonal drizzle, the room awaiting them at the *Double Locks Inn.*

'And where's home for you Gurney? Where do you live now you're an important academic in this not very important town?'

Over several flutes of chilled Chablis, he'd talk a little of the flat, the refuge it afforded a busy academic; his plans to turn the garden into something special...

'But it's still somewhere nice to return to, isn't it?'

'It's actually a maisonette ground floor, the guy above owns a Porsche. Dodgy websites I think. But we get on.'

'I bet it's tidy Gurney, you know shoes in a shoe rack, mugs on a shoe tree, books in a bookcase?'

He would pause and quote the great Gladstone,

The book must of necessity be put into a bookcase. And the bookcase must be housed. And the house must be kept. And the library must be dusted, must be arranged, and must be catalogued. What a vista of toil, yet not unhappy toil.

'Sounds like you live alone with your library full of the great words of good men never read except by those who never do, eh Gurney?'

A relentless film of drizzle was casting a lowering gloom over the *Open House* as he circled twice looking for an available space to park. He wondered if he really wanted to talk to Linden? If he had stayed a further hour at the University, he would now be in possession of a lengthy email from a veranda in Phoenix bathed in warm veranda light.

As he entered the pub his friend shot up from the corner table.

'Burma's out!'

'Burma?'

'Yes, apparently, she's ditched Burmese Kim, you know, the one on attachment to the Registry and she says after much thought she realises how fed up she is with him, and reckons that what she needs now is some stability in her life.'

Linden was clearly the most excited Gurney had ever seen him. He'd ordered no drinks or crisps but had an unfolded piece of paper on the table in front of him. The administrator placed his hands slowly upon the table as if commencing a séance, communicating with a spirit from a previous life. He spoke clearly and deliberately enunciating each word,

'The thing is Gurney is this: She. Has. Decided. She. Wants. To. Give. Me. A. Second. Chance.' Gurney was impressed.

It was out. Linden could safely breathe again. Refreshments could now be ordered. The university administrator, Mister Linden Arthur Slackly lent back and surveyed the half-empty room, a smile-cum-smirk playing about his lips.

Gurney wasn't sure what to say. He'd been brought up to treat public displays of emotion with caution. As his mother, would say, 'who knows where it might lead?' His father would look away or cough, something Gurney resisted as he offered to get in the first round. This was clearly going to be a long haul. He smiled and gave his friend a thumbs-up.

'Salt and vinegar or plain?'

As he headed towards the bar he tried to inject a little joy and happiness into his walk. He was genuinely pleased for Linden. Perhaps the evening would enable him to break cover and get some advice about the women who seemed to be crowding into his life: Amy, Alice, and if he was honest, gyrating Anne Angel who was clearly more salt and vinegar than plain. What was it with the initial 'A'? Hadn't someone written somewhere about the power of alphabetisation, children towards the end of the alphabet having to learn to be patient whilst the adorable Anne Angels of this world revelled in the knowledge that they would always be first? Even Slackly came before Sleep. It wasn't fair, though to be fair, he could have been carrying round the moniker, Yehudi Yanker or worse, Zahiri Zabriskie.

He carried the beers and the crisps back to their table. Linden picked up the piece of paper and theatrically cleared his throat.

'Dear Linden, nice to bump into you at the conference. Makes a change. I'll be brief as we have recently introduced a policy on the personal use of computers which I support. I have been thinking about what you said about Kim and the Myanmar regime's policy towards the Karen people's struggle for self-determination, and have decided that what is best is a period of stability and calm, and for me to be happy with someone who at least questions the Junta's human rights record. What I now realise, and hindsight is a great thing, is that what makes me happy is indeed peace and stability, knowing where you are and where we stand. I know I have said some unkind, albeit truthful words about you, but I'd like to give you a second chance. Why don't we wipe the slate clean, and make a fresh start? No matters arising. Regards, Lucy. P.S. I'm coming down to see Kevin next weekend. Drink?'

'Kevin?'

'She has a brother. Apparently, he's a policeman. Drives the Chief Constable around. Lives in Arundel just down from the castle, over an expensive photographic shop. What do you think? It is a second chance, isn't it?'

'Sounds more like she wants to give peace a chance.' He half-suppressed a snort blowing a nose full of pale beer over the spread-out email.

'Sorry, Linden, I couldn't resist it. Look, if I'd received an invitation like this I'd be more than happy. And you did say she looked good, the last time you saw her, didn't you?'

'Yes, she looked radiant, whereas I felt, and probably looked, a bit grubby.'

'And clumsy what with the kissing mix up.'

'And what I said about Avril.'

'Avril? Who the hell is Avril?'

He reddened slightly.

'I didn't mention it to you last time, but I didn't want her to think it was all going her way so I decided to tell her about Avril, our new appointment, who I told her is going to help with the international marketing drive. Avril Anstruther, on attachment from Estates.'

'Does she look like Lucy, that's the important thing?'

'No, she doesn't, couldn't.'

'Which?'

'Which what?'

She doesn't look like her or she couldn't look like her, though what matters here is that she doesn't look like her, not so?

'She doesn't look like Lucy. Lucy is probably the prettiest administrator who has set foot inside our office. *Couldn't* on the other hand raises both a semantic and a developmental question,'

'...anyway, she didn't mention this Avril Bunbury person in the email so probably she isn't jealous or more likely she's seen through my feeble attempts to lie and thinks I'm just trying to impress her like the last time.'

'Last time? You mean you've done this before, inventing girlfriends from Estates called Avril?'

'No, I mean, yes. Once after that disastrous first date I let it slip that after we'd gone our separate ways I'd bumped into an old flame on the way home, Chloe from Croydon.'

'Croydon?'

'Yes, I liked the sound of it, Christine from Crawley that kind of thing.'

'And she too doesn't exist?'

'Well, yes and I think she knew that too because she's never asked me much about her either.'

Before their conversation moved onto other more salubrious parts of south East England, Gurney went up to the bar and ordered a fresh round.

'So, what should I say? About next week end.'

'First, you want to avoid having a drink with the Kevin brother. By the way can we assume he does exist? I can't imagine what you'd talk about – you don't drive, he shouldn't drink, and anyway the last thing you want to do is get wrapped up in is a familial ménage a trois.'

Not that Gurney had any experience of such sibling relationships. He was after all, an only child, Amy had no brothers as far as he knew, and he couldn't imagine gyrating Anne Angel being related to anyone.

But this *was* big news and Gurney felt fatherly and protective towards his old friend. They'd sleep on it and meet again tomorrow night to make war plans for the weekend. He'd need to be careful though about being roped in to any social thing Linden might dream up, the idea of being outnumbered by two lovey-dovey university administrators didn't appeal, and anyway Linden needed to be emboldened and confident in his ability to strike out solo. He drained his glass. They'd had three pints and some crisps. Phoenix would have to wait.

'And the meeting tomorrow Any ambushes I should know about?'

'Nothing really except you need to know Williams is trying to link the Centenary celebration to the diktat from Finance to bring in more international students from outside the EU. Apparently, he's going to propose an action plan about visibility, 'courting private capital'. Williams is spreading the word that when it comes to recruitment the Department of Linguistics really can 'walk the talk'.'

Gurney groaned. Alice in the morning, this committee after lunch. And back here in the evening. He eventually found his car and noticed a fine scratch running from the driver's door to the petrol tank. It didn't matter, he could barely remember what the colour was let alone the state of the paint work, it was the targeting of him that added to his depressed mood. Either that or the e-numbers they put into the pork scratchings. His house looked dark and unlived in as he sloped up the cracked front path. For a moment, he wondered about connecting to his office computer and checking his mail, or even ringing his mother to reassure her that he'd dined well on slices of mince and pieces of quince.

Sleep needed sleep. As he stumbled the few feet to his bedroom door he tripped and cracked a knuckle against the frame. Too many packets of cheese and onion.

Chapter Six

We should not desire the impossible – Leonardo da Vinci

Each letter he had received from her had been carefully numbered from one to twenty-five, the final one telling him they had no future together, it was all over. He had read them all many times, particularly the early ones so full of affection and promise. There was even an occasion when he had lifted one of the envelopes to his nose to catch something of her, the unusual perfume she had liked to wear, and which he had tried in vain to find during the bleak days following her departure. Antelope, wasn't it? 'Discontinued' the blonde assistant at the perfume counter had told him, suggesting he might try a new fragrance called 'Desire'. If only it was that easy.

As his memory of her faded he had come to rely increasingly upon visits to the shoe box, reminding him of what he once had and worse what he had thrown away. His parents had tried to help but strangers to passion they could only offer parental banalities, 'There's always more fish in the sea, dear. Someone more worthy of you,' his mother had said.

His response was to stare into the middle distance and say, 'but it was that fish that I wanted'.

It had been the sea that had brought them together the autumn of his first term as a post-graduate student of contrastive linguistics. He had settled in remarkably well at his new and better university. His room was in Barton Place, a Regency house a little outside the town and dedicated solely for mature and international students. Rolling lawns, rooms with pleasant views towards the moor in the distance, it had a comforting and well-deserved Brideshead revisited feel about it. Though the Government of the day was playing havoc with the national school system, universities were left pretty much to themselves, so long that is that they recruited well and continued to produce research that made little impact upon Government thinking, another oxymoron Gurney noted with a growing sense of academic detachment to the world around him.

He unpacked the few clothes and books, threw away the sandwiches his mother had insisted he take, and looked around his room. Very nice. Ground floor, two large sash windows, and a slightly musty smell which augured well for a year devoted to the pursuit of a branch of linguistics that was considered *cutting-edge*. Just beyond his room was the hallway and a door which led into the shared kitchen and pantry, a relic of the days when apparently, Jane Austen had spent a summer there.

The house accommodated a dozen students following courses he'd never heard of – modern Islamic studies, critical ethnography, and one that seemed to teach you everything you might need to know about oil-rig platform design. From the murmur of voices and the occasional laughter the kitchen was clearly the social hub of the house. He'd rehearsed his introduction on the train down. Important not to be laughed at immediately.

'Hi, I'm Gurney' – the surname could wait – '…mine's the Morris Minor with the dent.'

'I'm Gok Wan, but everyone calls me Wok, coz I'm good at using one!'

'And I'm Gina doing an MSc in Oil Technology which is really boring unless like me you find it really interesting.'

Gok laughed. This was going to be fine, they all seemed really nice especially the Chinese guy who laughed shrilly at everything everyone said as if it was the first time he'd heard it.

They decided there and then to eat together that evening, and afterwards to wander over to the pub opposite.

'When the others arrive, we can ask them too,' Wok said, laughing freely at whatever was amusing in that. Gurney and Gina smiled in unison. Gok, Gurney and Gina. They awaited George and Gill or perhaps even a Genevieve? Names, he'd remind them over a second pint, the stuff of Linguistics, the scourge of yours truly, the poor laddie called Gurney or God forbid, saddled with an even worse surname.

'Which is? Come on Gurney, you can't clam up now. We're interested aren't we Wok? It's not Gok is it? Gurney Gok? That would be too much!'

'And even though it is a very common name from where I come from he doesn't look much like a Chinese,' Gok said,

'No, it's worse than that, not that being called Gok or even Wok is bad, it's just that even though I always say you won't laugh when I tell you people they always do.'

'Well we promise you we won't laugh Gurney. We didn't laugh when you introduced yourself as Gurney, and you can't count Wok because he laughs at everything, so come on tell us.'

'Sleep.'

'Sleep? Like, I wanna have a nice sleep now?'

'Yes, Gok, except that it isn't nice and I'd change it except that when I once suggested it to my mother she told me it would kill my father, who had just survived a minor heart attack'.

'Well we didn't laugh, did we?' said Gina.

'But you must admit it is quite funny,' she added, 'It could be worse. We had a teacher in my school, which was a posh girl's public day school who was called 'Frinny,' Miss Frinny. I think her first name was Eustace but everyone called her Miss Franny.'

At this point an intense artist with a large beard and a pipe called Rob entered. He shook hands with Gurney. 'Could have been worse. She could have been called Crunt.'

Gok laughed shrilly at this, suggesting they have another round and then if they were hungry he'd give them a demonstration of his Gok-Wok skills.

Gurney awoke the next day happy and in good cheer. A day for exploring in his trusty, if dented Morris. One of the reasons he'd applied to the university was its proximity to the beaches his parents liked to take him to when he was smaller. When he was ten they had found Brixham, a delightful fishing village which met the four exacting standards of his parents for being 'suitable': first it was in England, second, the food was likely to be English, third, the language they would encounter would be English, and fourth, they would be guaranteed an endless supply of English sunshine, except that is when it was raining which seemed to be quite often in June, July, and August.

But fifteen years later and he now had an opportunity to revisit a favourite beach, a cove in fact where he could wallow in a little nostalgia, and who knows perhaps to skim some stones?

Which is where he would meet the love of his life.

*

The fishing port hadn't changed much since the final visit with his parents when, his mother had unilaterally decided that the steep roads that framed the town were, 'really not suitable for your father's legs.' His father had coughed in agreement but had found an opportunity to slip away with his son and fly a kite on the headland overlooking the port, the crumbling Napoleonic fortresses providing a magnificent setting as father and son had wheeled the kite between the hillocks of gorse and clumps of thorn. His mother had stayed behind to pack and talk with Mrs. Pengelly who ran the small hotel with her never-to-be-seen husband Gordon.

From the harbour, he took the winding road up to the southern side of the town, cutting along Higher Ranscombe road, past a large community college, and out towards Kingswear which he remembered would eventually take you to the ferry and if you so wished to the elegant naval town of Dartmouth. But he had other plans.

The small lay-by he remembered came upon him suddenly. Not a lot had changed. A large green notice reminded visitors this was an English Heritage site and that the steep path down to the beach was not suitable for those with disabilities. He parked behind two other vehicles, an old Morris Maestro that looked in worse condition than his own and a new 12-seater minibus sporting the logo of the university he had just joined. It was one of those West of England days much-loved by tourist office and landscape painters who had made their home and their name in the fishing port around the headland.

Below the bright azure sky yellow gorse and ancient conifers covered the steep hills that protected the narrow cleave down to the cove below. As he set out from the car park a buzzard circled high above him, welcoming him back he imagined to a place where he too had experienced a momentary childhood sense of freedom. He'd forgotten how steep the path was and wished he had brought tougher footwear with him. After about half an hour of stiff walking the beach came into view. From what he remembered the cove was mostly shingle with rock pools at one end and the scatterings of flat shale tumbling down onto the beach.

About half way down he shielded his eyes to try and catch a glimpse of the people from the cars parked above. He could just make out a small group at the eastern end, probably from the mini bus, and at the other end near the rock pools what appeared to be three couples sunbathing on large towels. He couldn't be sure but it looked as if none of the couples were wearing any costumes. He frowned. What would his mother have said?

'They only need the breeze to pick up and they'll catch their death.'

A small stream ran down through the valley and on to the shingle where it broadened out before flowing into the sea. He remembered once finding a sheep's skull in the water and tossing it high over the waves. Around the gurgling water were the flattest and best skimmers, smooth and flat but with sufficient weight to give you an eight or possibly a nine.

He soon reached the stream and entrance to the beach. Nothing much had changed though he noticed more flotsam and a couple of discarded beer cans. He stopped and began to pick up the flat stones beneath the stream which he put in a plastic bag he had brought with him for this purpose. He glanced up and noticed that two of the mini bus group had detached themselves from the half dozen examining the cliff face and were skimming stones over the gentle in-coming tide. Time to show them how it's really done! Despite his father's short stature and aversion to any kind of physical exercise, Gurney senior had an uncanny ability at skimming stones.

'Success lies not in the throwing Gurney but in the selecting of the stones.'

You needed a good eye for the ideal piece of shale, heavy and flat enough to guarantee at least a dozen hops, some veering left or right, others powering ahead like one of those Barnes Wallace bouncing bombs. Gurney's shoes were now soaked from the stream as he crunched his way across the shingle towards the two skimmers who were frantically throwing stones towards the fast in-coming tide. Without saying anything he positioned himself a little to the right of the shorter student and with a flick of his wrist sent a stone bouncing six times over the waves. She turned to her right and looked directly at him.

'Pretty good! But watch this.'

She half crouched, curled her left arm back and cast the flat stone towards the sea. It bounced three times before disappearing into the first wave.

'Try the other hand, like this.'

His next skim was an improvement on the first, the shale bouncing nine or ten times before disappearing into the foam.

'I'm left handed in case you didn't notice.'

He moved closer and watched her throw once more, her stone skipping five times before being lost amidst the foam.

'Yeah, much better. You're getting the hang of it.'

She was short, perhaps just over five feet tall, with long dark hair parted neatly in the middle. She smiled at his complement and dropped the two stones she was holding in her right hand.

'I bet you can't throw one so it bounces more than ten times.'

She laughed and moved closer. He noticed the pale blue sweat shirt beneath a padded fleece that had clearly seen better days. Her fellow skimmer had wandered off to join the group who looked as if they were preparing to head back to the car park.

'And if I can - what's my prize?'

She continued to smile at him as she brushed the hair from her face.

'A drink. You do drink, don't you? A pint of whatever you like if you can bounce one more than ten times?'

'And if I lose?'

'Then you can buy me whatever I like, and I should warn you I have expensive tastes'. She laughed again.'

'But I get to choose the stone!'

Before he could protest she dug deep into her pocket and withdrew an almost perfect circular stone.

'I was going to put it in our bathroom but it'll do for this.'

She handed him the stone, her fingers brushing lightly against his.

'Bend low son. This is going to be magic.'

He crouched low and curled his index finger around her stone. With a quick glance towards the sea he flicked the stone just over the approaching wave. It flew fast and low, clipping the water at just the right angle, not too low which would cause it to sink and not too high which would result in a large bounce but nothing more. The stone flew on dancing five or six times before it skittered across the water with four small hops.

'Eleven or twelve if you count the last one. But definitely more than ten!'

She beamed at him and clapped her hands.

'A pint then. Oh, I'm Amy.' She straightened up and offered him her right hand.

'Gurney.'

She continued to smile. He looked up at the buzzard way above them. How small and insignificant they must appear to him.

'It's a buzzard. He followed me down here. If you're lucky you might see the occasional seal off-shore and in those rocks over there Peregrine falcons breed, though I haven't seen any.'

'You know this place quite well then?'

The rest of the group had paired up and were ambling towards the path that led up from the beach. Gurney and Amy were the last to negotiate the stream and manoeuvre their way through a broken gate that marked the boundary between field and beach.

'I used to come here every summer with my parents when I was a teenager. Well, more with my father who liked to skim stones, and if I'm honest get away from my mother.'

'What did *she* do?'

'We used to stay in this pretty run-down hotel in the town and mum liked to chat with the owner. In our first year, they kicked us all out after breakfast so we had to look for cheap ways to fill in the days. Somehow, we heard about this beach and skimming stones became part of our holiday ritual. If mum came she'd complain all the way down about the steepness of the path, as if it was our fault, and on the way up spend most of the climb telling my father to watch his legs.'

'And the buzzard and the peregrines, was it your dad who taught you all that stuff?'

'Not really. It wasn't that he or I were really interested in birds, more in the names of them if you know what I mean. Dad, like me, was interested in what things were called, though that's no excuse for giving me such a weird first name.'

She said nothing.

'In the second year, I bought the Observer book of British birds and started to tick off the birds I saw when we came here. But I was also interested in the others in the book, those with names such as the greater spotted grebe warbler named after ornithologists I'd never heard of.'

'And the tits! A real find for a boy entering puberty!'

'Tits on a naturist beach, your mother must have loved that.'

'They weren't here then and if they had been I don't think she'd have allowed us to return. She had strong views about things like that.'

'She sounds pretty formidable. Did you get on with her?'

'In a funny way, I did, her bark was definitely worse than her bite, but sometimes wish I'd had a brother or sister. It was all a bit intense what with mum overseeing everything and dad never really standing up to her.'

They had almost reached the top of the hill and the group were huddled together looking back down at the beach. It gave him an opportunity to pause and catch a good look at her. She seemed unaware of her beauty dressed in less than flattering clothes and wearing no makeup or jewellery which in his eyes added to her attraction. She smiled a lot too in an easy and infectious way. She had led the discussion with him happy to answer her questions and enjoy listening to her voice which had a slight burr, perhaps Bristol or somewhere further West? When they arrived at the bus she introduced him. There was a Tom, a Harry, a Ben, and a Jack. And two girls called Maggie and Emma. She wandered over to his Morris.

'Can I hop in with you? Do you know the *Nobody Inn*, at Doddiscombleigh? It's about six miles south west of Exeter but if you haven't been there before it's dead easy to get lost.'

She climbed into the car and immediately started fiddling with the radio.

'We haven't hijacked you have we? Anyway, I owe you a pint remember.'

He kept close to the mini-bus in front as it navigated the narrow high banked lanes He thought it was about time he said something to her.

'You're not at all sinister you know?'

'Sinister?'

She frowned.

'Left handed. From the Latin *sinistere.'*

'I forgot you are a linguist.'

'Linguistician more than linguist – I can only speak English, sadly. You?'

'French a bit. And some Devon dialect if you really push me, *my lover'*.

He laughed at my *lover*. If only.

By the time they had arrived at the pub she had established where he lived, why he was continuing to study something she considered 'a bit dry', and whether he'd enjoyed the afternoon.

'And what about you?'

'Here's me answering all your questions and I know nothing about you.'

'There's not much to know. What you see is what you get, I'm afraid.'

What he'd *got* so far, he liked, apart from the fleece which was giving off something that reminded him of a farm he'd once visited as part of some school visit.

'Well first, what were you doing down on the beach? You can't have gone down there to skim stones. You're not doing geography or something, are you?'

'Actually, you're not far wrong. Most of us or I should say most of them, are taking geomorphology as a final year option – all about rocks – but I'm doing history, and am with Ben, the one without the beard, but I thought I'd come along, and try out the pub again. Apparently, it has a bit of a reputation.'

'For what?'

'Devon dialect. They say there are a couple of old guys who speak it to each other when they're not pissed. I was also interested in the name of the beach which might tell me something about local place names and the dialect.'

With Ben.

He kept his eyes firmly fixed on the bus ahead. Damn the preposition *with*!

But it did seem a bit odd that she'd agreed to walk up with him from the beach and not be 'with Ben' in the drive to the pub.

'We're both interested in place names then?'

She turned towards him.

'Yes, I'm thinking of doing my final dissertation on Devon place names. Whether they're the last bastion of the dialect. My tutor, Jeremy's written a book about it which I really love and he's encouraging me to go for it.'

They'd arrived at the pub and tucked the car behind the mini-bus.

'Why's the pub called the *Nobody Inn*?'

'They say it got its name from an unfortunate episode concerning a deceased landlord way back? Perhaps nobody could find him, sounds spooky but they serve good beer.'

'And if you're interested it used to be called the *New Inn* in the 1830s, and in case you're wondering it has nothing to do with the Devon dialect.'

She paused.

'If you're wondering where I got all this from, there's a plaque on the way on the way to the ladies.'

It was his turn to laugh. Even *with Ben* he liked her. She was combative but not in a way that put him down or made him feel small.

The group had obviously been to the pub before and were comfortably huddled around two corner tables which they'd pushed together. He felt awkward about joining them without her and so tagged behind as she pushed her way to the bar.

'Your reward. What's it to be?'

'Whatever you're having which I guess will be a pint of the best?'

As she ordered he looked over her head and saw their reflections in a large mirror behind the optics. They looked like a couple to him, one standing slightly in front of the other, but to the barman just two rather scruffy students impatient for a drink.

Two days later he received his first purple-enveloped letter from her. It had been delivered by hand through the rarely used front door letter box. Letter number one.

'Gurney, I wanted to thank you for offering to drive me home the other night. It was sweet of you but I don't think Ben would've understood. As you say he can be a bit of a pain sometimes and, well, we had such a nice day I didn't want it to end in a scene.'

'But look, I'd like to see you again, one afternoon perhaps? Wednesdays are free for me so come over if you're free. Love Amy.'

His heart rose. No-one who was *with Ben* or with anyone else would take the trouble to deliver a personal invitation to see you again in a purple envelop and sign the letter, 'Love'. Would they? He propped the letter up in front of the toaster and sliced some bread. She was beautiful, friendly, had spirit, and possessed an ordinary name, a little too ordinary if he thought about it, but - and it was not an insignificant but - she was with Mister can-be-a-pain Ben. Gok was making an omelette. He looked sideways towards his flat-mate.

'Hi, you need omelette?'

'It's not what I *need* Gok, it's what I *want*.'

'I think you need a Wan omelette.'

He flourished a second small frying pan and dexterously began pouring the egg mixture simultaneously into the two pans.

'The secret is not to fiddle with it like you English do. Keep the heat up high and then flip it over like this, after one minute. Omelette will be crisp on outside and soft inside.'

'Yes, soft on the inside,' Gurney mused.

They carried their plates to the farmhouse table in the middle of the room and sat facing each other.

'You remember that beach mentioned I used to go to with my parents?'

'Oh yeah one with the hawk flying around.'

'Buzzard but, well, I went down there the other day and not much had changed, except it's used by sun lovers at one end. Must be bloody mad.'

'…And bloody freezing.'

Gok laughed.

'Anyway, I met someone I think I really like down there…'

'One of the bloody freezing?'

'No, you idiot, a student with her boyfriend looking at the coastline, some sort of field trip. We all went back to this pub and she and I spent the evening talking about everything including talking – she's very interested in how the locals talk in the old dialect.'

'You say she has boyfriend, must be 'bloody mad' if he lets her talk all the time with the likes of you'.

'That's it, I think she's going off him, she's sent me this note inviting me to meet up again. I should, do you reckon?'

'Meet up with her and fight the Mister Ben? You will fight for her, Gurney? In my country, we say, a hesitant man does not get the beautiful woman.'

'Yeah, we say more or less the same thing.'

For some reason, he felt dispirited as if he'd lost the fight before it had begun.

'Gurney, cheer up. Meet her in the afternoon like she says and tell her you want to be her good friend and that mister Ben can be your friend too. And we have another saying too: 'I make food, you clean plates.' He laughed.

*

Letter number two arrived a week later delivered in the same manner.

'Gurney, thank you again for suggesting you drive me home. I hadn't realised it was so late. At least you know the way now from the pub. I wanted to thank you for bothering to come all the way out to our place at Kenton and then being willing to drive all the way out to the moor. I loved the clapper bridge. Next time we go to the pub I'll tell Ben to drive that way. He'd be really interested. And thanks again for listening to my ideas for my dissertation. When I tell you I'm being a 'bit of a churn' you'll know what I'm saying, eh? My luvver? Thinking of Ben, I'd hate to hurt his feelings so I think we shouldn't meet for a while until I get a chance to sort out my feelings for him. I'll be in touch. Amy.'

How significant is a change in salutation from 'Love Amy' to just 'Amy' all in the space of a week? He numbered the envelope and placed it on top of the previous one. As he washed up the plates he realised that something important had changed. Something had happened to him unexpectedly and which seemed far removed from the accumulation of academic knowledge.

He had fallen in love.

Chapter Seven

Study without desire spoils the memory, and it retains nothing that it takes in –
Leonardo da Vinci

Gurney woke up a minute before the alarm and tried to remember where he was. He'd been luxuriating in that half-erotic dreamland in which the air is heavy with sexual promise. Whoever had been stroking the nape of his neck – Amy, Alice, or gyrating Anne? – had obviously stopped, no doubt dissuaded from honouring any promise by the drabness of his maisonette front room. His mood of *unrequited* lust soon gave way to one of *requited* foreboding as he struggled with his socks and remembered the schedule of events the day held: his briefing with Alice in the morning followed by the internationalisation committee in the afternoon. Both seemed to demand more of him than he thought he could deliver.

His breakfast was interrupted by a dull thudding noise coming from his small front garden. He opened the door cautiously and peered out. Across the street, a young labourer, supervised by three older on-lookers, was hammering a thick wooden post into the ground. Attached to it was a square metal plate informing the motoring public that this was now a designated disabled parking bay. He stared at the post. He had little to do with any of his neighbours and as far as he knew none appeared afflicted by any physical handicap, though Mrs Widdowson who lived at number 73 seemed particularly socially-challenged evidenced by her telling a neighbour to 'fuck off' when he enquired if her day was fine. Clearly, she had dreamt up this wheeze and in so doing had deprived him of one less parking space. He wondered what constituted a disability. A broken heart? Or perhaps sudden mood swings brought on by the irrational and cruel world in which he found himself. He closed the door and returned to his nut clusters.

Trying to remember where he'd parked his car was particularly trying that morning – the space opposite would help – but at least this disability gave him some sense of continuity. It was raining and only the wiper on the passenger side seemed to be working. The road to the university was surprisingly clear and he found himself with good time to spare as he approached the entrance to the campus. Overnight someone from Estates had erected a large blue sign which informed all visitors that you were now entering 'the South of England's most flexible university'. Half the car park had been fenced off with yellow crime-scene tape, a large paper notice advising that for the remainder of the week tree-felling would necessitate limited parking. Helpfully the notice concluded with the advice, to 'only use the car park if really necessary'. He wondered if going to work was indeed 'really necessary'. 'Was life really necessary?' He had just over an hour before Alice Hildebrand would bounce in all eager to be briefed.

Was it Aristotle who suggested that it is repetitive behaviour that defines the man? Gurney believed so: open the door, place keys next to the printer, turn on said computer, shake kettle to ascertain water level, boil kettle, remember to buy coffee, milk and sugar, read emails. His Aristotelian reverie was interrupted when he saw the mail. She'd written. He savoured the moment.

A familiar voice, not dissimilar to the dull thudding noise he had experienced at breakfast cut short his savouring.

' The last fucking straw Gurney, the last fucking nail in our collective departmental coffin!'

Williams barged in through the door and flung a crumpled sheet of paper over towards him.

'Bad news?'

'No, fucking good news you twat. Let me enlighten you my dear colleague for what passes for enlightenment from our esteemed Pro-Vice Chancellor with responsibility for entrepreneurial initiatives.'

Gurney tutted in what he hoped would be taken for solidarity and straightened out the piece of paper. Williams snatched the paper from him and revved up,

'Far from me to interfere with your advance plans...fuck him...but if I may could I share with you a few words of encouragement...screw him...with regard to the ongoing discussion you and your colleagues will be having concerning the Centenary plans.'

Gurney opened his mouth, decided against echoing anything profane, and tutted to indicate further agreement.

'This is the moron, Gurney if you remember who has had his facility for frontal thinking surgically removed and replaced by what I call a fucking random jargon generator!'

'Generator?'

'Listen to this, 'as you are no doubt aware, the University is anxious to facilitate increased opportunities to improve institutional performance with regards to corporate social responsibility. As such - and in line with our private long-term economic and social engagement – or PLEASE – strategy we consider it useful for all staff to develop initiatives, such as the Centenary, within such guidelines.'

'Does it mean anything?'

'No, it doesn't and - yes - it fucking does!'

'It's ambivalent?'

'No, it's fucking moronic Sleep - and it's fucking insulting.'

'So, I shouldn't take any notice of any guidelines when I meet Alice...?'

Williams turned on his heels and stormed out. Alone. Peace and quiet. He got up gingerly and walked over to the door and closed it. He returned to his chair and switched on the monitor.

She'd written. He savoured the moment. Again.

*

Gurney loved words, particularly those written and spoken by someone else. Somebody – why couldn't he remember who it was? – had said, 'young men learn the rules, old men the exceptions' - exceptions being the unloved words uttered by his mother and every noun, verb and particularly adjective uttered by Williams. Her words though were presented boldly in Times New Roman – romantic? – font twelve and were exceptionally seductive. There were ninety-seven of them - more if you counted a contraction as two - but he read them again.

'Hi Gurney, so lovely we are back in touch after so long. To cut to the chase I'm heading your way – or is it 'our'? - in three weeks' time to launch a new product onto the UK market – I'm into candles would you believe! – and after London we'll be off to Exeter, so I thought why not see if you are free for a walk down memory lane, some wine in front of a log fire? Let me know if you want to hook up? Love Amy.'

Three weeks' time. Of course, he was free. He involuntarily shivered at the thought of how powerfully ninety-seven words had transformed the morning. Him. His life. Recognition, and what's more, recognition from the woman he loved.

No longer a sharply dull academic pootling away at the foothills of learned academia but a beloved *recognisee* who could not only think but could feel! The Phoenix of love had arisen again, lit by a votive candle, from the ashes of his former life!

'Be calm Gurney. Don't fan the flames of destruction with a hasty response. Speak with Linden, your friend and counsel. Savour the moment but let that moment stretch for a few hours till you and he can agree what is best to do.'

His reverie was interrupted by a quiet knocking at the door. Clearly not Williams. Gurney read quickly over the e mail, savoured 'our way' and 'in touch', switched off the screen and said 'Yes?' with a suitable rising tone of one who has been interrupted in his great work. Whoever it was clearly hadn't heard him as the knock was repeated. For reasons to do with status he felt it wasn't his responsibility to move towards the door but for the knocker to hear and then come to him, the *knockee*. Gravitas gave way to irritation.

'Enter!'

Then he remembered who it was and leapt swiftly to the door.

Alice Hildebrand had her right fist raised, about to strike once more.

'I thought you weren't there.'

'Sorry, damned emails, full inbox, you know how it is.'

'I don't really as I prefer twitter or texting. Can I come in?'

She was wearing some of the clothes she had worn at the interview: crisp white blouse set off by the pearls but with her lower half now clothed in tight-fitting blue Levis.

'You are expecting me.'

'Of course, come in, take a pew. Congrats again on getting the post. You were, are, clearly the best person for the job.'

He smiled.

She smiled but said nothing.

'You're going to brief me?'

'Yes, and I'll try to be brief.

He laughed.

'Linguistics!'

She nodded in agreement.

'As this is our first formal meeting I thought we might just chat, get to know each other a little, and I could answer any questions you might have about the job.'

'Shall I nip out and get us a coffee?'

He nodded and waved a hand airily towards the door. After she had gone he was tempted to switch on the monitor quickly and read the ninety-seven words again but decided he'd wait till later. 'Delayed gratification' isn't that what it's called?

She quickly returned with two coffees in Styrofoam cups. Each cup had the words, 'I enjoy flexibility' emblazoned on them. Clearly the university had been working fast in its rebranding drive. Next week no doubt the message would be in Chinese, Malay, and South American Spanish. Gurney had another look at her as she put his coffee next to his computer. Something had changed. It was her accent. Gone was the strangulated vowels and in had come the modulation of a well-brought up girl from the home counties. Estuary had clearly been a nod in the direction of the university's equal opportunities policy, though he couldn't remember the time when a senior academic ever said 'innit.'

She was wearing the same sensible shoes.

'You don't take sugar, do you?'

'I do but I'm trying to give up,' he lied.

She smiled, showing that beautiful set of white teeth. An advertisement if ever there was one for giving up unsweetened beverages.

'What would you like to know? About me?'

He sipped his coffee and thought about this.

You're clearly an attractive woman Alice - you don't mind me calling you Alice do you – and I was wondering if you and I might continue this conversation over a glass of white later tonight?

He blushed and hoped that mindreading was not an additional skill she had acquired during her expensive private schooling.

'Do please call me Gurney. But let me clear up one thing. Boden? You mentioned you'd spent some time with them? I was wondering why they were called such? I assume they're named after a founder? Gottfried Boden or some such?'

'   No idea, but I agree it's an odd name.'

'And Hildebrand is not a name I've come across before. Not that I can talk'.

'My father's very proud of it, and his Austrian roots.'

'What does he do?'

She looked up from her Styrofoam cup.

'He's a life peer. A Lib Dem. Lord Hildebrand of Frome. In the county of Somerset to be precise.'

She giggled.

'Why Somerset? Weren't you brought up in Surry or Hampshire, a Home Counties girl?'

'Yes, I was but his father, grandpapa was a prisoner of war here and basically stayed on near where he was held, which was just outside Frome. I think the camp was demolished in the early 50s. Anyway, he met a local girl and the rest, as they say is history. Daddy was born in Frome but spent most of his life working in London, and mummy was from Wimbledon and wasn't awfully keen of doing rural. Anyway, when he got ennobled he decided to return to his roots, even if they are a bit shallow – the roots that is.'

She tossed her cup expertly into the bin next to his chair.

'Grandpapa still lives in the village. Grandmama died a few years ago, but he's happy, even more so since daddy bought a small place in the village, next to the old castle.'

Gurney couldn't remember the last time he'd had such an engaging and revealing conversation, and certainly this was a first time in this particular room.

' And what about you? Do you hail from some *sleepy* village somewhere?'

She giggled again at her joke. He wondered what was in the coffee.

'Sorry, you must be truly fed up with people making jokes about your name.'

'To be honest I am, but I've more or less got used to it. What is worse though is having an awkward first name coupled to a laughable second one.'

'Your parents have a lot to answer for.'

He tossed his cup towards the bin and missed.

'Should we discuss the job?' he said, keen now to steer the conversation away from his parents and the list of things his mother had to answer for.

To thwart the inevitable questions from her about what the Centenary might involve, and more specifically when it would be held, he suggested a good start would be for her to do a library-based trawl of everything connected to the linguistics department over the past hundred years, and, in particular, its genesis and antecedents.

The pale October sun broke out from behind the clouds and streamed into the room. They'd been talking for about forty-five minutes, longer than he had anticipated. She had captured his attention and had absorbed his thoughts to an extent that it was not until she'd left that he remembered the email awaiting his attention. He switched on the computer, the edge of his excitement blunted a little by his encounter with his new research fellow. For a moment, he forgot about the thrilling ninety-seven words he had received earlier. There was a red-flagged message from Linden.

'Gurney! Great news! Lucy is coming down at the end of the month. I know it's three weeks away but I'm thinking about what we might do together, us and you? Let's meet up tonight, if you're free, and plan.'

Three weeks' time? He opened the mail from Phoenix and re-read the message. Gurney considered himself secular, rationalist, and sensible when it came to matters of superstition, religion, or emotion and yet, he acknowledged the coincidence in Lucy agreeing to meet Linden when Amy would be visiting him. Why not bring these four star-crossed lovers together for a weekend of conjoint romance? He chuckled benignly to himself – no, no. no! These four star-crossed individuals had nothing in common apart from university administration, an interest in contrastive linguistics, Votive candles -and in the case of Gurney and Linden - sex. And anyway, wasn't the purpose of the weekend an opportunity for both men to consolidate with their respective better halves, and then conjoin away from the distraction of the other? Quickly he replied to Linden that he would meet him tonight usual place, usual time. He wrote 'confirm' on his pad followed by *could, would* and *must*.

The telephone rang. Since the advent of email, he rarely received any calls on the device. He liked to use it as a paper weight. Students had no concept of the landline and as far as he knew no one, including his mother, had his office number. Who could it be? Nervously he picked up the receiver. Perhaps Mrs Widdowson had reported him for lobbing a banana skin over her front wall? He glanced at the computer screen and the alluring ninety-seven words. 'Hook up' and 'free' swam out from the screen in an oxymoronic haze. The voice, which sounded East Coast American, was male and educated.

'Professor Sleep?'

'Yes and no.'

Brits. Could never decide.

'I'm calling you to congratulate you on behalf of Marquis Who's Who in Contrastive Linguistics for your inclusion in our latest edition of the world-renowned publication'.

He paused, his pleasant easy-going accent reminding him of a young Harrison Ford

'Professor Sleep?'

'It's actually Doctor Sleep and Yes, I am here. I'm to be included in this book? Er...thank you.'

He paused unsure what he was expected to say next. Harrison stepped in quickly. Slow on the uptake too.

'That's great. What happens next is that our editorial team will send you a draft resume of your career, achievements, and vocations after which we would ask you to approve and suggest any amendments.'

'Vocations?'

'Yeah, things you like to do away from work such as baseball, ice hockey or walking in the Catskills.'

Gurney vaguely remembered a very distressing film about two hillbillies living in a caravan in the Catskill mountains. Apart from lots of drinking and the manufacture of crystal meth he couldn't remember much about the Catskills that he liked. Perhaps Harrison Ford had been one of the men?

'And now Professor may I ask you about which level of service you would prefer?'

He looked at the screen. 'Happen in Exeter' and 'into candles' were what he would really prefer.

'...the bronze service consists of your entry mounted upon velum and posted to you in a secure tube, the silver your entry framed in one of several polished mahoganies or limed oak frames, the gold a deluxe mounting in gold or silver.'

A second telephone rings. The caller speaks impeccable English with a Swedish accent,

'Professor Sir Gurney Sleep will you hold please, I have Mister Lars Larsson of the Nobel Committee who wishes to confer with you and to ask if you will accept the award in person....'

He put the receiver down before Harrison had an opportunity to mention the small matter of cost for the honour bestowed upon him.

Deflated and distracted, he decided to call Linden.

*

He read the ninety-seven words again. Call Linden? Was he mad? Why wasn't he composing his reply to 'wine', 'fire', 'hook' and 'love'? He knew enough about himself and academic life to recognise classic displacement activity: draw up a list, pop over to the library, search for that one remaining reference, grab a coffee, or even just stare out of the window lost in thought. Linden could wait even if it meant delaying an opportunity to hear his usual useful advice. Yes, he'd call him and postpone their meeting. His answer machine was on (why didn't he have one?) and told him that he was 'in conference' - probably planning the *desired outcomes* of the internationalisation committee with the chair. He left a message about hooking up and returned to Phoenix.

His telephone rang again. This was getting beyond a joke. Perhaps the server had gone down. Whatever next? A porter arriving with the internal mail in little brown envelopes always too small for those committee papers or late student essays? He let it ring. But what if the server really was down and this was Phoenix bringing forward the weekend? He picked up the receiver as if it was unexploded ordinance.

'Yes?'

The line buzzed and fizzed, a voice half-strangulated and possibly half-pissed repeating what he had said,

'Yes?'

The static increased suggesting mobile to landline or possibly field telephone to HQ via the pipeline-under-the-ocean.

'Yes?'

This time the line suddenly cleared.

'Is that you Gurney?'

He agreed it was.

'And who are you?'

'I'm Albert Noakes, you won't remember me but I live next door to your mother. Lovely lady…'

'Yes?'

The static returned.

'…not to worry…fall…Royal Infirmary.'

Gurney said 'OK' this time and replaced the receiver.

He remembered Albert now from the party his parents had arranged when he had received the official news that he had gained his doctorate. For most of the evening he had tried, with difficulty, to explain to his parent's neighbour that, whereas he was now a Doctor of Philosophy, the GP up the road was better qualified to deal with a nasty attack of neuralgia.

Albert continued in the same vein, however informing Gurney that his dear wife, Doris had long suffered from 'funny turns' brought on he was sure by her sister's chronic sciatica. Gurney had never met Albert's wife and for a moment wondered whether she did in fact exist. Albert hadn't left a number but Gurney vaguely remembered the hospital, it was where his father had spent his last days, situated at the back of a Lidl and not far from his parent's home.

Instinctively he knew he had to drop everything and rush to his mother's bedside, assuming that 'fall' referred to some sort of collapse. But dropping everything now would mean missing the internationalisation committee during which he'd be nominated to take forward whatever inanities the chair saw fit. And what about Alice and her expectations of follow up? He thought for a moment. Once she'd heard he'd dropped everything to be near his fallen mother she'd see him in a more extended light: caring son who puts family before career. Computer off, keys secure, door closed. Find the car and he was done.

Chapter Eight

Wellness: the quality or state of being healthy in body and mind, especially as the result of deliberate effort. – Dictionary.com

The journey to the hospital was familiar to Gurney: slip road out of the university to motorway, slip road onto the second motorway linking to the orbital motorway, then slip road past the cul de sac where his parents and he had lived, and then finally along a congested dual carriageway to the nearby suburban town which housed the hospital, once a private girls' school and before that once an insane asylum. He parked in a narrow street a few minutes' walk from the hospital, noting the terraces of well-maintained homes with names that seemed redolent of holidays way back – *Miramar*, and *Paxos* nestling next to a *Witterings*. One of the larger houses was called *Nice* – proper noun or adjunctive? He assumed the former and resisted the temptation to knock on the door and ask. Shortly after he'd arrived at the university, the pro-VC (marketing) had established a committee to explore the idea of a university re-branding. The suggestion was that rather than be called simple after the city in which it was located, potential customers – as applicants were to be known – would be more attracted to a name such as the 'University of the South Coast'. This plan was hastily dropped after the other university of the South Coast threatened to sue over the use of the definite article. As Williams reminded the pro-VC at the time, linguistics does have its uses.

At the entrance to the hospital he saw his way barred by a semi-circle of protesters clutching placards, one of which read, *Death by a Thousand Cuts*. Another said *Over my dead body* which he thought appropriate and yet offensive depending on your reason for visiting. He noticed that most of those holding placards were junior doctors.

Once inside the building he looked around for a reception desk which was prominently to the fore but unoccupied. Next to the desk he saw an elderly man peering at a large notice board devoted to sexually transmitted diseases and the reorganisation of health trusts into GP managed health consortia. There was also an advertisement for a radical new treatment for bipolar disorder. Gurney walked up to him and tapped him on the shoulder.

'Would you happen to know where the new admissions go?'

'I'm Albert Noakes. Saw you walking in and knew it was you.'

Gurney was impressed. Clearly, he was in command of all his faculties and only reading the notice board to pass the time.

'How is she? What happened?'

'Third floor, Murdoch ward. She's fine really, considering'.

'Considering what?'

'Considering, she's well getting on and considering she was up a step ladder talking to my Doris when it happened. Soft underfoot. Was telling my Doris only the other day. Not that she was on a step ladder at the time.'

'She was standing on the ladder to talk to your wife?'

'That's right. The fence we put up over the summer was – what - this high and what with everything, and it being soft underfoot and our Doris being not what you'd call tall...'

Gurney felt no great inclination to delve into why neither woman had invited the other into her home to have a neighbourly conversation or what Albert was doing at the time.

'To be honest, Gurney I think your mother, bless her, is just having one of her funny turns...'

'Funny?'

'Well strange. And when I say strange I say it with great respect and affection. But you must admit taking a step ladder out into the garden when it's soft underfoot does strike me as strange, wouldn't you say?'

By this time, they had arrived at the third floor. His mother was sitting up in a bed next to the door, the other three in the room empty. She was engrossed in what looked like an old copy of the Radio Times.

'Mum?'

She looked up and smiled a watery grin that reminded him of his father. He moved swiftly to her bedside and kissed the top of her head. She smelled of soap and fresh violets.

'Mum, are you OK?'

She peered closely at something on the page.

'If I'd known this was on I'd have watched it.'

Albert Noakes had followed him into the room and clearly saw his role as interpreter.

'I think she is telling you about something she wished she'd seen on television.'

Gurney decided to ignore him. She looked fine, wasn't in traction or hooked up to a life-support machine. He felt slightly cross and deceived.

'Mother, what is wrong with you?'

His urgent tone seemed to energise her and at the same time silence Albert Noakes.

'The doctor says it's my back Gurney. Observation, he says, to see if I've done something to it.'

Gurney felt relieved and annoyed in equal measure. Clearly his mother wasn't paralysed from the waist down and equally clearly, she was enjoying the experience of being cared for, and something he acknowledged had gone from her life since the death of his father. He felt a pang of guilt. As he was there it seemed only politic and polite to spend some time with her. He sat down on the plastic chair next to her bed.

'Gurney?'

'Mum?'

'I'm worried about you dear.' He felt this was something he should be saying to her.

'No need to be mum, I'm fine. Work is good, as usual, and I'm eating well.'

They were both silent.

'I think your mother is wondering about your future Gurney.'

He had forgotten all about the grey presence of Albert Noakes.

'My future?'

He wondered if the two of them had some satellite link up with Professor Williams or worse Grand Canyon Candles.

'I think she's worried - if you don't mind me saying so Gurney - that you might not really be interested in girls at all.'

A large Afro-Caribbean nurse who was about to enter the room immediately turned tail and walked off.

Gurney withdrew the Smith & Wesson from the inside pocket of his tuxedo and pumped three bullets into the chest of Albert Noakes.

'Would you mind if I had a few words in private with my mother Mr. Noakes?'

After he had gone Gurney wondered what he was going to say.

'You don't really think I'm gay do you Mum? You remember Moira, the Scottish girl. And that lovely woman I told you about when I was doing my MA. Amy?'

'You never brought her home, Gurney. We never saw her. She could have been a figment of your imagination for all we knew. You should get in touch with her again, Gurney. Rekindle an old flame.'

His mother's choice of metaphor was more apt than she knew. Gurney had long ago learned that in listening to his mother the best strategy – or was it a tactic? – was to occasionally agree with something important to her but inconsequential to him such as his need for a hearty breakfast or a parking space opposite his house. Then he could get on with navigating his own way through the choppy waters of life.

'You're right Mum. When I'm in touch I promise to let you know and bring her home. For Christmas'. This rash promise both surprised and thrilled him in unequal measure.

'Thank you dear.'

A sudden ghastly thought struck him: his mother and the clearly interested Albert Noakes welcoming him and a rekindled Amy into their home with a warm glass of Amontillado. His mother might be physically incapacitated, though there was no evidence of that, but she'd lost none of her ability to mind read.

'Don't worry about Albert dear, we're just good friends, me and him and his Doris. He needs someone to help him when she has one of her turns.'

Gurney felt a familiar fog of confusion descend upon him whenever his mother provided any analysis of her behaviour. Wasn't it she who'd had a turn? Perhaps one funny turn deserved another? He swallowed a laugh.

'It's not funny dear, lying here with nothing to do.'

On the way back to the university he remembered he'd forgotten to thank Albert for calling him. No doubt he'd see him again if his mother or Doris took a turn for the worse.

If his car had been fitted with one of those female Japanese voice-activated warning systems it would have reprimanded him five miles from the university.

'You make mistake Mister Gurney in not filling up with petrol at last service station'.

Instead the car gave two warning lurches and slowly shuddered to a halt, giving him just enough traction to slide onto the hard shoulder. A few drops of rain splattered onto the windscreen. The wiper on the driver's side was still not working. He'd read somewhere that it was imperative to get out of the vehicle immediately, walk to a nearby emergency telephone, and then stand shivering by the side of the road whilst large and speeding articulated lorries thundered past. After that it was imperative to try and remember why you hadn't signed up to a roadside recovery organisation. The roadside telephone hadn't been vandalised though and when the voice answered it sounded remarkably like Albert Noakes.

As he waited for the arrival of the 'fourth emergency service' he decided it would be pointless to return to the university, however seductive the pull of the email, and anyway he hadn't composed a reply yet. *Life on the hard shoulder.* How apt! He was almost tempted to shed tears of frustration on this hard shoulder at his mother, Noakes and himself at being thwarted at every turn to do something he really wanted to do. *But man up, Gurney! Reply, reconnect and rekindle. Onwards and upwards! Blue-sky thinking!* A glimmer of blue had penetrated from behind the rain clouds. Perhaps his mother was right, his future had been looking bleak but ninety-seven words had changed all that. By the time he was back on the road it was getting dark with more rain clouds hastening him towards his home.

The encounter with his mother and Albert Noakes had unsettled him. His mother seemed to have more going for her than him. Noakes was clearly no figment of the imagination and he'd done nothing to advance project Arizona. He resisted the temptation to park in Mrs. Widdowson's exclusive disabled bay, reconciled to a good mile's walk from wherever he could park and what passed for his home. The walk did him good, however, cleared his head of morbid thoughts so that when he entered the house he felt light in spirit, jolly almost. He hadn't eaten. Omelette cooked al la Wok-Gok. How appropriate!

He found some new potatoes and left-over French beans from the weekend. There was even a bottle of wine chilling in the fridge. His kitchen was small, described by the estate agent, as a kitchen-cum-breakfast bar. Presumably living alone types like him ate dinner out?

He ate and composed at the same time. He felt on fire, scribbling down, then crossing out, then topping up his glass with more white. How different her ninety-seven words were to that fateful twenty-fifth letter. On an impulse, he went into his bedroom and extracted the letter from the pile in the second shoe box.

'Gurney, I'm sorry to have to write to you like this and on a day I've enjoyed. But I think you know as well as I do that it isn't going to work. I tried in the pub today to talk to you but lost my nerve, and now I am writing to you like a coward. It is about timing Gurney, our careers, where we each want to go, the things we want to do. And I am being honest in saying I've loved the times we've spent together, have loved being with you, skimming stones even! But I think it's best we break now and remain friends. Who knows perhaps we'll meet in years gone by and I'll regret today? Please forgive me for hurting you and I'm sorry if I've raised your expectations. Can I come by tomorrow and pick up my things? Love as ever, Amy x'.

He placed the letter carefully back in the box. Things were changing. Past imperfect now present. Tense.

Chapter Nine

Double-blind study: an experimental procedure in which neither the subjects of the experiment nor the persons administering the experiment know the critical aspects of the experiment; 'a double-blind' procedure is used to guard against both experimenter bias and placebo effects - The Free Dictionary

Gurney arrived first. He was late and surprised to see the pub empty. No Linden looking mournfully towards the door; but time to rehearse the good news and arrange his face into something not resembling a gloat.

'Drinks are on me, dear Linden. Pray take a pew old man and allow me to enlighten you of my good fortune'. Why was he sounding like a bit player in a Dickens Christmas Carol? He felt avuncular and paternalistic towards his *dear friend* Linden, who did possess something of the Bob Cratchet about him. By the time Linden arrived Gurney was half way through his second pint and feeling slightly pissed.

'You're looking merry. Good news?'

'Wonderful, thank you Linden. Let me get them in my good man. Sit! Pray Sit!'

At this he stood a little unsteadily watched by Linden who looked alarmed and excited in equal measure.

'I've been a right old fool Linden I don't mind saying, worrying myself silly over what I should write, whether what I did write would be rejected, and what have you...'

'What have you?'

'Another pint, boom boom!'

Linden forced a weak smile and accompanied his friend to the bar. They were the only drinkers in the place, the *Open House* serving nothing in the way of food apart from crisps, peanuts, and pork scratchings.

'Last night I re-read every one of the twenty-five letters she wrote to me, every single one, looking for some clue, some inkling of the mistakes I had made, and more importantly what to avoid as we rekindle our relationship. I had intended to read just the final missive Linden, but you know what?'

'What?'

They had returned to their corner table with four pints – 'I insist' - plus an armful of crisps and packets of yellow wheat snacks that looked alarmingly as if they had been made from *Sunny Delight*.

'It suddenly dawned on me at about three in the morning that it was clear what I should and must say.'

'Which was?'

'...that it was fantastic news that she was coming over in three weeks' time, that I'd book us – that is her and me, not you and me – a room and that I loved her, always had, always would.'

'That's it? That's what you wrote?'

'Not quite all. I signed off, 'Love, Gurney.''

'You haven't sent it, have you? You're getting plastered because you've written it – in your head anyway – but you don't have the courage to send it, have you? Is that it Gurney, is that it?'

Linden had never been quite so forthright with anyone before but it was necessary given his friend's extraordinary behaviour. He also had an aversion to alcoholic excess, a social ill he felt contributed to much unhappiness in the world. He also felt mildly protective towards his friend.

Gurney was starting on his fourth pint and second packet of yellow peril.

'That's where you are wrong, Lind, wrong. Sent and what's more received and replied to.'

At this the lecturer in contrastive linguistics produced - with a flourish worthy of a Victorian melodrama - a single sheet of paper from the inside pocket of his jacket. He waved it aloft a little like Neville Chamberlain after Munich.

'Book a room overlooking the river Gurney. It'll be great to spend time together catching up on old times. I've got loads to tell you. Love as ever. Amy x'.

Linden was impressed and allowed himself to imagine his own response to receiving a similar invitation from Lucy. Clearly it wasn't the moment to turn the conversation towards the outcomes of the internationalisation committee and the unanimous decision to co-opt the absent Gurney onto the working sub-group charged with encouraging rich alumni in the United Kingdom to sponsor an international applicant from a poor country. And the imminent weekend with Lucy? Linden felt deflated and out-manoeuvred by his friend's high spirits. What had she said? 'I'm coming down to see Kevin at the end of the month'. Unlike Gurney he hadn't booked a room in a love nest overlooking the river, thinking more along the lines of a meal at the new Italian next to the Lidl.

Gurney had spread the piece of paper on to the table held down by four empty beer glasses. Linden remembered Gurney's idea of joining them for a quick drink before he and Lucy savoured the delights of spag bol.

'And you did agree, didn't you?'

Now it was Gurney's turn, emboldened by ale, to be assertive.

'Yes, we've agreed, didn't we, that I'd join you for a swift half before you and dear Lucy launch into the linguini'. Linden knew that when he was in this sort of mood, it was best to try and steer his friend home.

'I think we've all had enough Gurney. You didn't drive, did you?'

With a sense of obligation and grace Linden steered his friend home, returning the way he had come to the bus stop where fortune rewarded him with just a five-minute wait for the number 6B.

Gurney woke the next morning and wondered where he was and why a familiar large industrial hammer was lodged between his ears. He swivelled his eyes around the room half expecting to see his friend Linden Slackley asleep in his easy chair. Wasn't it the Liverpool poet Rodger McGough who penned the immortal lines, 'Woke up and put my hangover on?' He'd clearly never attempted to place two long cotton socks over two unwashed feet without bending down. And then he remembered: today was the first day of the rest of his life! Today was the day he would book the room with a view, check out the train times for the West Country, and if he had time pop, into *Past Times*, the high street *Old Worlde Shoppe* famous for Victoriana. They'd had a window display of pretty cotton nightgowns last Christmas and he could think of nothing better to bring with him. And the sort of thing he felt sure you wouldn't be able to buy in a downtown shopping mall in Phoenix. Think of it: in just a little more than three weeks' time he'd be gazing out of the attic bedroom of the Double Locks Inn with his long-lost love lying by his side.

He tucked into his bowl of slushy cereal and tried to remember what he could of last night. Good old Linden. Linden and Lucy. Perhaps he should buy them something from *Past Times*, a kind of welcome-back-together gift? It was the least he could do given the circumstances. His mobile rang. It had to be mother or Albert Noakes telling him she'd had another fall.

'Yes?'

'Is that you Gurney? It's me. I've been told by that nice black nurse you met that I can go home today. Gurney, are you there? ... Albert is coming by taxi which should be here soon. I thought you should know.'

'Thanks mum. I must rush. Work and all that.'

He put his cereal bowl into the sink and let himself out. The front of the house had once been painted magnolia but now looked a little like those properties estate agents euphemistically call 'tired'. But he was far from tired, if a little exhausted from the night before. He'd put the flat on the market. He remembered a flash new property shop a couple of doors down from *Past Times*. He felt emboldened, a new man, born again. Even the walk to the car seemed shorter. He'd keep the price low and by Christmas - at the latest - he'd find himself in a little bijou place somewhere in the centre of town. At times of stress Gurney liked to fantasise. And being happy was certainly stressful. He felt unsettled, out of the ordinary, disquieted. Correspondingly, he behaved oddly, striding towards his car singing loudly the only song he knew, the aria from Nessum Dorma.

On route to the university he was cut up sharp by a black transit van with the logo *Springboard* emblazoned on the side. Though a rational unhappy man might err against drifting off into an erotic reverie whilst hurtling along a dual carriageway, Gurney - the reasonable and reasoned academic - was far from rational. That had been her name, Springboard, Arianna Springboard! She of the second-hand Laura Ashley frocks, Greenham Common peace camp and reheated mung beans eaten off tin plates in a small bedsit she shared with a fellow PhD student called Patricia who seemed never to be there, which suited them just fine.

The affair had only lasted a month but it had been vivid, at times heady, and at the start and end decidedly disquieting. He laughed; yes, his quiet had been well and truly dissed. Not since argumentative Moira had he realised how different he was to other people, particularly those he slept with. As a linguist, he was scornful of hackneyed clichés but the expression 'attraction of opposites' seemed apposite when he recalled Arianna and himself.

Arianna Springboard! She who had sprung forth into his life in a most unexpected way and when he had least expected it. He'd only been an undergraduate for a couple of weeks and had taken it upon himself to attend all the professorial inaugural lectures. Who knows he might learn something, and there was always free wine and canapes afterwards. The first one was on ageing and was being given by Arianna's supervisor, an aged academic who had devoted a considerable number of years to the subject of Werner's Syndrome, a condition that resulted in a twenty-year-old looking like Sitting Bull. He'd met her over canapes after and she'd told him she was researching something to do with the life span of free radicals, a research area Gurney suggested that seemed appropriate for a left-leaning university. His error and her bafflement had brought out something unexpected in both of them, and before the night was out they had agreed to meet up the following day. Her flowing auburn locks, off-beat clothes, and attachment to women's causes, he discovered, masked a deeply conservative thinker. Arianna was a scientist and as such held to three cardinal rules:

1) Science is the saviour of mankind - or in her case *personkind.*

2) The Arts and Humanities - and she included linguistics in this group - were all very well when going on holiday and looking for a light read to occupy a few hours on a beach, but not the stuff of serious stuff.

3) The scientific method of identifying a hypothesis and then confirming or refuting it by means of procedures such as double-blind testing was the only way, you could ever arrive at the truth. And that was the serious stuff of serious stuff.

As she had said this she'd leant forward, her wavy brown hair framing her delicate face. Truth? For a moment, Gurney had felt intoxicated. No-one in his department had ever talked of truth. Contrastive linguistics, after all, was founded upon the idea that what mattered was the relative, one word or phrase in relation to another. And each lexical item in relation to the culture from which it came. There was nothing *true* about this relationship, only what he and others found *meaningful.* Arianna would have none of this dismissing his explanations as the postmodern shilly-shallying of people unable to take a stand, be robust, and possess *rigour.*

Looking back, it had been a good month, a steep learning curve, and though they had argued a lot, she had been rigorous in bed and he robust. And he'd enjoyed himself, a truth he could not deny. On his door was a yellow post-it note from Professor Williams,

'Have been here since eight trying to catch you. When you arrive come to my office.' Gurney could only imagine it had something to do with the Centenary and Williams' increasing paranoia that it was being hijacked by the suits on level five. He'd ring Linden first; he'd know what was up.

He had a solitary e mail in his inbox which was odd. He telephoned the IT helpdesk and listened to a recorded message - from someone he guessed hailed from Solihull - informing him that the university server was being upgraded, normal service being resumed on Saturday. That explained the post-it and no doubt any angry messages on his answer phone. Didn't the professor have better things to do, or more importantly, a home to be in at breakfast time?

He read the lonely email which was from the lecturers' union branch secretary, Charlie Hickson. Gurney liked Charlie and admired his persistence and resistance towards the management's belief that a better university was a private one. Why not outsource the maintenance of the car parks, student hostels and catering services? And while we are about it why not give 'due and proper consideration' to examining cheaper ways to 'develop the institution's core human resources', which was code for 'pile 'em high, teach 'em cheap!' Though Gurney had never actually joined the Union he felt a comradely sense of solidarity with Charlie and his besieged desperadoes, and if the Centenary did go belly up he might need the services of their legal department.

The latest communiqué from Hickson concerned the disturbing news that the Socialist Workers Party was leading a Trojan Horse attempt to derail the Union's decision not to boycott academic contacts with a growing list of countries eager to send valuable fee-paying students to the UK. Gurney cast his eye down the list of repressive governments, noting three were possible summer holiday destinations. The email urged him to attend that afternoon's Union AGM when a raft of *key votes* would be taken on the Trojan virus, opposition to the latest round of cuts, and the encroaching privatisation of university events and services. The meeting was to be held in the small seminar room of the Blair building.

Gurney was about to delete the message when he remembered something Linden had mentioned in passing at the pub. Something about Bundy outsourcing departmental public events, and care that would be needed in making sure that it did not include the Centenary. Who was Bundy? Gurney found three in the university address book: Edward, a third-year criminology student (appropriate), an Elizabeth who worked in the new information services complex (once known as the library) and a third, one Tristan Bundy, business development and enterprises director. It had to be him. He'd bring it up when he went over to Williams. His well laid plans to take a leisurely drive into town and sort out his train tickets, the *Past Times* purchase, and put his place on the market were now well and truly scuppered.

At least the land line was working. He dialled the hotel and asked for the room with a view of the river.

I'd like your best room overlooking the river for myself and my lovely bride Amy, she of the willowy limbs garlanded in Old times Victorian cotton...

This thought was interrupted by the soft burr of Devon dialect asking him how she could help. Yes, the room was available, yes, he could reserve it, and yes, he could place an order for chilled champagne and strawberries to be waiting upon arrival.

Next, he rang the train company and found it surprisingly easy to book a return ticket which included a front-facing window seat with a table. His call to *Past Times* was answered by a young woman whose accent he placed somewhere east of Bratislava and west of the Urals. It was one of those husky alluring voices very appropriate for a discussion about the availability of feminine night wear. They were awaiting their Christmas order but if it was 'urgent' he might try David Nieper, 'purveyor of classic nightdresses, camisoles, and dressing gowns'. Gurney did just that, and without flinching, ordered a long-sleeved Regency-style silk peignoir he was assured would, 'charm the lady in question.'

Whatever the question, he felt sure he had found the right answer. He decided against calling up the estate agents lest he be carried away with the moment and be persuaded to put down a hefty deposit on a newly renovated 'love pad' which has just come on to the market. At least he could now face Williams with a raft of good news below his belt.

The professor had long dispensed with what he considered to be the niceties of informal conversation. Not for him the time wasting 'hello' or 'good morning', rather he preferred to cut to the chase and get to the point, particularly if it was to his advantage. On this morning, he made an exception,

'You look like shit, Sleep. Not getting any?'

'No, I mean yes.'

'We've being fucking hijacked Gurney, fucking hijacked!'

Unless he was mistaken Gurney failed to see any imminent 'clear or present danger', a maniacal Al Qaida terrorist about to leap out from behind Williams' over-sized metal filing cabinet that occupied most of the room. If anyone was in danger of being seized by a deranged egomaniac bent on world domination, it was him.

'It's that egomaniac Bundy. Have you seen this?'

It was a communiqué from the VC, 'touching-base', a follow up from the previous Monday's brown bag lunch confirming that henceforth all university external activities were now to be commercially costed, rigorously driven by market economics - and if necessary - down-sized and out-sourced. Gurney wondered where this rant was leading.

'Have you ever heard of the Stockholm Syndrome, Gurney?'

'I think I have. Wasn't it something to do with Patty Hearst the newspaper heiress falling for her Symbionese captors, presumably in the Swedish capital? If I remember she went on to rob a bank.'

'It was indeed and ...'

'We're going to rob a bank?'

'No, you twat, I have decided that the only way we are going to beat them at their own game is to join them. I - or rather you - are going to hoist them with their own petard!'

Gurney stared at his mentor.

'Don't look so bloody worried, dear boy, what I have concocted is to agree with Ted fucking Bundy and that you are going to develop what he calls a 'departmental business plan'. 'Apparently to achieve this intellectual feat we need to speak the crap he speaks something that can be facilitated by one of his beloved away-days.'

'I'm going away?'

Williams glanced at his computer screen.

'Yes, and more precisely away to somewhere which calls itself a country hotel in a place called Weston-under-Penhard outside the town of Ross-on-Wye, which is presumably in the county of Somerset-under-milk wood in the good country of England-out-of-Europe.'

Gurney looked aghast. Please not in three weeks' time.

'And before you say no, you might like to know that when I said 'you' were going I was using the second person plural, you and our newly arrived eye candy, Ms. Alice Hildebrand will be joining you, for the purposes, so Mr. Bundy informs me, of 'building critical mass'. I've spoken to Bundy this morning and he's agreed to stretch his largesse to include two places, two second-class rail tickets - and in case you were wondering - two rooms.'

Gurney continued to stare.

'Whatever Bundy may think our aim will be to write exactly the kind of business plan that says everything he wants it to say, but crucially delivers exactly what we want.'

'Which is?'

'A centenary celebration Gurney that is run by us, is for us, and the profits, intellectual and financial are kept firmly within our grasp.'

'But I don't know anything about economics; it's hard enough trying to understand my own bank statement let alone strategically plan for anything.'

Williams looked hard at his computer screen.

'I have just sent you the on-line application, Gurney, fill it in, and remember, this is our chance to run the whole bloody show and keep the forty, fucking percent.'

'Forty percent?'

'Top slice boyo, stop the thieving buggers in admin from creaming off what is rightfully ours.'

Gurney wandered back towards his room wondering about what he had just had thrust upon him. At least he'd have Alice for company - and her sensible shoes – and it would take his mind off the Double Locks weekend. And who knows perhaps Alice would pack a *Past Times* nightdress?

The rain was falling in a steady drizzle now as Gurney and Alice ran from the taxi up the winding, leafy drive of the Country Hotel. They were both laughing at the absurdity of it all. As they ran into the hotel lobby she grabbed his arm. 'My key, Gurney, I've left it at the pub.' It was late and the receptionist had long gone. Gurney laughed. She looked like the most attractive drowned rat he'd ever seen. 'My room. I've some scotch, perhaps we can dry off in there?'...

His reverie was cut short by the sight of the very subject of it hurrying towards him.

'The weekend! Great news. Let's talk later about it.'

And she rushed past him in the direction of Williams' room. Williams had obviously enjoyed being the deliverer of good news and he wondered how he had sold the event to her. The on-line application form had been designed for a teenager to complete but one well-versed in log-on, password culture. Eventually Gurney reaching the final question which asked for a succinct reason for participating in the away weekend. 'Bullied into it' just about summed it up but Gurney tapped in, 'an opportunity to fine-tune our draft development plan' and pressed *send*. He sat back and tried to conjure up the rain, whiskey, and laughter as they ran down the corridor towards his room.

The euphoria of the morning had given way to a familiar feeling of anxiety at his inability to stand up to Williams, and worrying feelings about the shifting loyalties of his dream world.

Chapter Ten

Symposium: a conference or meeting to discuss a particular academic or specialist subject
Origin: originally denoting a drinking party: from Greek 'sumpotes' or 'fellow drinker' - Wikipedia

The hotel's brochure was right about one thing: it was secluded and was cut off from the hurly burly of modern life, which went some way to explaining why the taxi driver had to ring his HQ for more explicit directions hindered also by the fact that he was Bangladeshi and still finding his way around this corner of the English countryside. Gurney had always enjoyed discussing matters of language and idiom with taxi drivers, particularly as to date, he had never encountered one who was an indigene of the United Kingdom. Yet another paper waiting to be written on the linguistic interface between driver and passenger in a globalising marketplace.

Alice hadn't uttered a word during the lengthy detour from the railway station to the hotel which Gurney assumed she preferred to joining in his lively discussion with the driver about what constituted the difference between 'left' and 'right'.

The hotel drive was impressive, a cattle grid followed by a curving track leading up to the grand Georgian house fronted by lions rampant and a huge cedar tree.

'We're here', Gurney muttered redundantly, thanking Ali for his time and trouble. They were welcomed at the door by a tall Indian-looking man resplendent in a silk suit and a scarlet turban. He carried their bags into a large reception area that could well have graced a Mister Darcy or at least a Mister Hugh Grant. They were met by another imposing looking gentleman.

'I'm Andrew Johnston your host and facilitator for the weekend.'

Gurney shook the proffered hand, noticing the carefully prepared casual country look – brown corduroys, open neck check shirt, well shined brogues disguising a probable military background and razor-sharp intelligence. Clearly George Smiley incognito. As he took their bags towards their rooms he nodded towards an open door to the right of the hall.

'The David Stirling room. There's talk, mostly in the village mind, that this is where he dreamt up the idea of the Special Air Service, over so they say, a large malt. And, as you no doubt know, we're a stone's throw from Hereford where, so they say down in the village, Afghan and Iraqi Special Forces ops are planned down to the finest detail, and toasted over larger glasses of good scotch, not that we ever see any of them.'

Alice was in between Johnston and Gurney and was caught in the crossfire of the conversation.

'Daddy was in something like this I think, a boat service or something.'

Their host stopped and swivelled round to address her. 'The Special Boat Service, Paddy Ashdown's lot, and great bunch of lads I must say. Is your father still with them?'

'No, he's in the Lords now. With the Lib-Dems.'

'Ah, the Lib-Dems...'

They had now arrived at their adjoining rooms which Gurney noticed were named after legendary military leaders, he in the Clausewitz room, she the Blücher. As expected they were briskly handed a manila folder and ordered to report at the bar in half an hour. Presumably to be briefed, synchronise watches, and set up an ops room? For a moment, he wondered whether the taxi driver had made it out in one piece. Alice seemed to have brightened.

'All rather jolly don't you think Caruthers?'

'Miss Moneypenny, I'll have you remember we are here incognito', he managed with a very passable impersonation of the great Scot.

Through the wall of Clausewitz, he could hear Alice next door, humming what he thought was the march from 633 Squadron. Yes, this might be fun, as long as they didn't take it all too seriously and returned with something that pleased Williams and Bundy. She had stopped humming and he could hear the jangling of coat hangers. Perhaps her bed was just beyond the partition wall that divided Clausewitz from Blücher? When he arrived at the bar he saw Alice had not only arrived much before him but had changed into the outfit she had worn for the interview. She was also absorbed in conversation with a tall, gangly young man hanging on to her every word.

'Gurney, this is David from the new University College of North Norfolk. His place is just a few months old and he's wondering if we can tell him what he should do in ninety-nine years' time when they run their centenary.'

At this the young man took a gulp of his warm white wine and asked Alice if she'd like a re-fill. Before Gurney could speak he returned with two large glasses of wine and a gin and tonic which Alice tipped merrily into her glass. Her white blouse, grey pleated skirt, and the pearls gave the impression that she might easily have appeared in *Fatal Attraction* or *The Girls of St. Trinians*. He realised he hadn't said anything yet to Alice or the David person.

'And where are you in North Norfolk?'

'Well Wells...'

'Well Wells ... the reduplicative?'

'Wells-next-the-Sea, actually. Nice place on the coast not far from Blakeney, which is not far from Sheringham, which is not far from Norwich, which is not far from civilisation. We're a sort of outpost of the University of East Anglia, bringing learning to a benighted, socially-deprived corner of this fair land, which – and I've only been there a year – I'm actually enjoying.'

It was the first time in a long time that Gurney had encountered an academic - and a young one at that - who acknowledged he actually enjoyed his work. Enjoyment, Gurney had learned early on, like truth, was the first victim of the academic culture. Enjoyment was something you did after work. Enjoyment was decidedly un-cool, light weight, and unproblematic. It had no *reach* or *significance*. Enjoyment was the *Double Locks* in just under three weeks' time. It was also the first time in a long time that Gurney had experienced the very modernist pang of jealousy. How dare this young bearded fool regale his research assistant, his colleague with banter about enjoyment! His murderous thoughts were interrupted by Johnston beaming at the assembled drinkers with what looked like a set of Balinese wind chimes in his right hand.

'Charge your glasses my charges and raise them please for our wives and lovers – and may they never meet!'

Clearly Smiley by name and Smiley by nature. Perhaps he would relax over dinner and get into the mood? Alice was clearly ready and willing to make a go of it. With any luck *rain clouds, lost keys, drying off in his room awaited...*

Alice and the David man had moved on from the geography of North Norfolk to Richard Dawkins's latest book, *God, no.*

Gurney decided to try and join in the discussion.

'I was just thinking, David, that Dawkins has clearly never been one to enjoy his work as you seem to.'

'I'm sure he enjoys the royalties and the bashing he gives the Jesus army', Alice said to his surprise. As they passed out of the bar Andrew Johnston handed them each a pack of papers and a playing card. Gurney had the Jack of Hearts, Alice the Queen of Spades, and David the King of the same suit. It looked ominously that after dinner they'd all be encouraged to discover their *true* Jack or *real* Queen or some such idiocy. Gurney waited for his bowl of consommé and glanced at his pack of papers. The programme appeared to consist of opportunities to eat and drink interspersed with *plenaries, breakout sessions*, and something called *working work-outs*. He thought about Amy and the *Past Times* nightdress.

'Good to see you smiling Gurney, what's the joke?'

'Consuming consommé, a curious alliterative interplay between verb and noun'.

Gurney was seated to her right, the gauche bearded lecturer from the University College of Wells-next-the-Sea appropriately to her left.

*

After the fourth and longest *breakout session* Gurney felt ready to do just that. It was five in the afternoon and they had spent the first day *storming, norming, forming* and *reforming*, something that had included speed dating, walking around the grounds with their eyes closed, and finally *being a bit of a card*, an activity that involved Gurney encouraging the rest of his group to discover his inner Jack of Hearts. *Deforming.* If he was honest some of all this had been fun – bumping into Alice behind the Lebanese cedar and telling David the bearded one that he clearly enjoyed being king of his own castle-next-the-sea. But there was just so much mindless diversion he could take. Standing at the tea urn was Alice looking bright-eyed in his direction.

'I'm not sure about you Gurney but I don't think I can take much more of this'. Gurney was surprised as she seemed to be well into the swing of things.

'What do you suggest?'

'That we leave.'

'Leave?'

'I don't see why not. Tomorrow looks like more of this followed by presentations which, I don't know about you, but I don't have a clue what I should be saying.'

'But where would we go?'

'We could call a cab and go and visit daddy.'

'Daddy?'

'Yes, we're not far and I called him last night thinking it might come to this.'

Gurney was impressed.

'We're not far and he said he'd pick us up from Ross-on-Wye whenever we want. And I want it now!'

Gurney agreed and thought about how much he too *wanted it now*.

She linked her arm through his and guided him towards the door.

'OK Gurney let's give Jerry a run for his money! Back here at 18 hundred hours, sharp!'

Gurney gave her a mock salute and walked briskly and lightly towards his room.

It had been remarkably easy to slip away, the turbaned doorman even helping them carry their bags to the taxi. They waited at the taxi rank in Ross-on-Wye. Gurney wondered how he should address him. 'My Lord' sounded too *toastmasterish* yet 'George' too familiar. Alice must have been reading his mind.

'He likes being called George by the way. Only mum calls him 'my Lord' and that's when she wants him to do something.'

'But do ask him to show you his picture of him being introduced to the House in his finest ermine. He's very proud of it.'

'Oh, and I think you're sleeping in my room.'

Dawkins was wrong. There is a God.

'I'm sleeping with you?'

'No, sorry to disappoint you...,' she laughed and clutched his arm.

'...you'll be sleeping in my old room. I'll be up the corridor in the old au pair's room. It's on suite. And I need a bath.'

Gurney liked George from the moment he roared up in his short wheel-base Landover, leapt out and threw his arms around his daughter.

'You must be Gurney. I'm George, and if you want to be formal, you can call me George.'

And so, George it was. In the two days Gurney spent in the noble Lord's company he heard nobody address him any differently. The journey from Ross to the village passed quickly, Alice's father regaling them with a series of anecdotes she had clearly heard before but which nonetheless provoked gales of mirth from both father and daughter. From the tone and content of the more risqué stories it was clear the Liberal Democrats were working hard to secure the vote of the philandering classes.

'It helps that most of the lower House constituencies are in the Celtic fringe, need for a pad in town, that kind of thing. It's all about deceit and the greasy pole, Gurney – and God forbid, I know enough about that.'

'Deceit Daddy?'

They both roared with laughter.

'No darling, the greasy pole. Remember that MEP from Warsaw we invited down who took a real fancy to you even with a 'very understanding wife' he told us who toiled away at home raising their bonny children?'

'You must excuse my father, Gurney, he has an advanced imagination. Just remember that only fifty percent of what he tells you will approximate to anything like the truth.'

They soon arrived at the house which appeared to be in darkness. As they stepped out and crunched their way across the gravel towards the front door Gurney felt the fresh air of the countryside and heard what sounded like the distant sounds of a gurgling stream. What a grand decision they had made to give Johnston the slip and come here. He soon found himself standing in a large well-lit kitchen – clearly hidden from outside – sipping large a glass of single malt whilst Alice's mother threw what looked like large prawns and mussels into a steaming wok.

'We've heard a lot about you Gurney from Alice.'

Lady Araminta Hildebrand was an attractive woman - part Bohemian, part Women's Institute - but clearly a shrewd match for her husband and daughter.

'What have you heard, Araminta? Remember I sit on the university disciplinary committee and Alice is still on probation.'

Gurney was equidistant between the old wood-burning stove and the wok that was now emitting a pungent aroma of fish and coriander.

He felt relaxed and happy, and relieved to be able to converse in a language he understood. The lady of the house smiled at him,

'She thinks you're brilliant but a little lost. But isn't that the fate of most academics these days?'

'Mum. You're like dad, hopeless, and anyway I didn't say he was brilliant.'

Alice put her hand on Gurney's sleeve.

'Remember Gurney that anything and everything anyone says here is only half true. And that's if you are lucky.'

'Lucky?'

'Words, Gurney, words. Daddy and mummy like to use them for fun, to play around, and I think to embarrass me and my brother, especially when we bring people home. It entertains them, the problem is, that it also entertains me. Must be genetic...'

They all laughed at this, and with steaming plates and bottles of very expensive looking white wine moved the short distance to the large oak kitchen table. After the meal Araminta had suggested they stay for two nights, he could ring in to the university and plead illness - laryngitis caused by an overdose of management speak.

'And an opportunity for Alice to show you the village – where's where and more importantly who's who. And where they park the Bentleys.'

It had been an enjoyable meal. Washed down with several bottles of – or so he was assured – a rare white Chianti.

'A little man I know, outside Sienna, has a small vineyard, most of the nectar he produces disappears down the throats of the locals but he owes me a favour, and well you know how these things work.'

Gurney nodded though completely mystified about how 'these things worked'. The noble Lord then regaled them with family holiday disasters, all of which cast a poor light upon him but a positive one upon the two women in his life. He was clearly practised in the oratorical skills of self-deprecation mixed with just enough pride in the accomplishments he had accrued in what seemed to Gurney had arrived more by chance than by design. At a lull in the conversation, Gurney pitched the question he had been wanting to ask all evening.

'George, do you enjoy your work in the Lords?'

'Interesting choice of words, Doctor Sleep. You could have asked me, as many do, about whether I find my work rewarding or useful or even preposterous. Let me think.'

He rubbed his chin in a mock rueful manner.

'Let's think for a moment, *enjoy*? Before I answer I should say that I don't really consider what I do as a job, as I'm not sure I actually *do* anything. But if I do I would say that what I am concerned with is much more a matter of moral philosophy.'

Alice, who was sitting directly opposite him, fixed her pale blue eyes upon his. And you, Gurney?

'I'm not a moral philosopher, Alice, my field - if you can call it that - is more the muddy back yard of contrastive linguistics.'

'And there is no moral dimension to that?'

'Don't divert attention from what I asked George, I want to hear why he considers any Parliamentary work he does do, moral philosophy?'

'It's all about mistakes, Gurney, the importance of making mistakes, something undervalued in philosophical thought, and of course unthinkable in what passes as political thought, an oxymoron if ever there was one.'

He paused - as Gurney laughed - and topped up their glasses. Both Araminta and Alice remained at the table, silent but attentive.

'We learn by our mistakes, and God forbid, I've made a few, but I have come to realise that what's important about politics is the very opposite of what motivates most to enter in the first place, doing what is right. For me, most of what I have achieved has come from learning from doing what was wrong and then learning from the experience. Certainty, in my view - and I might be wrong – this is the curse of the lower House, the braying self-righteous attached to some cause, socialism, the markets, or those wretched Greens, for example, forever looking to tell the nation what they believe - in the public interest of course – whilst this particular nation collapses around us.'

The two women began to clear the plates, each returning swiftly with a loaded cheese board, fruit, and a large bottle of port.

'But what about you Gurney? Are you in the same game or can you teach doubt and error? 'I suspect not from what Alice tells me about her new place of work, no offence intended I am sure.'

'And what did I tell you about the University, Daddy?'

George smiled indulgently at his daughter. He went on quietly and with a more serious note in his voice.

'Oh, you know, that they are either rich playgrounds like Oxbridge where you can have fun for three years before following daddy into the firm, or poor playgrounds, like your place, Gurney where you can also have fun for three years before following daddy into the jobcentre plus or whatever it's called. Not that it's your fault Gurney, God I don't envy you the task of trying to teach the young anything serious, and it'll get worse now they are having to pay higher fees for the privilege of being cajoled into something I suspect most see as an interruption...'

Gurney recognised the accurate portrayal of university life but felt he ought to take issue with the suggestion that nothing serious occurred or was at least was intended in the teaching of the callow and the young. And what of his own research? Was that not serious? Was the Centenary not a serious endeavour aimed, if Williams was to be believed, to communicate the very seriousness of his department's contribution to the shaping of the nation's linguistic, if not social, fabric?

'What you say about serious, is serious George, and rather than leap to the defence of my research, an aspect of which concerns the use of modal auxiliaries in common speech – don't laugh - I should say that unlike you I do have serious doubts. For example, I might be wrong about whether anything I do, centenary included, could remotely be called serious or to have anything to do with moral philosophy.'

Alice spoke.

'But isn't the Centenary serious Gurney? Certainly, at the interview I got the impression from Professor Williams that if it wasn't serious it was at least important. My father, here, considers himself important, like most of the people in this village, apart from the folk who run the shop and deliver the newspapers, but I don't think he is really serious, and if he was I don't think he'd like us to really think he was, would you daddy?'

'Yes, you're right as usual Alice, in that most of the MPs I work with recognise that you be important and entertaining, especially on Radio Four, but if you try to be serious, you'll inevitably be dull, unless you are David Attenborough who manages to be both important and serious. And I fear, the perception is that most universities are stuffed full of rather serious people who would like to be regarded as important but are in fact rather dull and not particularly important, though of course they think they are.'

Alice was drinking sparkling water. She offered Gurney a glass.

'Daddy, from what I know, which isn't much, for the Centenary to be a success, I reckon it is going to have to be serious and important, reminding people who come to it that there are some serious things still left in life, OK they might at first seem a bit dull – and you're too hard on yourself, Gurney - but they are important...and ...'

'...at least self-important?'

Alice and George laughed at Gurney's joke.

'No, I'm serious...'

At this Araminta joined in, the shared laughter diffusing the possibility of sourness creeping into the conviviality and alcohol of the evening., the long-lost love he was seriously in love with, and Alice the serious girl he was not in love with but who was an important player in his drive to gain recognition and promotion. His third ambition, sex could wait for the delivery from *Past Times* and the upstairs room at the *Double Locks Inn.*

Bed. His last thought was of the empty Chianti bottle and the map of Brazil.

Chapter Eleven

Truth - Above all, don't lie to yourself. The man who lies to himself and listens to his own lie comes to a point that he cannot distinguish the truth within him, or around him, and so loses all respect for himself and for others. And having no respect he ceases to love – Dostoyevsky, The Brothers Karamazov.

He awoke and for a moment wondered where he was. His head hurt. She was right, he was a little lost. From downstairs, he heard a deep male laugh followed by a chorus of applause. When had he or his mother ever applauded his father, or come to that anyone? Certainly, he had never received such an ostentatious show of appreciation from anyone, and had certainly never given one. At the end of one of his better lectures a couple of years ago a visiting Chinese student had bowed towards him and had followed this with three claps of his hand. There was a small tap on his door.

'Coffee downstairs in five minutes Gurney. Then I'll show you the village whilst Ma and Pa do church.'

He mumbled assent, hoping he gave the impression he was up and dressed. He quickly straightened his duvet and headed for where he thought the bathroom was, which turned out to be a study lined floor to ceiling with box files, books, and several half empty bottles of malt. A coffee mug inscribed, 'the lord help us' was on the desk next to a silver letter opener. The room overlooked the garden which meant that Alice's new room must be next door, the opposite room at the end of the corridor had to be the bathroom. Resisting the temptation to have a peek into her room, he entered the bathroom to discover it contained just a bath, shower, and wash basin. No loo. George looked up and smiled as he entered the bright kitchen.

'Loo? Ah the lavatory. There is one up near your bedroom but no one can ever find it on their first stay. There's another over there.'

He waved towards the back door.

'Interesting name, don't you think lavatory? Like 'napkin', a preserve of the middle class.'

Gurney remembered a paper given a few years ago, at his own university by a barking Marxist, whose theory was that the middle class kept the working-class children in their place by using an *elaborated code* that apparently only they knew. A senior army officer, for example, had told him that applicants would be automatically disqualified if they asked to go to the loo, and presumably wiped their hands afterwards with a serviette?

It was a lovely late Autumnal day. He felt relaxed and anonymous, he had an attractive companion beside him, , and had the prospect of a pub lunch ahead. He almost felt happy.

'What are you smiling at?' She looked up from the paper.

'You, and how much you are like your father, and wondering whether there's much of my father in me.'

'Would that worry you if there was?'

'I suppose it would depend on what I'd inherited, I don't know, his indecision perhaps.'

They had left the house and were now walking towards the village. George and Araminta had gone ahead. Something to do with flowers, she had said, and a little 'local difficulty,' George had added with a chuckle. So far Gurney hadn't seen anything resembling a Bentley, clearly one of George's exaggerations. At that moment, a Rolls Royce silver cloud glided by. Alice clapped with glee.

'That's the first one, Lord Tresize, lives in a bungalow outside the village, lost his money on Black Tuesday or something but couldn't bring himself to sell the Rolls.'

'Who owns the other Bentleys - assuming George was right about the number but wrong about the make?'

'Viscount Templeton, a dispossessed Irish peer owns one, and does have a Bentley, but he's also an atheist so it's unlikely we'll see him this morning. And the other one is driven by Sir Vikram Patel, who made a pile from lime pickle, and is angling to join daddy in the House, if his increased levels of donating to party funds are anything to go by.'

There was clearly more to the village than met the eye. They were strolling down Horn Street which consisted of two rows of attractive stone cottages. There was *Weaver's Cottage* next to *The Spinners*, names that spoke redolently and distantly of the village's long past commercial life. Just over the stone bridge, was an impressive ruin of a building that seemed to be making its mind up about whether it should be a Fourteenth Century ruin or Victorian folly built to look like one. Beyond the ruin - but in sight of the castle - was the *George Hotel* outside which the Silver Cloud was parked. Next to it Alice's father was leaning his bike up against a wall. They wandered over and looked at the tariff framed behind a pretty glass window box.

'£100 per night? Bit pricey don't you think?'

Alice seemed to think the cost reasonable.

'It's for the Americans who love coming here. If you know William who runs it he'll readily offer you a very good rate, especially if you stay for more than a night. Daddy also thinks it's popular with what he calls the rumpy-pumpy set from Frome, retired from the City at sixty and with time - and their secretaries on their hands.'

Gurney rested a hand gently on the warm bonnet of the Rolls.

'Lord Templeton is presumably just calling in for a spot of lunch?'

Again, he was surprised.

'No, he helps behind the bar. Parks the car here as a piece of free advertising. 'Ringing the changes,' he says'.

Gurney laughed and whilst doing so reflected upon the fact that he hadn't laughed so much in such a short space of time. At some point, they'd have to address the decidedly unfunny matter of the Centenary action plan. She read his thoughts.

'We'll need to concoct something for Bundy by the time we get back?'

Gurney agreed and added that it was Bundy who needed to be convinced. Williams was on their side along with the whole department who would agree to anything so long as it didn't involve any effort on their part. Alice turned her face to his.

'We'll be fine just as long as we can show we're on top of things.'

Gurney looked at his research assistant. He hadn't realised just how blue her eyes were. He thought of the no doubt pink bedroom at the back of the George – all coaching inns had them – and how reasonable one hundred pounds was if you checked in with a pretty girl who was 'on top of things.'

'Penny for your thoughts?'

He blushed and pointed towards the church.

'When do they come out? And you're quite right we should cobble something together to convince Bundy that the retreat was in fact an advance.'

Mid-day sunshine sparkled on the stream that gurgled past the church, a mother duck and her brood heading purposefully across the road.

'Bundy would approve.'

'He would?' he asked.

'Ducks in a row. It's one of his favourites along with 'listen up',' she continued to look directly at him.

'One of the things I learned at Boden's was work out quickly who is the most important person you work for – and that is not necessarily your boss – and then to write up all your reports in the language they speak. Powerful people not only love the sound of their own voices but they like to read it in print too. Sort of validates them, makes them feel that the slippery climb has been worth it.'

Gurney wondered whether he was 'the most important person' she worked for. And whether he was in fact her boss? Technically he was her line manager, a concept full of positionality but bereft he suspected of any authority. He looked at her with admiration.

'We'll brainstorm it on the train, then we can shape it up when we get back.'

'Not *we* - Dr Sleep - but me, it's my job remember to assist you.'

He said nothing suddenly worried the lead duck might end up under the wheels of a speeding Silver Cloud. George waved at them from outside the church. Araminta seemed nowhere to be seen.

'Are you two joining us for lunch? At the George.'

Two bottles of Argentinean Malbec accompanied Sunday roast, followed by a dessert of apple pie and custard. They could certainly live like lords in this place.

'Her ladyship's hoping to join us once she's sorted out our little *local difficulty.'*

Gurney was seated next to Alice with George opposite them. For a ludicrous moment, he imagined whisking a diamond ring out of his pocket and asking Alice for her hand in marriage, blessed by the benevolent smile of the noble *pater familias*.

'You are about to ask me something?'

Gurney put down his fork and lent forward.

'When you say *local difficulty*, might it be connected to the chap I see entering with your mother?'

Before he could answer Araminta advanced smiling accompanied by a tall, wiry man who looked a little like Mervyn Peake, a glum expression suggesting that if he was the *local difficulty* it wasn't *little*.

Gilbert was the curate of the church which he told them was nine hundred and ninety-nine years old, though there was a small group of parishioners, led by a retired professor of history, who considered it to be older, and were therefore adamantly opposed to any plans to celebrate a tercentenary that should have been celebrated two years ago. George turned to Gurney.

'Gurney, you're experienced in these centenary things and so we thought it would be good for you two to discuss strategy and whatever. We're having Gilbert over tonight for supper and we'd like, for once, to encourage our guests to talk shop, and that includes you Alice given you are in on all this too.'

The curate brightened up at this, though Gurney wasn't sure if it was the prospect of Alice rather than the prospect of a discussion about strategy that lightened his mood. Gurney wasn't sure he liked the look of him. He spoke with that forced sincerity vicars seemed to use these days and he was clearly a cleric on the make, his curacy here a necessary stepping-stone to an urban bishopric. The fact that he was young, mid-thirties, held two degrees from Oxford, and was a member of Synod clearly marked him out for the fast track. Other than that, he appeared arrogant, overbearing and possibly, the more he talked, irreligious, something that would clearly be no impediment to higher office. He seemed gilded. And glib. But Gurney possessed enough self-awareness to entertain the possibility that he was just jealous of this cleric's assumption that it was just a matter of time before he would receive his earthly reward.

They left the pub and Alice suggested a walk up along the river bank to a large hill that she promised offered spectacular views from whence they had come, and the opportunity to walk off their heavy lunch. Perhaps she'd tell him a little more about Curate Gilbert and what she thought of him. Instead they walked in silence along the river bank, Gurney thinking about Alice and her blue eyes. Since they'd left for the away-day weekend he hadn't thought about votive candles or the not too distant tryst with an old flame dressed in a flame-resistant Victorian nightdress. He looked back towards the village and for a moment thought he saw Alice and himself walking slowly towards them. This time they were walking hand in hand.

*

They gathered for pre-dinner drinks in the large reception room at the front of the house. It had a coolness that often accompanies rooms rarely used. Araminta had changed into jeans and an expensive-looking pale blue silk shirt with the collar turned up. Her daughter was similarly attired in a tartan shirt set off by a row of dark stones around her neck. Gurney was relieved to see George wearing pretty much what he had worn the night before; he reduced to recycling a white shirt he'd worn on the first night of the retreat. At least the antiperspirant was new. The curate was yet to arrive with or without a Mrs. Curate. Gurney doubted there would be a better half, clerics these days tending to be either celibates or closet gays.

They each held a glass. Araminta said, 'Gilbert will be along shortly. He's still working on resolving his *little local difficulty* which seems to involve everyone wanting to help but no-one willing to work with anyone else.'

'Sounds familiar,' boomed George who was looking for a corkscrew in the bottom drawer of a huge Welsh dresser.

'What about the universities, Gurney? Co-operatives or a nest of vipers?'

'Nest of vipers I'm afraid George, though there are one or two of us, Alice included, who hang on to the idea of the collegial.'

'You are miles away Gurney, what are you thinking?'

He was helping Alice lay the table for dinner before joining Araminta and George in the front room for more drinks, she the crockery and cutlery, he the condiments and sauces.

'Nothing really, just musing on the linguistic sources of sauces.' She laughed and for a moment he wondered whether his tendency to be flippant in her presence was an altogether appropriate response given their professional relationship.

They were into their second drink when the curate arrived. Alone. He was dressed as if he spent extended periods of time in draughty parlours, wearing a woollen roll neck of the kind popular in the 1970s over which was a well-worn Harris Tweed jacket with leather patches on the elbows. They were sitting around a beautiful circular dining table in one of the chilly front rooms. Gurney was sitting opposite Alice with the curate to his left, Araminta opposite him with George at the head of the table.

'You're looking thoughtful Gurney. Your work perhaps? Hope Araminta and I are not keeping you from it?'

'Not at all George, far from it. In fact, as we are all here may I take this opportunity to formally thank you, first for rescuing us, and second for your much-appreciated hospitality.' They raised their glasses, Gilbert and Alice clinking theirs for a second time.

'And to your tercentenary, Gilbert. Hope it's ten times as successful as ours!'

Gilbert gave Alice a warm smile which Gurney interpreted as conspiratorial. Perhaps they shared a torrid past? But wasn't he new to the village?

The curate looked towards Gurney.

'The trouble is that I'm not convinced that any of our parishioners, apart from the meddling professor, know or frankly care about what it is we are supposed to be commemorating. Ivor Trezise who has offered to chair our planning committee, for example, is keen to exploit the event for its tourist potential, 'put us on the map' whereas I, and I think George and Araminta here, have a different, perhaps higher purpose.'

Alice spoke. 'Which is?'

He twirled the wine is his glass and looked thoughtful.

'If I am honest - and I'm speaking in a personal capacity here - I'd say it is less to do with what we can make from the event, or – and this is where the professor takes issue- even less with what occurred back then; for me the celebration should be more about what we stand for now, a statement if you like of the enduring Christian values under threat from our secular media, militant atheism, scientism ...'

George looked towards Gurney.

'I'm not sure what scientism is Gurney but no doubt your university is on Gilbert's list of pernicious influences?'

Gurney paused and twirled the wine in his glass.

'Gilbert's church has certainly seen greater change in its purpose, raison d'être, attendance even, than my department has in the hundred years since its foundation. What links the two institutions of course - and I would suggest the decline of one has led to the rise of the other - is the Enlightenment, rationality, the spread of education, Man's search for evidence in what he has experienced of the world rather than being told what to believe.'

George interrupted him.

'But don't you do the same thing Gilbert? Instruct your young undergraduates in what to think, which explanation is worthier over another, which meanings are currently in vogue? In other words, which version of the enlightenment to believe in?'

The curate was quick to speak which was a relief to Gurney who wasn't sure of his ground.

'In one sense, I agree with Gurney, one enlightenment founded upon what are called scientific principles which has resulted in the diminution of another, an older Enlightenment, one based not upon evidence of what we can see or touch but rather on what we feel or know to be true.'

It was Gurney's turn to interrupt.

'You speak of truth Gilbert, something rarely spoken of in a university old or new. But it's not that we neglect the search for it – whatever it is - but rather what differentiates my Enlightenment from yours is *certainty*; once one of us discovers a truth you will find a queue of our peers waiting to shout him or her down, to pick holes in any certainty, to enlighten us if you like in the errors of our ways, to cast doubt upon our evidence and to shine a light on what we have missed or misunderstood. This enlightenment – which is more of a process than a product – is what lies at the heart of academic life, it is surely what our centenary should be celebrating.'

He hoped Alice was paying attention for he was sure to forget what sounded to him a convincing rationale for the Centenary. He had surprised himself. He had forgotten a time - if ever there was one - in which he had been called to defend the purpose of a university or more specifically his field. He dimly remembered an occasion, perhaps when he was talking to Albert after he had got his doctorate, when he had launched into an explanation of the relationship between cultural anthropology and contrastive linguistics: the pivotal role of culture in creating forms of representation – words, phrases, idiom – that were surely shaped by modes of communication – music, art, poetry – which in turn were organised and used to generate meanings, different 'ways of seeing' - to quote Berger - the evidence for which was provided by the painstaking gathering of how different cultures used their own evolving language system to provide legitimacy for their world views. It was *evidence* not *belief* that mattered; what a researcher felt or believed to be the case mattered not a jot, what was important was the evidence collected, collated, analysed and then published; which in turn would then be scrutinised and questioned by the next generation of *uncertain* researchers.

George had been listening closely to what Gurney had said but turned to Gilbert.

'Is there room for doubt in your enlightenment Gilbert? Room to learn from your mistakes? I ask because as these two unfortunates know from our discussion last night, it is an interest of mine.'

'And it is an interest I share,' said Gilbert helping himself to more wine. Araminta and Alice had begun to talk quietly to each other. He went on,

'C.S. Lewis, probably our greatest religious writer, embraced the concept of doubt in his journey of faith, and more recently I've been reading a chap called Ward who takes on Dawkins in his, 'Why there almost certainly is a God'. What is interesting to me -an uncertain believer if you like - is the conclusion that probably there is likely to be someone or something out there. That fills me at least with hope, whereas Dawkins fills me with, what? Regret I suppose that he can't see any bigger picture.'

George clearly relished this kind of discussion.

'I think you'd find, too Gilbert that if he'd titled his book 'Why I believe in God' it would probably have sold a few copies on the religious retreat circuit but he'd have had little chance with a broader more sceptical audience. And isn't it very British to hedge one's bets, to err on the positive, don't you think? It's the 'almost certainly' that will appeal to the British reader. Says a lot about our culture and our faith. Makes me think there might be mileage in a memoir, 'Why there almost certainly is social democracy', the only trouble being - and I talk as a convert – is what's left of social democracy now has to be dressed up as the Third Way or some such vacuous sound-bite dreamt up by Alistair Campbell on the wet Wednesday afternoon. It's almost as if we're embarrassed to talk straight when it comes to politics or religion in this country, preferring to relegate it to the purely academic. But I'll stop before I start becoming very dull...'

He winked at Alice and moved over to the sideboard to open two more bottles of red.

Chapter Twelve

Extenuating circumstances has different meanings in academia and law. In general, it refers to circumstances that excuse somebody from a punishment they would receive under normal conditions - Wikipedia

There were hundred and thirty-nine emails awaiting Gurney when he arrived back from the weekend. He settled down to read them. He wasn't exactly happy but he felt good. The ghastly retreat only served to make what followed more enjoyable; the meeting with Araminta and George, the walk along the river, even the dinner with curate Gilbert who turned out to be more interesting than Gurney had given him credit for. And Alice? Perhaps the main source of his inner wellbeing? Half the emails originated from the owner of a Morris Minor, a lecturer in fibre-optics, who insisted - contrary to the evidence of many who had walked past his car - that the lights were *not* left on but rather gave the appearance that they were was the result of an optical illusion caused by the late Autumnal sun. A further ten emails then followed from the same lecturer apologising for the previous emails with a suggestion that the university invest in a fibre-optic vehicle early warning system currently being developed in his lab.

Two messages were from students of his Saturday occasional class asking whether he was likely to miss any more of them, another from the conference secretary of the Linguistics in Europe Society (LIES) asking him if he would consider presenting a paper at a conference in Oslo the following week. Apparently, a key speaker had dropped out at the last minute and if he could make it they'd pay all expenses. Tucked away at the bottom was a mail from Phoenix tagged, *our weekend*. She was coming! It was on! Now he felt more than good. And a freebie to Oslo too! The future was more than conditional.

There were also two mails from Linden, one flagged as urgent. And a final message from the owner of the Morris Minor apologising for using the intranet for the purposes of self-promotion but would any colleague like to buy a motor vehicle? He heard the heavy tread outside his door and tried to look busy.

'Ah! You are here at last boyo. Prepare yourself for a shock'. He thrust his pelvis forward into the face of Gurney who had swivelled around to greet the professor.

'But a fucking pleasant shock I must say! It's Bundy, or should I say, Bunking Bundy whose run off with half the university's reserve fund, and to rub salt in the wound has taken lovely Lucy, Second Year English. Blonde, blue eyes and very ...'

'Lovely?'

'Yes, and fucking rich too, if she decides to stick with Bundy.'

Gurney found himself once again trying to work out the mood of his senior colleague who was clearly enjoying the news.

'How do you – we – know he's disappeared with the money and the student?'

'His dear wife, bless her, is so worried about his state of mind, that she thought it only decent and proper to share with the Vice-Chancellor the contents of a brief text her loving husband shared with *her* before he, and his lovely bag carrier, embarked upon their EasyJet flight to one of our nearest tax havens, and presumably a destination with no extradition treaty with this benighted Isle.'

'I haven't seen the note but that nice temp in the VC's office tells me it runs along the lines of 'My dearest Margery - blah blah blah - being in love is different from loving - blah blah blah - can't wait to get into a younger pair of knickers, yours ever Bundyikins or whatever endearment he chose to sign off with. I never liked the guy, as you know, but you have to give him some credit for going out with less of a whimper and more of a bang. And let's not forget the 'reluctantly-given' taxpayer's money.'

'And we know the money's gone and that he took it?'

'Well that's a moot point but I think it was Lord North who famously said, 'why let the truth get in the way of a good story'; however, what we do know is that Bundy recently persuaded the University to open an off-shore bank account somewhere in the Caribbean over which he had sole- signing rights, a fact that has left the VC rushing about in crisis mode, saying to whoever will listen 'Wot me guv? I know nothing!''

'And us? The Centenary?'

'Good question, Mycroft, good question. From what I hear from the fifth floor it'll probably go ahead but given the speed of the university's legal services, we've been told to expect a green light but to organise something much less grand, on-the-cheap in other words. Which'll mean warm glasses of in-house bog standard white unless somebody can come up with a benefactor riding in upon a Linguistic white horse.'

Something 'much less grand' might also have implications for Alice on her temporary contract. He liked Alice and the last thing he wanted now was to have to organise the Centenary by himself, 'less grand' or otherwise.

'And what about Alice? Her contract's for a year, isn't it?'

Williams looked thoughtful an expression of faux concern on his face.

'Ah Alice, yes and your have-it-away weekend. By the way how was it and did you?'

Before he could reply he turned towards the door.

'Given the circumstances don't bother producing your report for Bundy, unless that is you know of a cheap flight to the Cayman Islands. I'll get back to you later when I hear more about what the men in suits are doing but for the moment rest assured about Alice. She is safe in your hands.'

And with a smirk he thundered out of the room.

Gurney re-opened the Phoenix email. She had signed off, 'in haste. Love A'. There was a soft knock on his door. Alice entered carrying two Styrofoam cups and what looked like flapjacks on a small plastic tray. She beamed at him, clearly unaware of the impending crisis. Gurney had learnt from his parents that bad news is better delayed, concealed or even better never mentioned. Though this increases the negative consequences of the news when it does surface, it makes the present moment at best ok. Aren't storm clouds always on the horizon? his mother had told him. Like all pessimists, Gurney felt that if everything was bound to end badly and so it was only reasonable to delay as much as possible the arrival of the awful.

'Have you heard about that Alan Bundy running off with that student, Lucinda somebody or other?'

'Lucy, actually.'

'It's all over the university. And there's a rumour he was seen last night trying to find her in her hall of residence, telling some people in her corridor that he had something important to share with her and that he had to find her immediately.'

Alice was wearing a pair of blue jeans he remembered from the weekend with a white hoodie emblazoned with the university's logo on the back. She looked younger. He swallowed a large piece of flapjack and nodded in agreement at what she was saying, and at what he was thinking. They agreed to meet later in the day to review plans, to think less grand...

The landline rang. It was Amélie, a temp. from the Departmental Office who clearly is surprised to find him sitting at his desk.

'Glad to have caught you. I received a phone call yesterday from a gentleman called Albert who rang to say you should call your mother on your return and not to worry.'

Not to worry not to ring her? Or not to worry about the call to ring her? Or perhaps not to worry that Albert had called him and not her? Gurney decided not to worry about his worry and to call her later.

He looked at the Phoenix email again and checked the date of the weekend. Two weekends from now. It could end well, couldn't it? Success, after all, didn't have to be delayed failure, did it? The past weekend was a good example and let's not forget Alice's chaste kiss outside his bedroom door. The next weekend away offered the possibility of more than that - and from the other side of the door too. Gurney wished he was like George, certain of his doubts, content to be wrong, eager to learn from his mistakes; or like Gilbert, fighting the good fight with the trusty sword of Christian principles. But then these were confident men certain about their uncertainties, aware that they were important people capable of even being dull in an important way. Who had said, 'if we want things to stay as they are, things will have to change'? Whenever he wanted things to change, they always stayed as they were.

His Outlook diary reminded him that in one hour he was due to teach the third-year elective module, *taboo language in a globalised age*. It was rated 'popular, interesting and fun' by last year's students, something he thought he might need if the Centenary collapsed. He hated being unprepared or more what it would say about him – 'Gurney Sleep? Nice chap, but rather a second ranker don't you think?' Inspired he jotted down: 'shit', 'wank' and 'fuck' next to which he wrote, 'Anglo-Saxon sexual connotations, feminist critique?' Plenty for a good twenty-minute plenary after which they could pair up and exchange personal levels of offensiveness drawn from their own experience. At the end, he'd use up at least fifteen minutes reprising the module assignment which he'd decided would involve the content analysis of a popular television programme which relied for its popularity on the excessive use of taboo language. The previous year most students had opted to write about one of Gordon Ramsay's programmes which had met all the assessment objectives but had cast little light upon the deeper theoretical issues. Perhaps *Woman's Hour*?

He arrived on time to find the lecture hall empty, not even the Chinese student had remained. Bastard. Perhaps Charlie Hickson had called an emergency down tools and he hadn't heard? Or more likely word had gotten out that he too had done a bunk and it wasn't worth making the effort. On route back from the lecture hall he passed the door of the departmental assistant head of school which was slightly ajar. Gurney liked Graham Steer whose major responsibility was timetabling, room bookings and internet maintenance, duties that had earned him promotion to senior lecturer. He was younger than Gurney and made no bones of the fact that in two years' time the baton could be passed to him if he so wished - or was so deluded. Graham also knew what was *going on* and would be a reliable for current news of the Bundy debacle. He was also a champion of the cross-disciplinary, inter-disciplinary, even multi-disciplinary combinations of degree subjects such as medical technology and ethical studies, or the intriguing 'journalism in the new age' coupled with media studies, the latter an innovation the Vice-Chancellor liked to trumpet as one that not only guaranteed undergraduate recruitment but also a job at the end of it. Not that any graduates so far had found their way into the BBC or mainstream press, those organisations still preferring to recruit Oxbridge graduates with degrees in Latin or Greek.

Graham liked to consider himself a 'touchy-feely sort of guy', in touch with his self, keen to communicate, convinced that academia was a poorer place without an emotional stream running through it.

Gurney pushed open the door to find the room empty though the computer screen glowed with a picture of a wallflower with the caption, 'even wallflowers are loved'. Gurney left a post-it on the screen asking for any news of Bundy, and more importantly, the Centenary budget. Graham was a reliable source on both counts.

He drifted back to his office. As he entered he had, what Albert might have described, as a senior moment. In other words, he asked himself, 'why am I here?' Or more critically and more bitterly something along the lines of, 'so far today, the tax payer has forked out about two hundred quid – what he estimated he was paid for a mornings work – for me to read and delete a bunch of emails, then listen to the demented ravings of my head of department, then inadequately prepare for a lecture no one attended, then have coffee and flapjacks with a research assistant I possibly fancy, rounded off with a non-meeting with another colleague, the purpose of which will be to glean gossip about a potential university scandal that might cost the institution a considerable amount of money. No wonder the budgets are being cut.'

He looked at his Outlook Diary. Long ago he had decided that leaving any hour blank left him open to charges that at some point in the working day he wasn't 'doing something', 'something' being defined by the university as 'teaching, scholarly activity or research.' The first was self-explanatory, the second was supposedly any activity that involved getting up to date by reading the latest journal, and the third – and most important – the holy grail of academic life: the 'output.'

The trouble was that Gurney felt 'put out', listless and unproductive. He thought about the Oslo conference. Perhaps his mood suited the theme of this year's meeting, 'emotional globalisation'. He hadn't a clue what it meant but he was sure he could find some links to his perennial interest in the modal auxiliary verb? Williams had once told him,

'Gurney boy, never expend more time before the conference on producing your paper, than you spend afterwards in the bar forgetting about it. And first don't delude yourself that they're there to listen to your words of wisdom – its networking and finding out who is doing what to whom, that has drawn them to some god-forsaken hole south of the perma-frost.'

In the end, he did what every academic did: re-read what was generally regarded as his best publication – delivered two years ago at an obscure meeting in Malta – gutted it for dross, re-dressed and re-tuned it with the new theme in mind, re-titled and updated references to include at least one by the conference chair, changed the font and then bobs your uncle conference paper and potential publishable 'output'. He was on a roll. What else did he have to do? Meet Alice, ring Albert, re-schedule the missed Saturday lecture, contact Linden, and think about Phoenix. And send a thank you letter to George and Araminta.

He leant back in his chair. It wasn't such a bad life. He could hardly complain. OK, so he wasn't recognised or promoted but unlike other poor sods who were on fractional or temporary contracts he at least had tenure. And with the Centenary he was getting there – the LIES conference might lead to something, he could offer to turn the proceedings into an edited volume, perhaps even offer to host next year's bash here? And OK so he wasn't in a relationship but – hey - hadn't he just spent a very enjoyable weekend with a very attractive woman - and let's not forget Phoenix, whose flight was imminent.

Lunch. Gurney trolled over the new refectory in one of the wings. The canteen had just been voted the 'sixth healthiest refectory on the South Coast' and were offering free chips with every salad to celebrate. Talking of health, Gurney was a little concerned at his recent increased in-take of alcohol.

Universities might 'be fountains of knowledge where students go to drink' but he needed to be careful if he was to arrive at the *Double Locks compos mentis.*

With a commitment to drink a maximum of two pints, he left later that day for his appointment with Linden at the *Open House.* They settled at their table in the far corner and whilst Linden went over to order their usual pint, Gurney considered what he wanted to discuss with his friend and the order in which the various topics might be prioritised. News of Bundy first. Apparently, Linden had the low-down from the fifth floor.

'His biggest mistake was to take the student with him. From what old ma Bundy has told the VC's office, she's having cold feet now she's twigged that she might be regarded as an accessory after the fact.' He took a healthy swig of lager and beamed at Gurney.'

'Which is?'

'Which is, what?'

'The fact that she might be an accessory to?'

'Well, what we do know from Mrs. B, who seems to be in touch with the student the student, is that she thinks it's all been a terrible mistake and that if she takes the next plane home can she claim extenuating circumstances regarding her assignment which I understand is due in today?'

Gurney crunched a pork scratching.

'Did she say where she was?'

'No, but her mother says she heard an airport announcer mention something about Port of Spain which tells us they are in the Caribbean somewhere. Trinidad, isn't it?' Or Grand Cayman?

Gurney laughed and washed down his scratching with a generous mouthful of beer.

'And even if he is apprehended we may never get our money back. These off-shore havens aren't exactly paragons of virtue when it comes to even admitting any ill-gotten loot has ended up in one of their off-shore accounts.'

Linden nodded. It was time to move on to more pressing matters. The weekend. Or rather his weekend. Gurney's weekend with Amy could wait. He looked across the table at Linden. Linden. A good mate. A good bloke. A buddy. A colleague. A fellow linguistician. An ally. A fellow weekender. He tried saying 'fellow linguistician' aloud and realised he was getting well and truly pissed.

Time to discuss *the* weekend He has alternated pork scratching with gulps of lager before launching into his interrogation.

'Remind me when she's agreed to come down, Lind?'

'As I said, we agreed on the weekend after next. She'll visit her brother on the Saturday morning, after which she'll swing by and we'll hook up in town.'

'Then what? Early film and meal or bite to eat and then the late film?'

Gurney smiled benignly enjoying the rolling of his chosen words. Choices - that's what Linden needed.

'And then back to your own place or an overnight somewhere romantic? But be tasteful.'

It was Linden's turn to smile.

'I've taken the best room at the *Globe* - which if you remember - is walking distance away from the Bombay Brasserie which has a special on at weekends.'

Gurney drained his beer – he could do with an Indian now – and walked over to the bar which was filling up with what looked like junior bank executives ordering pints of Guinness and whiskey chasers. He steered his way back past two lads and a beefy type eyeing his empty chair.

'I'm not sure about the curry, Linden. With no disrespect to the millions and millions on the Indian sub-Continent, but I'd steer clear of a hot curry - there is something a tad cheap about the Brasserie, and though I'll admit that the 'Eat as much as you can' is a good deal, it's not likely to curry favour -if you'll excuse my words - with a rising star of the Registry. And anyway, you can't drink wine with an Indian, and wine is the romantic drink of the Saturday evening when you're on the pull.'

Linden seemed impressed not only with his dextrous use of common parlance but also the logic of his argument.

'So where would you suggest?'

'Have you thought about cooking a meal for just the two of you at your place? M&S have a great deal on now that includes a bottle of wine. Or you could cook your signature dish?'

'Salmon in a white wine mushroom and tarragon sauce, but I haven't made it in a while and you're forgetting that I've booked the room at the *Globe*. I can hardly say, 'let's leave the washing up Lucy and head over town to a little bedroom I've booked' when we've got my own bedroom just above the kitchen. Sounds a bit odd, don't you think?''.

Gurney agreed.

'True, you might as well stay where you are but if your place is like mine it's hardly what either of us would call romantic.'

Linden decided it was time to move the discussion on, something he found increasingly difficult when discussing anything with an academic.

'Wherever we do decide to eat - and it isn't important now - I was wondering if you'd still like to meet up with us for pre-dinner drinks? Give you an opportunity to say hello.'

Gurney ordered another round of drinks despite his promise to be limited to a couple. They eventually agreed a plan: they'd meet up at the *Welcome Inn,* after which Linden and Lucy would walk to the refurbished dining room of the *Globe* where, after a candle-lit non-curry-wine-drinking romantic meal, they would repair upstairs to the best room at the back of the Inn, and he would stop downstairs for a swift half. Linden wasn't sure.

'And where does Lucy think she might be staying on Saturday night? Not with her brother I assume? Presumably she hasn't arranged to just have a meal with you and then call a cab to take her off to one of her female friends?'

'What do you mean?'

'It's crucial Linden that you've thought through all eventualities, have a sense of what she's expecting, and what she might agree to when the moment of decision arrives.'

'Moment of decision?'

'Yes, when she agrees to forgo the dessert and trundles up with you to the bijou bedroom furthest from the car park.'

Linden looked downcast. Brutal but necessary. Like a mock examination, it was worth the pain *now* if his friend was to reap the gain *later*. He agreed with Gurney that it was essential he covered all bases and – yes it was a good idea to send Lucy a brief email confirming the weekend and suggesting too that they push the boat out and stay at the *Globe*. 'Should he book a room '- note the use of the singular? 'Avoid drinking and driving, the responsible option?' As Gurney reminded him, a way to a woman's heart was through her social conscience.

The weekend. They agreed. It was on. And more important, Linden getting it off was also on. The definite article.

Chapter Thirteen

A conference is a formal get-together where people talk (or "confer") about a chosen topic, like when your office holds a conference to talk about the problem of snoring during meetings - Vocabulary.com

A s he sat down the telephone rang. When he stood up it continued to ring. The coffee on arrival had done little to defuse his post-hangover sense of hopelessness. It was from Amélie in the office, would he ring a certain Albert who had called again. Nothing urgent. About his mother. His, not Albert's.

Gurney stirred his coffee with a pencil. What if it was in fact *very* urgent, his mother lying on her death bed pleading with limpid eyes to her one and only caring neighbour to call her only child, her rasping plea fading away, her last thoughts being of an ungrateful son too busy to meet the last wishes of his dying mother? He felt the tears coming to his eyes as he leafed through his diary for Albert's number. He would ring him first and ascertain where his mother was, and possibly the reason that lay behind the call. He dialled the number. If Gurney was to list his top ten irritants of the communications age, at the top would be those who answer a call with *Yes?* Gone are the days when etiquette demanded name, rank, and number. And anyway, what does 'yes' mean? 'Yes, I am here' – patently obvious – 'yes I am hearing you?' Or perhaps, 'yes, I have agreed to continue this conversation?' Or more likely these days, 'yes but you're not getting anything out of me. Just because you I have acquired a means of communication don't expect that you can take liberties and expect me to tell you who I am.' As he mother liked to say, 'don't give anything away on the telephone dear, you never know who they might be or what they might want.' Thus, his parents were proud owners of a telephone through which they received very few calls.

An older female voice – presumably Doris - appeared to have answered the phone.

'Yes?'

'It's Gurney. Mrs Sleep's son. I've received a message from Albert that I should call...'

Silence.

'There's nothing wrong is there?'

A shorter silence.

'I'll call Albert, he can talk to you.'

Now Gurney felt a tremor of worry.

Death bed, last thoughts, ungrateful son.

A deeper voice.

'Yes?'

Gurney resisted the temptation to ask who it was

'Hi Albert, it's me Gurney.'

'Oh...'

Being a teacher, he had come to realise that carries with it the temptation to educate the public at large, people, like Albert in particular, in the niceties of telephone usage. As he had learnt when he had remonstrated once with a telephone caller about her misuse the past perfect tense, the English as a rule, do not take kindly to correction - or education come to that.

'Is mum all right?'

'Ah Gurney, yes, she's fine but it wasn't her I was ringing about - it was you.'

Gurney coughed twice to remind Albert he was still there, whilst he thought.

What on earth did he mean? Was he about to enter into some sort of *pater familias* role and chide him for his absences?

'The long and the short of it lad is that this year, what with your mother being frailer and all that, Doris and I thought it best if she spends Christmas with us, which brings me to the purpose of my call.'

His plan, which Gurney readily agreed to would be that he and Doris would host his mother on Christmas day, and of course, he was welcome to come as well, and to bring along 'your lady friend...'

'...my lady friend?'

Albert clearly knew more than he was letting on or more likely was just being polite in extending an invitation to a partner. It was the *your* which suggested a particular female friend. Perhaps his mother had told him about Moira or more worryingly he had mentioned Amy or Alice during his last visit.

*

The President of the Linguistics in Europe Symposium (LIES), Professor Rupert de Waal was a large man sporting a domed forehead, fleshy hands, and flashy clothes - yellow spotted handkerchief in top pocket, matching bow tie and scrupulously polished Oxford brogues. He extended both hands towards Gurney. His only weakness - amongst his many strengths - was his lisp which manifested itself is his tendency to turn an 'r' into a 'w', something he had decided to accentuate, to turn it to his advantage. LIES. Academics love acronyms, they hint of power lost to management and those with real jobs, a code known only to the initiated, an opportunity to create something new, something witty, something memorable.

As Gurney welcomed the slightly warm, though damp, hands into his own he wondered if he might buy a spotted cravat at the airport on the way out. Rupert liked to greet all newcomers to the conference and therefore to himself personally, hence the situation he now found himself in.

'Welcome to Oslo Doctor Sleep, welcome, dear boy, welcome - or may I call you Gurney?'

Standing next to de Waal was a slight diffident looking man his hands clasped behind his back a little like the Prince Philip. Rupert de Waal extended his arm leftwards.

'Walph here will provide you with all you need to know.'

'Walph?'

'Yes, our membership officer. Marvellous scholar and teacher of the first wank.'

'Wank?'

There was not a flicker of disquiet from the membership officer who appeared genuinely bored by the encounter.

'Yes, absolutely first-wate.'

The professor prided himself on several things, the most oft repeated being that he had only ever worked with the metropolitan belt of the M25. Denied a chair from Oxford - his alma mater, a hurt that still rankled with him - he had vowed never, *ever* to seek an appointment anywhere other than at a university within the sound of Bow Bells. Thus, he had, at various times, been London's Benedict Cuthbert Professor of Applied Linguistics, the Basil Bernstein Professor of Elaboration, and was currently the Norbert Sieffert Professor of Contrastive Linguistics at one of those new universities just south of the river.

He was also unmarried. Wives he realised at an early stage in his career offered little in the way of advancement, few women at that time sitting upon appointment committees or grant-awarding bodies. No, it was better to be alone, free of the domestic scene he considered at best a hindrance and at worse 'ghastly'. The speech impediment he adduced was a likely result of the tendency for the de Waal's to have inbred in the particular corner of Wallonia from which they originated. He also secretly harboured the view that a de Waal was really only ever to be attracted to another de Waal.

But he was not without his charm. In fact, he understood his duties as president of the Symposium was to lavish affection and praise upon all those who toiled beneath him, thus guaranteeing the success of this annual event. For those who had the misfortune to stand in his way he preferred to look the other way and simply refer to them as 'ghastly'.

Though pleasingly regarded as a workaholic, Rupert de Waal had established a reputation as a knowledgeable and highly effective wine connoisseur. He considered himself an expert on New World reds and especially the much-underrated Argentinean Malbec, a full-bodied, affable little number now increasingly to be found upon the shelves of the better supermarkets. De Waal had even gone as far as researching and writing a well-regarded paper on the grape's origins (Northern Burgundy if you ask) and its successful translation to the wooded hillsides of Chile and Argentina.

Before Gurney could say anything, de Waal had gone, his whinnying voice exclaiming to a new arrival, 'dear boy, so glad you could come, welcome, welcome.

Gurney looked around hoping he might catch sight of someone he knew, aware that he looked like a new boy in the school playground. Everyone appeared to be streaming out after de Waal, leaving Gurney to try and remember where his room was and, more importantly, why he'd agreed to come to this thing.

He quickly unpacked and headed out in the wrong direction of the bar. For some reason the dimly-lit carpeted corridors of the hotel reminded him of his mother. The walls were lined with lithographs of great Norwegian explorers of which there seemed to be far too many. He felt little like Scott must have felt - so near and yet so far - laughter and shrill cries coming from the bar crowd close by and yet tantalisingly out of reach.

Mother. He was never surprised by anything she said let alone asked. As a child, she was fond of telling others that he was a strange boy, always ready to ask the most ridiculous questions. Her favourites were paraded before the occasional visitors: 'mummy, where does the wind come from? Why do the floorboards squeak?' and her favourite, to which he still waited for an answer, 'who chooses our mummy and daddy?' her answer, 'God, does dear' neither satisfying the curious young child of nine or the university teacher of thirty-five. He would call her when he returned from this Nordic outpost.

It wasn't that his mother was unintelligent or lacking in any interest in him, his questions or what he had become. It was that she had become unsurprising. She was predictable. She Lacked in any kind of spontaneity, as if the burdens of marriage, childbearing and family life had squeezed out anything of the young girl who might, in an earlier age, have asked similar questions.

As he decided it was best to retrace his steps back to where he thought his room was, he recalled one occasion, shortly after he had been appointed to the university, when his mother had shown an interest in where he was about to work. Interestingly she had been more curious about his working environment than anything he might do in it.

He had been careful to invite her on a Friday afternoon - when most of his colleagues and certainly all his students - were unlikely to be around. If he avoided the office and the photocopy room, with any luck she wouldn't run into anyone. He wasn't sure why he felt less than thrilled at the chance that his mother might meet colleagues or administrators, some anxiety perhaps that she might expose his humble roots - or worse - that she might ask someone a rare question that would reflect badly upon him and his upbringing.

But she was clearly impressed by the eco-friendly spaciousness of the building and the fact that it had a coffee shop within it.

'Reminds me of Reading Station forecourt dear. Wouldn't be surprised if there isn't a W.H. Smiths in here as well.'

Gurney wasn't surprised either, the university recently deciding in favour of the installation of a branch of a local building society. She looked at his office, the view from his window, and his name on the door. Everything was *nice*.

'Very nice dear.'

It was then that she did something out of character and surprising. She asked him a question.

'But what *exactly* do you do, dear?'

Good question. And one he been asking himself for some time. He looked directly at the small woman sitting opposite him in the coffee bar.

'What do you think I do mum? I'm interested to know.'

Now it was her turn to look surprised, startled at the directness of the question, something she considered - if she was honest – well, impolite. But she was enjoying this opportunity to find out a little more about her son's work. His hair hadn't changed over the years, the small tuft that stuck up at the back a reminder of who he really was beneath the important person with his name upon the door.

'You teach students, dear, and write books. You gave me one after you passed your exam. I'm afraid I haven't had time to read it…'

It must have been the bound copy of his doctoral dissertation he had presented to his parents shortly after his successful defence. He didn't blame her for not reading it. Writing it was bad enough. He remembered seeing it placed in pride of place in the front room along with Stephen Hawkins book on time and another about an Edwardian Lady who collected plants. At least her book was full of beautiful illustrations, though it too had remained unread. Books were not part of the weft and weave of the Sleep household, they were something you took on holiday, and then for her it would be a Jean Plaidy or perhaps an Agatha Christie.

As he headed in the direction of the bar – the laughter was growing in intensity – he smiled to himself. Be honest, when was the last time he had been asked a direct question? Contrary to what the public might think, academics are some of the least questioning people he knew, unwilling - or in some case incapable - of asking anyone any question, for wasn't that the prerogative of the ignorant? A more useful approach when given the floor was to ask yourself a question and then provide the answer to the very same question in such a way that showed whoever was listening that you were an extremely clever chap well worth listening to. At the bar, he ran into the treasurer of the first wank. He seemed to recognise him this time.

'Ah Gurney, long time no see. How is it going in your little place by the sea?'

Before he had a chance to answer he was presented with both the answer to this question plus a series of further questions and answers that somewhat proved his point, though only to himself.

'Had an opportunity to examine down your way. Dreadful hotel and if I recall dreadful student. But at least you get to see parts of the country you wouldn't necessarily visit. You ever get to Cambridge?'

He said no.

'We must invite you to the little college thing we do each year, very informal'.

Gurney nodded and made to move past and on to the bar.

'Can I get you a drink?'

But he had gone. De Waal had provided an open bar offering a surprisingly good Chardonnay, a Malbec for those who preferred red, and beer for the rest. Gurney asked for a beer, took a frothy sip, and used the opportunity to glance around.

'And who are you?'

He was surprised he hadn't seen her when he'd entered.

Before he could say, 'Sleep – Gurney Sleep' she added,

'I am studying here in Oslo. Human Rights Education and Gender.'

She was leaning on the bar drinking what looked like a large glass of white grape brandy.

'I can't buy you a drink – they're free until we're called for dinner – but let me at least ask for one for you. What are you drinking?'

'I think I can do that for myself, thank you, but as you ask, Polish vodka 100% proof.'

Her accent was lilting, her looks dark, Italian, or perhaps Portuguese?

'Andrea von Hofmann, and before you ask, German.'

She said this with some pride.

'My father is from Berlin and my mother from Slovakia. She is a Romany who fled to Germany to escape persecution and instead found my father.'

He wondered what he knew about Romany gypsies or come to that persecution.

'They don't get a good press here, particularly with the recession, unemployment, coming over and stealing our jobs, that kind of thing.'

'Who, the Romanies or the Germans?'

'Well both I guess now I come to think of it. Tough times to be an outsider, unless you are paying overseas fees to a British university then of course you are most welcome.'

He laughed in what he hoped was a combination of sardonic with world-weary. She also reminded him of Moira. The room was filling up with delegates remembering the free bar had a shelf life of strictly sixty minutes.

'We can continue to talk over there? If you like?'

She pointed to a corner of the room which was poorly lit but blessed with two plastic chairs that looked like they had been stolen from an art gallery.

'I'll get us a top up if you bag those chairs.'

She seemed genuinely interested in him. Within a minute or two – was this borne of experience of speed dating? – she knew about where he worked, his mother's illness, her desire to spend Christmas with him, and the Centenary. He carefully avoided all mention of Alice, or Amy, or Moira preferring instead to give the impression of busy academic squeezing pint pots into half glasses. He put his own down upon the small round table and asked her about her work and why she was attending a conference that seemed to have little to do with her master's degree.

'I'm here to meet people, perhaps someone from home, and...' she laughed in a particularly Eastern European way reminiscent to him of a Bond girl in an early film involving gypsy dancers and swirling dirndl skirts, '... and to escape my roommates who only want to talk about going off on the *piste.*'

Gurney had no idea what she was talking about but enjoyed the way she talked and her unaffected, open demeanour. He felt protective, wise, a fatherly figure but also one jaded and past its sell-by date. Her hair and teeth were faultless. And she had asked him several interesting questions and had allowed him to answer and he had reciprocated. Now he felt they were friends, *off-piste* and ready to go into dinner side by side - Emma and her Mr Darcy?

The Norwegian hosts had helpfully set out several small round tables seating exactly eight delegates. A bottle of white and red was opened in the centre of each table along with sparkling and still from a famous spring somewhere in the frozen north. It turned out Andrea had a good first degree in English from the University of Birmingham.

'Edgbaston not Alabama.'

'Thankfully you didn't pick up the accent.'

'I did for the three years but once I returned home it gradually disappeared and the old me returned.'

Once she had completed the masters she planned to apply for a doctoral scholarship from the German Ministry of Higher Education.

'And they will give me one because I am good. I work hard and will bring back to Germany valuable lessons from my field.'

'Which are?'

She looked surprised. A first course of shrimps and lettuce on small squares of crisp bread was placed before them.

'You are certainly confident which is good, given the completion for these things. Where would you like to study?'

'If you are thinking of your university, then of course if the programme is first rate, and they accept people regardless of gender or ethnicity or race, then I'd be happy to...'

Gurney butted in,

'...For a doctorate, what matters, of course, is the supervisor, more I would say than the university or its reputation. If he has time for you then with some good organisation and hard work almost anyone can be successful.'

'Why do you say 'he'? Haven't you forgotten I am studying gender?'

She spoke lightly, delicately lifting a forkful of shrimps to her perfect von Hofmann mouth.

'No I say 'he' deliberately in that in my field anyway most senior tutors are male, and if there are any women they tend to get the undergraduate work leaving the more flexible doctoral stuff to the professors.'

He hoped he continued to sound worldly and sardonic and not bitter and resentful. A main course of salmon and dill with new potatoes and green beans improved his mood. Good drink, fine food, and good company. Even the welcome address from de Waal, when it came, was surprisingly light on erudition and heavy on in-jokes, banter about the state of Scandinavian linguistics, and a running joke that seemed to revolve around opening a tin of rancid fish at a Russian airport customs desk.

Perhaps he had been uncharitable in his assessment of de Waal? Gurney smiled to himself and nodded benevolently to the half German - half Romany student who had agreed to join him for the plenary the following morning.

*

His mouth was dry, his head felt heavy and lop-sided, his neck pencil thin and about to break. He was waiting in line to board the inexpensive Norwegian Air flight from the extremely expensive Gardermoen airport to the extremely inexpensive version at Stanstead. He'd just downed an extremely expensive glass of *Rignes* lager. He really should see someone about his drinking. A barman perhaps? A month's salary and he could probably buy a pint of the local brew.

The plane was full of rich Norwegians doing a little Christmas shopping in London plus a handful of conference delegates who were attending another conference in Crewe which he vaguely remembered being granted university status along with Bognor Regis and Scunthorpe.

At the end of the symposium he'd agreed to meet Andrea at the Munch museum. Looking at *The Scream,* he felt an affinity with the artist. Painted after his application for a senior paintership and no doubt been turned down for the third time? A flight attendant offered him a glass of beer and some peanuts. Something of the Nordic gloom seemed to have entered his bones as he wrestled to open the nuts. Oh, what was the point? Schlepping all that way to a cold grey city to be closeted for forty-eight hours in a drab hotel with a bunch of people most of whom he'd either met before or couldn't remember meeting. Andrea was the exception. Her looked out of the porthole window. A good example of a redundant word, *window*, aka all port holes were, by definition, a type of window – one of those a proud Norwegian had told him had been given to the English, along with. *maelstrom* and *quisling.*

He perked up. It had been worth coming. His re-hashed Maltese paper had been politely received and, more importantly Andrea had chosen to attend his session, afterwards telling him it was interesting, 'not that I know anything about these modal verbs'. He wondered who was paying her conference fee and accommodation, and hoped it wasn't de Waal. They had parted on a good note too. He'd read over her PhD application and – funds permitting – she'd try her best to come to his centenary.

Amy, Alice and now Andrea. Three sirens about to lure him onto the rocks of recognition, promotion, and…sex? But if anything like that was to happen he had to be more assertive. He moved the paper tissue from beneath his glass and wrote:

'From today Gurney, you will be proactive and not reactive; you will summon up your courage and fortitude and pursue what you want. And when you do that, you'll get what you want – and soon - under the eaves of a small bedroom at the *Double Locks Inn* not far from the fair city of Exeter.'

Chapter Fourteen

Vacation: the action of leaving something once previously occupied - Oxford
Dictionary

*T**he past is a foreign country.* Whoever had said that knew a thing or two
about life, and in particular, travel by train. As soon as Gurney boarded the
5.15pm from Paddington he had the distinct feeling he was leaving behind
a settled, if chaotic present and journeying back, towards a foreign but
recognisable past. He found an empty seat as far away as possible from the toilet
and took out his reading material for the journey, Friday's edition of The Times
Higher Education Supplement. He went straight to the appointments pages.
Though he had no intention of moving he liked to indulge in the fantasy of
starting afresh, wiping the slate clean. And there was some truth in the view that
he'd be more likely to obtain promotion if he was applied for somewhere else
rather than internally through his own university. A new place that wouldn't
know what you were really like.

He scanned the advertisements for anything remotely connected to
Linguistics. Nothing. It seemed the word was out that the word was out. Well his
centenary would soon change all that! The various jobs on offer seemed totally
foreign. The University of Derby, for example, was 'actively seeking' three
lecturers in *Applied Informatics* - whatever that was. The nearby University of
South East Lancashire took up a quarter of a page with an announcement that the
university – 'You've tried the rest, now try the best' – was eager to appoint an
internationally recognised Professor of Tourism Studies. Find the university and
no doubt the job was yours.

The rest of the Supplement – the news section if you like – carried several
articles relating to a current Government initiative to inject into the sector ideas
from the business world in general and marketing in particular. As to be expected
the greatest howls of opposition were coming from the Business Schools who had
spent a considerable amount of time and effort escaping from the very world they
saw encroaching on their turf. Gurney stuffed the paper into the grip at his feet
and settled down to enjoy the journey.

Exeter. Back onto his turf, his manor. And it could be a lot worse. On the
10 O'clock news the night before he had heard that Merthyr Tydfil had more than
a quarter of its residents claiming incapacity benefit, and a third of its young
people leaving school with no qualifications. But looking on the bright side, with
no prospects of a job - and so no likelihood of recognition or promotion - their
sex lives were probably much more rewarding than his.

The train was nearing Reading. Linguistics at Reading? It was thought.
Perhaps he should jettison the weekend, alight here and find himself teaching the
discourse of reading at Reading? It had a nice ring to it. *Plumbing at Bath* or
Electrical Wiring at Leeds? The possibilities were endless, but no, he was happy

where he was. It would be a couple of hours before they arrived at St David's in Exeter, time for Gurney to review the plan for *the* weekend. With any luck, he wouldn't be disturbed by new passengers joining, for as far as he knew the train didn't stop until it reached the West Country. He would arrive at the station about an hour and a half before she would fly into Exeter City airport from Paris where she'd have had a short lay-over from the States. If he took a taxi it would involve fifteen minutes at most from station to the *Double Locks* and to *their* room. What a marvellous thing a personal pronoun is; *their* room, *their* bed, *their* weekend.

He looked around worried his thoughts might have been seen. To distract himself he thought of Linden and *his* weekend. It would all kick off for him tomorrow and if he played his cards right - and kept to the script – he too should be enjoying the fruits of the personal pronoun *their*, and of course the crucial preposition – *with*. They'd agreed to swap notes when he returned from the West Country. And when Linden had realised that with Gurney being in Devon it would mean he couldn't join him and Lucy for a quick drink on the Saturday, he'd been secretly relieved. The last thing two administrators want is for an academic to spoil the show. They had enough of that at work.

His reverie was interrupted by a new arrival who had joined the train at Reading and was looking for a quiet carriage. She was a youngish student-looking type not dissimilar to Alice. Even the grey pleated woollen skirt and crisp white blouse could have been lifted from her wardrobe. She settled opposite him and opened a magazine which appeared from what he could see to be something called *Heat*. It looked a lot more interesting than the THES. He wondered if it had an appointments section at the back.

Alice. Let's think about her. They had had a brief briefing meeting the day before during which she had presenting to him with a new slimmed-down action plan. Apparently, the whole thing could be done on a shoe-string if several 'stakeholders' agreed to participate *pro bono*. Williams had already agreed to chair the week of activities - and he cost nothing – and he had promised that he would secure the active participation of the three most important officials within the university, namely: The Vice-Chancellor, the Pro-Vice Chancellor (Entrepreneurial initiatives), and Ted Sikes, in charge of staff parking and the tow-away vehicle. Ted's numerous other duties included 'knowing where everyone was' and making sure the university estate was 'fit for purpose'. Alice had reminded Gurney too that the Centenary wasn't until the final week of the academic year which meant they had a good six months before it all kicked off.

The Alice Lookalike opposite clearly found the contents of *Heat* absorbing, not saying anything until the train drew slowly into St. David's their final destination.

'My stop.'

He nodded and replied that he too was getting off. As far as he knew the train was going no further. For a moment, he wondered about gallantly offering to share a cab from the station but if she was going to the same hotel - and she was dressed as if she might - it might look as if he was on the pull. Which he was but not with her.

There were no taxis at the rank and not a bus in sight. If the past is indeed another a country, then this country is a third world one at that. Slightly irritated - but keen not to dampen his mood - he picked up his grip and walked slowly in the direction of the canal and his hotel.

The Double Locks Inn was reassuringly unchanged. Even the swan gliding towards him looked familiar. There was a note waiting for him at reception. It was folded in half and handed to him solemnly by the receptionist who looked Iranian or possibly Iraqi, not quite what he expected in a quintessentially English hotel. No one apart from Amy knew where he was and so it had to be from her. Nonchalantly, but worried, he opened the note.

There, were three sentences.

'Gurney why isn't your cell switched on? My mother is in Frome General Hospital where I'm diverting. Join me there if you can. Love Amy.'

Four sentences if you counted 'Love Amy,' which was technically a phrase. He re-read each sentence. The first: he hadn't switched his mobile on because he had deliberately left it at home, having no need, or so he thought then, to be reminded of work and his mother. Second: he had no idea that she possessed a mother let alone one who was alive, or perhaps soon not to be. And third: of course, he could, and would, join her there - wherever Frome was. Frome? Hang on a minute, wasn't that the place outside the village where Araminta and George lived? What on earth was she doing in Frome? As far as he could remember Amy had not only never mentioned a mother but certainly as far as he could recall hadn't ever mentioned Frome.

The receptionist was waiting for instructions. From the expression on this new guest's face he was expecting bad news, a room cancellation at least. Gurney thought for a moment. If he high-tailed it back up to St David's it might just be possible to catch a Frome-bound train in time to rescue something of the evening or night depending on several factors that were outside his control.

'Would you like me to telephone the railway station sir and enquire about the possibility of a railway train taking you to your required destination?' Clearly the standard of the teaching of English as a foreign language in Baghdad or Tehran far exceeded that taught in the land of its birth. The Iranians might indeed be enriching weapons-grade uranium but clearly, they were also capable of turning out first rate hotel receptionists. He felt cheered.

He spoke quickly into the mouth-piece of the telephone and turned back to Gurney.

'The booking clerk at the railway station informs me that if you can arrive there in fifteen minutes you should be available to catch the fast train to Bristol where a connection to Frome will arrive exactly seven minutes later, which will result in you arriving at your preferred destination at 10.19.'

'And the room? Must I pay for the room?'

Expecting this question, he retreated into a smaller room behind the lobby and emerged with an older woman who reminded Gurney a little of an older version of Andrea. She spoke with a similar Eastern European lilt that under different circumstances he might have found attractive.

'I will be quick Dr Sleep as I understand you must return to the railway station post haste.'

As she spoke he noticed her colleague speaking once more into the telephone to whom he hoped was a taxi driver.

'We will give you a credit note which can be exchanged for a future booking at any time, apart from the Christmas.'

For a moment, he toyed with the idea of ringing Alice and suggesting another away-day weekend nearer the Centenary, until he remembered he didn't have her – or come to that -Amy's number. He looked at the note again. Under, *love Amy* was a set of numbers. *Focus, Gurney, focus*. He dialled the number. It was quickly answered by a voice that sounded like a cross between Theresa May and Oprah Winfrey.

'Is that you? Amy? It's me, Gurney.'

There was a long pause and what sounded like an echo. Was this call going out to Phoenix and then being bounced back via the Ascension Islands and then on to where he was now?'

'Have you found your phone Gurney? Are we no longer disconnected?'

He resisted the temptation to explain the difference between dis- and un-connected and said,

'Yes, I'm using the hotel phone and no I don't have my mobile because I didn't think I'd need it. But, where are you? Is your mother OK? I didn't realise you had a mother.'

'We all have mothers Gurney, in fact I remember meeting yours, but we'd better be quick because this will be costing you a fortune. We need to communicate rather than just talk.'

Gurney was impressed. She had clearly retained an interest in linguistic terminology.

'Hang on a minute Gurney...where am I? I'm in Pomeroy ward, Gurney which is on the top, the third floor of the Frome General which...how far is it...which is five minutes by taxi from the station. See you later.' There was a fainter echo.

'...I could do with some moral support.'

If she hadn't cut off she'd have heard him say he was 'on his way', would be there shortly after ten, oh and where was she staying? Cash payment for the room, handshake, taxi, grip thrown onto back seat, speeding back to the station. Who said academia was a spectator sport? He felt alive and in action. He made the train with five minutes to spare. Once onboard he ordered a Foster's premium strength lager – 'shaken not stirred' - and glanced out of the window.

At 10.20 the Great Western train pulled into the small Somerset town of Frome. The taxi drivers of this delightful town were clearly involved in some sort of secondary action with their Exeter colleagues, and so he decided to walk to wherever the town's general hospital was located. It began to rain.

Chapter Fifteen

Relational: relating to relations; friendly and peaceful – Wiktionary

Long ago Gurney had come to realise that the English have little idea of where they live or even at any given moment where they are. Five minutes from the station he stopped and asked an elderly man who was inserting a key into - presumably his own front door - the name of the street he was walking down.

'Don't know mate, haven't lived here long.'

Two young girls who looked about fifteen - and were supporting each other - came lurching towards him.

'The General Hospital?'

'Do you mean the General Hospital in Frome?'

By chance he had, in fact, been walking in roughly the right direction. The other interesting trait of the English he noted was the tendency to tell you where *not* to go. The taller girl wisely decided she knew where he wanted to go.

'Walk up the road, then once you reach the KFC on the corner you'll know you've walked too far. Turn back and you'll see a small road on the right. That's the Longleat Road. Don't go down there but take the next one which is called Bridge Street I think. The General's up there on the left.'

He thanked them both and made his way in the direction of the Kentucky Fried Chicken. Which reminded him that he was feeling hungry - but that could wait.

At the hospital, he approached a huge glass door above which was written 'Accident and Emergency'. The story of his life. The door slid open and he found himself inside a well-lit reception area. It reminded him of his mother's hospital though, clearly the sick and malingerers in this part of England expected a higher standard of decor. The welcome desk was empty. He waited. He was always tempted when asked his name in a hospital to say, 'Dr Sleep'. In that way, someone might take you seriously. But when he had last done this he'd been mistaken for a cardiac consultant who had apparently been helicoptered in from St Barts. Hadn't she said the third floor? He gripped his grip and walked in a dignified manner towards the lift. As he approached – as if by magic - the doors opened and there she was looking as lovely, beautiful, gorgeous, *liftable* as he remembered her on that day on the beach in South Devon.

Ten years had passed and she looked the same, unlike himself who he was sure looked older than he should have. Perhaps it was the Stephen Hawking effect - that time was relative - or the Richard Dawkins effect - that evolution somehow slowed the ageing of women, thank God, in direct relationship to the speeding up of men? Once males had served the purpose of procreation they had outlived their usefulness? Not that Gurney had any experience of that. Yet.

She seemed hesitant to disturb his thoughts until she realised that the lift doors were about to close. Then she advanced, held out both arms, and caught

Gurney who lurched forwards, forgetting his grip which came between him and her. They locked arms in a clumsy embrace half-in and half-out of the lift. For a moment, he wondered if the band would start up a waltz. He stepped back and looked at her.

'Amy!'

'Gurney!'

She smiled at him fondly. He returned the smile hesitantly aware that her teeth were a lot whiter than his.

'Amy!' What marvellous things names are!

'I think we have established who we are Gurney, so let's sit for a moment and I'll fill you in. By the way, I'm sorry about the weekend but it's all been pretty ghastly really.'

Now on English soil he noticed she was quickly sloughing off her mid-Western drawl and replacing it with an accent he thought he remembered. There were two grey plastic chairs arranged next to a large fire extinguisher. They chose a chair and turned them towards each other.

'It's good to see you Gurney, it really is.'

Now it was her opportunity to look over this man who had once instructed her in the science - no art - of stone skimming and who she had agreed to spend a weekend with.

'You look older... but she added quickly ...in a good way.'

His face fell.

'You know wise and experienced, as a university tutor should look.'

She clapped her hands together as he remembered and continued to smile at him. What is with America and this desire to smile at everyone?

'But let me tell you about mum and what I think is going on.'

At this she leaned closer towards him as if about to reveal a great secret. He too leant forward taking in her unlined neck, *broderie anglaise* blouse with pretty neck line, and musky perfume. His voice was quiet when it emerged.

'Yes?'

'I was about to board at JFK when I got a call from my uncle, that she'd had a fall, and a bit of a shock which seems to have caused the fall.'

Gurney leant closer in sympathy with her story and his desire to inhale more of the musky aroma. She was indeed - and always had been - lovely, gorgeous, beautiful, and now *musky* - adjectives that seemed redolent of who she was, who she had been, and who she would continue to be. He grimaced at the clumsy constructions.

'You're right Gurney it hasn't been easy, and I feel terrible for messing up our weekend.'

Our. A pronoun, a single word, but what a word!

'So, Amy what happened? The shock and the fall, in that order, was it?'

She had stopped smiling but took one of his hands which allowed him the opportunity to look at her solicitously and with compassion, overlaying deeper and lower, baser feelings. He squeezed her hand and expressed his worry on her behalf. Her right ear lobe seemed slightly larger than her left. He thought for a moment about his choice of adjectives.

If she was 'lovely, gorgeous, and beautiful etcetera', what was he? Certainly, 'passionate and determined' but also extremely 'uncomfortable' in the grey plastic chair kindly donated by the friends of Frome General Hospital. He turned on his interior monologue,

Isn't there somewhere we can go, perhaps to the one remaining hotel room possessing one remaining double bed where we can possess one another under crisp Egyptian cotton sheets?

She resumed her smile.

'You're as sweet as ever Gurney, let's indeed go for a coffee. I think there's a WRVS kiosk around the corner which is a start.'

They were about to close but Mavis, who served the refreshments, told them there was time for a quick cuppa. She smiled at the couple. Though he looked older and more care-worn, she surmised they were in love. Another good reason to provide them with some tea and her last four-finger *Kit Kat* which they could share. If things had been different she might have been a senior staff nurse, in charge of a ward, providing real service, but then everyone had a role to play and she had found hers.

Gurney waited for Amy to speak. He'd read somewhere that over 80% of conversations between men and woman are initiated by the male.

'Gurney, you're miles away.'

'Sorry I was just thinking.'

'You don't need to apologise, it is your job, isn't it? Thinking?'

'Yes, though we all think don't we, about lots of things.'

He'd liked to have asked her what she was thinking but it seemed too early and they hadn't shared the *Kit Kat* yet.

'You do look a bit older Gurney, which isn't surprising really, but I'm sure you're just the same underneath.'

Underneath he was wearing an expensive pair of Calvin Klein boxer shorts bought specially for the weekend. He blushed.

'Like every well brought-up Englishman I try and change what's underneath at least once a week.'

She leant towards him and kissed him lightly on the cheek. Whoever had designed Viagra had clearly never encountered the heady mix of broderie anglaise and musky scent.

'And mum, Amy, tell me all. The shock and the accident and Frome? Why here of all places?'

He offered her a chocolate finger. She placed it delicately between her lips and drew it in slowly.

'Well, to start in the middle of the story Gurney, mum doesn't live in Frome, though I think she'd like to, but the house prices and all that - anyway her brother George does and she sees him occasionally along with granddad - their father of course, who lives here to -, though what with mum falling out with dad a few years back family visits are all a bit awkward - her wanting to see George but not gramps.'

'Gramps?'

'Yes, more grumps really - and being German probably didn't help.'

'Being German?'

She took a sip of the scalding tea.

'Gurney, you once told me how irritating it is when someone repeats the end of a sentence.'

She took one of his chocolate fingers, broke it in half and swallowed a piece whole.

'Sorry. But your uncle George, what's he like?'

She widened her smile.

'Oh Gurney, he's just the sort of person you'd like, will like – clever, witty, and not at all stuffy.'

She devoured the remaining half of his finger.

'I'm starved but I hope we can eat later.'

Gurney remembered his earlier resolve.

'Your uncle George would not by any chance be a Social Democrat member of the House of Lords, Baron Hildebrand of Frome?'

Her bedroom eyes met his waiting-room gaze.

'You know each other? But that's amazing, incredible? How come? Don't answer Gurney because you can tell us all later when he comes and rescues me, us. He's very good at rescuing people is George.'

Gurney thought quickly. Etiquette and strategy demanded that he continue to ask about mother and the shocking fall but there was also the small matter of Alice ensconced at Hildebrand Manor and he and Amy homeless in Frome.

'But more important Amy, is your mother. Is she OK?'

'Gurney she's fine, well she is now, but when Uncle George rang me in the States it was a bit touch and go. To cut a long story short mother was down from London where she lives, visiting gramps and George, when she decides to visit gramps first, and when he doesn't answer the door -which is never locked - she goes in and finds him sitting there bolt upright in front of the television dead as a post.'

'What was on?'

'EastEnders, they think, but the doctor reckons he'd been dead for a while so it was probably Jeremy Kyle that finished him off.'

She laughed, clearly no love lost between grand-daughter and gramps.

'And your mother?'

'Not as you might think - a heart attack on finding her father dead - but when she turned around to leave she tripped over the welcome mat he kept inside the front door and knocked herself out on the plastic miniature of Ulm cathedral he kept next to the door.'

'Ulm Cathedral?'

Yes, he always said it reminded him of home, even though he came from some tiny village miles away. It wasn't until Mrs Jones the cleaning lady came in a few hours later to check on the old boy that mum was found well and truly out for the count.'

'And gramps out forever?'

She smiled at Gurney, something she'd learnt early on in her career in sales, the United States being formed on the twin principles of freedom and persuasion. Smile and they'll be more likely to be persuaded to buy whatever it was being sold.

'She's pretty much right as rain now but the doctors thought it was better she stayed in overnight.'

'Should I go up and say hello?'

'It's sweet of you Gurney but given you've never met I wouldn't bother, and she might get confused about who you are.'

Gurney agreed, though unsure if what she had just said diminished him somewhat in her eyes. Mavis had closed down her WRVS station. At half past ten the rest of Frome was also clearly shutting down, which might well apply to any hotels in the vicinity.

'You said George was coming to rescue you, what happens then?'

She delved into her smart Gucci bag and extracted an expensive white mobile telephone.

'I'll ask him, hang on.'

Disconcertingly she moved away and cupped her hand over the mouthpiece.

'Everything is well Gurney. George will be here in five and we can stay with them. Seems Alice has had to fly back to work to fire fight some emergency.'

At this she giggled.

'Something about some boss running off with a load of money and Alice holding the fort.'

Gurney attempted a nonchalant short laugh. Who would have thought?

'But at least we'll have 'till Sunday afternoon together Gurney when I've got to scoot to my big launch preparations which are happening in London on Monday. Not quite the romantic weekend we'd planned but you'll like George and Araminta and they'll be other times, won't there?'

She kissed his cheek once again. The same one. It seemed to unbalance him. Should he ask her to kiss the other cheek? He felt lost within an aroma of musk and desire.

'Amy!' A familiar voice boomed out behind them. George grabbed his niece from behind in a huge bear hug after which he released her and extended his hand towards Gurney.

'Doctor Sleep if I am not mistaken!'

Before he could reply Amy had whispered something to him and he darted towards the lift. Amy and Alice - but at least not under the same roof assuming she had left before they arrived. Like most academics, Gurney preferred to compartmentalise his life, it avoided complications. George returned carrying a large and expensive Gladstone bag. They walked out towards a deserted car park.

'Gurney, my boy I hadn't realised you knew Amy. You must tell us all but not until you are out of those wet clothes and into a dry Martini.'

Gurney laughed, his despondent mood lifting. If Alice was away firefighting then it was a conflagration lit by Bundy not him, and besides there was nothing he could do until Monday.

George, like all successful politicians, immediately took command of the conversation and on the route home regaled them with a long but amusing story about Ulm Cathedral and a Tory grandee with a particular fondness for the cathedral's choirmaster. Whilst George guided the car into the garage, Amy took Gurney's hand and walked towards the front door.

'And Alice, how do you two know each other?'

Gurney liked to think that a guiding principle of his life was to be truthful at all times. Wisely he decided this was not one of them.

'We work together, in fact the emergency George mentioned is something Alice and I thought might crop up, and well, it has, but I'm sure she can take good care of things 'till Monday.'

'And there's nothing you can do here is there Gurney, and anyway so perhaps we can rescue something of the weekend and enjoy ourselves?'

And enjoy himself he did even if at times it felt a bit like a re-run of his weekend with Alice. Surprisingly no-one mentioned the coincidence that he was, the boyfriend of one cousin and the boss of another.

It was just after eleven when they all assembled in the large kitchen for a late supper of bread and cheese and red wine. As he drank Amy regaled them all with the trials – some even before a grand jury - and tribulations of life in the fast lane of American corporate life. Like George, and Alice, she clearly enjoyed being the centre of attention, unwilling or unaware that she had reduced Gurney and Araminta to a nodding audience. She had developed a girlish way of talking, a something that she must have acquired from some self-help in-service course unless Gurney was listening to a woman who bore no resemblance to a voice he remembered from way back. He frowned at the thought.

'You look worried Gurney?' It was Araminta who had spoken causing Amy to halt her account of what happened when she asked a hotel receptionist if she could be 'knocked up' early the following morning.

'I wasn't frowning at your story, Amy. No, I was just reflecting on how I had forgotten what a pleasant voice you had.'

It was now her turn to frown.

'Well, I think my voice has always been the same thank you Gurney, though I acknowledge it might have picked up a slight drawl.'

It was later as he helped clear the table that Araminta said, 'she's a little like Alice don't you think?'

'Yes, I can see the likeness particularly in her love of language, and her love of an audience.'

She packed away the last plate and looked at him thoughtfully.

'From what Alice tells me you two are working well together rescuing the Centenary from one calamity after another.'

He wondered exactly what she had disclosed to her but agreed it was a fair summation of their relationship. She continued to observe him with her pale green eyes.

'She's quite fond of you I think Gurney, as I am sure Amy is.'

Gurney liked to believe that a strength of a *comparativist* was the ability to compartmentalise yet to be able at the same time to establish an objective basis for both comparison and contrast. If it worked well for his discipline it would surely provide him for the appropriate intellectual tools now. The problem was not the complexity in the case of evaluating one cousin with another but the fact that the basis for comparison was anything but objective. He tried to project a disarming man-of-the-world smile in return.

'Amy and I go back quite a long way Araminta, and I am indeed fond of her, whereas I have only known Alice for a few months, but you are right we do seem to have hit it off quite well which is just as good considering the mess we continuingly seem to be having to clear up.'

George had returned with another bottle of wine and a clutch of clean glasses.

'Gurney dear boy, she's just trying to tease out a little bit of a declaration from you. My advice to you is keep your cards close to your chest and you'll be fine. It's worked well for me right up to the moment I sat her down, next to the river Arun, if I remember rightly, and told her she'd got it all wrong and it was her I wanted to marry, and not whoever she thought I had my eye on.'

He poured himself and Gurney a large glass of wine as Araminta laughed and said she'd sort out the rooms and the beds.

Midnight and once again he found himself outside the bedroom door, kissed lightly on the cheek, and bade a fond goodnight. Once again, he lay and looked up at the empty Chianti bottle and the map of Brazil wondering if he'd risk it and creep down the corridor to her room and present her with the *Past Times*? As he drifted towards sleep he marvelled at the power of words, each distinctly different, one vowel or consonant differentiating one thing from another. 'My dusky, husky maiden with the musky perfume' he whispered slowly to the bottle above.

*

He awoke refreshed. The aroma of coffee wafting up from downstairs convinced him he was not at home or alone. George was sitting alone, however reading the *Daily Telegraph*.

Gurney knocked lightly on the door.

'I thought the *Guardian* was the paper of the progressive left, George?'

'It is old boy but I'm not reading this for pleasure rather to find out what the other side are up to and more to the point, what they say we are up to. Coffee?'

Gurney accepted a cup and helped himself to toast and ginger preserve. 'George, did Alice mention to you exactly what the emergency at work entailed?'

He hoped he had kept any sense of alarm out of his voice.

George looked up and shielded his eyes from the sunlight streaming in from behind his guest.

'Surprised you haven't asked before; but no, though she didn't seem too worried. Something to do with one of your chaps arrested for fraud in Miami of all places, I think she said. Just bloody well hope he wasn't a donor to our party; you can't trust anyone these days, and I include my fellow lords and ladies I'm afraid. Seems we're all driven by an easy buck.'

So, Bundy had been caught. But why then had Alice had to rush back when all was more or less settled? He was half-tempted to call her but then what good would that do? Better to enjoy the weekend and face any music that had to be faced on Monday, not that Gurney felt remotely responsible for anything Bundy might have done. It was the predicted fall-out for the Centenary that worried him.

'Eggs?'

He was hungry which was a good sign. A diet of cheesy *wotsits* and pork scratching was no way to live, even if washed down with pints of the very best ale. His mother was right, he needed a woman to keep him on the straight and narrow. Then he'd be well fed, contented and consequently happy? The question was – which one? Whilst George ambled off to cook up two omelettes, Gurney poured more coffee and occupied the time reflecting upon his present state of semi-happiness which looked likely to last for at least a few more hours.

Why was he so useless at being – what was the word? – *proactive?* It did seem to him that his immersion into academic life had come at some of cost: a loss of instinctiveness, an inability to live in the present, robbing him of, what? To be able to empty the mind of all thought, lie back in the golden sunshine, and do what? Nothing? Was it possible to switch off all thought and act like an animal, responding to whatever stimulus turned up to frighten, provoke, or give pleasure? It hadn't done Williams any harm. But then surely it was the act of remembering pleasure *later* that was an essential part of it, laying up foundations for something that could be enjoyed, relished even, long after the event had occurred. Why else did people keep a diary or take photographs on holiday?

He wished he had brought his notebook down from his room to record these thoughts. If he was honest he gained a great deal of pleasure in remembering as much as he could of what he had experienced, even if few of these experiences were remotely enjoyable or memorable. What was enjoyable was that he had survived to live another day more. He refilled his cup and decided to turn the question on its head: if he couldn't find happiness here - this weekend - in this warm and hospitable household far removed from the university in the company of a woman he felt sure he still loved then, when and where could he? A good example of a scientist's null hypothesis, though he didn't like the sound of that, and when you think about it when did you ever see a scientist enjoying themselves?

He looked around the comfortably furnished room. How did you get all this? The rambling house? The Aga? Lovely Araminta? The *settledness* of it all? There seemed to be no bridge between his humdrum and squalid living conditions – even being a university lecturer with a doctorate –and this world of *agreeableness* What had he done wrong? Or more precisely what had he not done right? He sighed and consoled himself with the self-evident truth that even though he earned about the same as a senior customer sales assistant at the local supermarket, things could be worse. He could be Bundy awaiting extradition in some Miami jail or worse Mrs Bundy learning that not only was your husband a crook but a philanderer as well.

In his reverie, he hadn't seen George return with the eggs and a pair of vicious-looking secateurs. 'After we've eaten this I'm going to be cutting out the dead wood, something I don't get much of an opportunity to do in the House'. Gurney agreed. Perhaps he should start living in the *now*? And so, what if he couldn't remember it later?

Which is in fact how the rest of the weekend turned out: a forgotten series of interconnected events involving wine, walks, warmth, and women, with Araminta playing cupid whenever the opportunity arose. So, Gurney left on the Sunday evening unable to recall whether he had kissed or had been kissed, whether he had arranged to meet Amy again – though she said she'd remind him by later that, yes of course she'd support him, and - yes really - the Centenary sounded well worth the flight from Phoenix. If the hangover he awoke with the following Monday morning was any indication, then he had indeed had a very *happy* two days in a small village on the outskirts of Frome.

Chapter Sixteen

Sexuality: the quality or state of being sexual a) the condition of having sex b) sexual activity c) expression of sexual receptivity or interest especially when excessive – Merriam-Webster Dictionary

He felt happy even as he drove in the pouring rain on a dark and gloomy November morning towards the university. As he neared the car park he saw Graham standing morosely at the bus stop presumably returning home for something. Gurney slowed and rolled down his window.

'Everything OK?'

'I'm fine thanks, Gurney, nipping back home for a bloody file.'

The estates vehicle behind him blasted him twice. Gurney accelerated and thought he heard Graham shout what sounded like *dingle* after him. He parked carefully and tried to remember if he had ever travelled to that part of Ireland. Didn't it have a peninsula? Perhaps he meant *dangle* which seemed odd for a Monday morning. Then he remembered. *Dongle*. It had to be that. A couple of years ago the university - in its efforts to improve efficiency – at that time 'the seventh most efficient university in Southern England' – had decided to issue all members of staff with the latest in electronic gadgetry: answer phones, laptops and of course *dongles*. Whereas the university justified the expense on grounds of efficiency – 'always able to keep in touch' etc. - certain unionised members of staff i.e. junior lecturers on temporary contracts, viewed the initiative as yet another nail in the coffin of academic freedom i.e. 'who is keeping in touch with whom?'

Gurney decided to ring university telecoms, the provider of the dongle. He was put on hold by an electronic keyboard rendition of Beethoven's Pathetique sonata. After a few minutes a voice with an easy Southern States drawl answered.

'Dr Sleep, it would appear... ' the drawl became more pronounced, '... that when you made use of your dongle recently in Oslo, you ran up a bill of one thousand, one hundred and one pounds...'

Gurney listened wondering at the curious repletion of the number *one*.

'Doctor Sleep?'

'Sorry, I mean yes, I have heard what you said'. He decided that North American drawl required Standard English precision.

'But forgive me but I cannot see how there can be any correlation between my use of the said electronic device and what appears on the surface to be an outrageously high bill, particularly given the fact that I was only in the aforementioned Nordic capital for approximately 48 hours, and then rarely using my computer with the said dongle attached.'

His reservoir of weekend happiness had emboldened him. Drawl stopped talking and appeared to be listening.

'Were you roaming?'

Gurney thought about his meandering around Karl Johannes Gate before settling upon a small bar which sold beer at only four times the price he'd pay at home. A pleasant roam from home if ever there was one.

Drawl interrupted him and suggested he discuss the matter with his line manager.

He opened his inbox. There were a large number of messages, several of which were flagged. None were from Alice which surprised him but there was a message from Amy, between flights sent via her blackberry. She obviously knew the dangers of the dongle.

'It was lovely, lovely, lovely Gurney. We must do this - and that! -again. Until March, A. xxx.'

Reinforced happiness but with a small niggle. Clearly living in the moment had been marvellous, a huge boost to his love-sick immune system but like a drunk after a particularly successful party, he wanted some reassurance that comes from some recollection of what had *actually* happened. Clearly, she could remember the difference between *this* and *that.*

He tried to remember what had happened. *This* was easy, it obviously referred to the weekend in general, *that* was more problematic. Surely if it had been more than just a goodnight peck on the cheek, more than just holding hands, down by the river, more than just a declaration of undying love in the Castle ruins he would have remembered it? The reference to *that* as opposed to *this* – and the effective employment of the exclamation mark – implied something specific, something *exclamational* had occurred within or without the bedroom door?

She had clearly enjoyed whatever had happened. He couldn't really ask for further details lest it suggested he had forgotten what had happened, though it had clearly been 'lovely' and 'xxx' to the power three, whatever it was. He had no alternative but to reply.

'Yes, it was lovely for me too. Roll on March and you coming to the Centenary. Love G. xxx.'

Suitable keen but not too desperate. He pressed send. Smiled. Logged off. Job done. Hey! This living in the moment thing was fun! He then wondered about Alice. No news seemed to be good news but it seemed out of character for her not to be in touch. He wanted her to see his smiling face before it wore off.

His landline rang. It was a Mrs Bedoe from Human Resources who wanted to set up a meeting between him, her, and the Dean to discuss his use of the dongle. Without uttering the word 'misdemeanour', it was clear that he had some explaining to do or he might find himself one thousand, one hundred and one pounds out of pocket. The problem from her point of view was finding a 'window of opportunity' in the Dean's heavy schedule of 'wall-to-wall meetings'. He was busy but given the 'gravity' - her word not his - of the situation she would send him a 'doodle', whatever that was.

Not even this could dent his aura of happiness. Like Tom Cruise at a Scientology gig he felt the need to smile at all and sundry. 'Bring on the dongle doodle, he could take all they could throw at him!' He was good. His inner being was well – his whole being suffused with *wellness*.

There was a knock on the door. 'Pray enter, sweet Alice', he called. Linden entered and sheepishly apologised for not being her but told him that she was off sick with some sort of bug she must have picked up on the train home. As he relayed this unfortunate news he too beamed radiantly towards his drinking friend. Clearly, they had much to discuss. To share. To flag up. Gurney suggested they catch up at the *Open House* at eight. 'But no junk snacks Linden, I'm a new man!'

*

As it turned out they were out of pork scratchings but they could rustle up two lamb curries with all the trimmings.

'On me Linden.'

Whilst they waited for the lamb to be rustled up Linden carried over two pints of lager and two packets of honey-roasted peanuts. They were sitting at their customary corner table. Linden managed to get one quick beam in before he started talking. He'd had a haircut and was wearing a grey woollen suit that made him look quite dapper. They sipped their beer in unison. Linden broke the ice.

'Lucy.'

Gurney took a thoughtful sip and looked up professorially.

'And I always thought you were called Linden ...which is no doubt what you said to her?'

They both laughed. This was going to be a good evening. And clearly the weekend had been a beaming, rip-roaring, honey-coated success for both of them. Linden cleared his throat.

'We met as you suggested, in the front lounge of the *Welcome Inn* at six. She arrived at two minutes' past and apologised for being late...'

'That's assistant registrars for you.'

'And female assistant registrars at that. Anyway, she looked gorgeous: cream blouse, cream skirt... cream skin?'

'Yes of course and let's not forget those deep blue eyes...'

'And you were wearing? That suit perhaps?'

'Indeed, I was, kind fellow, acquired in preparation the day before.'

'So, she was in cream and you in grey?'

'And before you ask Doctor Sleep - for I see where this is going – we did indeed look the perfectly matched contrastive couple!'

They both took further large mouthfuls of lager.

'And you talked about?'

'Patience my friend, patience! First, I must inform you that when we met we kissed, no peck upon the cheek, but a proper mouth-to-mouth I was at first thrown a bit.' Gurney decided it was best to move on.

'And then what happened?'

'Well, after we had sat down she edged her chair closer to mine, looked at me directly with those cornflower blue eyes, laid her hand over mine and started to tell me how wrong she had been, how Northern men - and one in particular from Moss Side called Alfred - are such brutes, how Southern men are so much more thoughtful and considerate. And the more she talked about this Alfred and Moss Side and the Registrar - who was also called Alfred - the more she seemed to want to confide in me Gurney, but not like some older brother but more as a friend, an ally, a lover...'

'She didn't actually say that, *as a lover*?'

'No, but I sensed it Gurney, sensed that she had indeed changed, and that things were now looking up.'

'I'm sure they were Linden but pray pause in your tale young man whilst I replenish our drinks.'

At the bar, Gurney was told that he had been wrongly informed about the availability of lamb curry but that the house could offer more honey-roasted nuts and the possibility of a sandwich. Gurney returned with more pints of Theakston's Old Peculiar and two packets of nuts.

'And had you discovered at this stage where and with whom she was intending to spend the night?'

'I didn't even need to ask, Gurney for right at the start of our conversation she'd looked around the lounge, said it looked nice, and enquired whether this is where we were spending the night?'

'In the lounge?'

'Yes and no, but I'll come to that.'

Linden continued to smile but a little more normally.
'We decided to eat at the Brasserie...'

'The Bombay? All you can eat for £9.99? Red hot curry and she in a cream outfit? Killing combination.'

'Yes, I know but the only thing she had liked about one of the Alfreds was his liking for a bhindi bhaaji on a Saturday night. And again, Gurney, she laid her hand on mine, and told me what a changed woman she was. Changed inside as well as out, she said.'

'The best kind of change – creamy on the outside and purer on the inside?'

'Yes, no hard edges she said, more loving and more able to give and take love she said. And she looked downcast at this point and said in a quiet voice, 'no chance now of making it to Registrar'. If I'm honest I think that's what upsets her most, to come to the realisation that if you want to reach the dizzy heights of university registrar you're going to need more than just purity and cream.'

They both paused at this point to ponder an essential truth about recognition and promotion in the heady world of university administration.

'And so, where did you go after the Brasserie? Back to the *Welcome Inn*?'

'This is where things take an unexpected twist Gurney. When we stepped out of the Indian it was tipping down and so I suggested we make a run for it...'

'Back to the *Welcome Inn*?'

'Yes, but then she grabs my hand and says the flat's just around the corner opposite the pound shop. Imagine we're tripping along in the best rain the city can offer giggling like two schoolgirls on a day out!'

'And the flat?'

'Turns out it belongs to a friend who lets it out to rich Arabs but inside it is spotlessly clean, beautifully done, sort of unlived in feel, lovely walls...'

'Cream again?'

'Yes, though more off-white walls, pale sofas, white scatter cushions, a carefully assembled vision of purity, virginity almost.'

'That last bit doesn't sound promising Linden, what happened next?'

'What happened next surprised even me Gurney, and as you know we university administrators have seen it all. Well, given that we didn't have an umbrella we were soaked through...'

'But there was no-one else there so you...?'

'Yes - I mean no - there was no-one else there, just us dripping puddles of rainwater on the cream carpets...'

For the first-time Gurney felt a pang of envy for his friend and what he was sure had happened. No doubt fluffy white towels were about to be introduced into the story. Which indeed were - along with glasses of chilled Chablis, more giggling and holding hands, and a suggestion that he 'stay over' given the awful weather – 'and it seems such a pity doesn't it to stop now considering we are having such a good time...'

'There was just one bedroom which contained one of those huge emperor-sized beds...'

'Are we still in the yes or no zone, or am I correct in thinking, Mister Linden Arthur Slackley, that we have firmly entered the affirmative area?'

At this point, Linden leant forward and touched Gurney's arm.

'Imagine, Gurney, you are lying in bed, still in fluffy bathrobes, next to the most beautiful woman you've ever met with blonde hair, blue eyes...'

'...and a creamy complexion...'

'... who is now ready to give and take more love...'

'...and is willing to start with me...'

'...which sounds to me Linden like we are a million miles from the no zone'.

'...but we are not Gurney, we are not, for once you are blessed to see that the categories of 'yes' and 'no' are not so far removed from each other, that they sit in a consensual relationship side by side...'

'...like bathrobe to bathrobe? But be honest wasn't it more you wanted 'yes' and she preferred a no?'

He almost added, 'that's women for you', but held back not wanting to stop his friend now he was *on a roll*. They were now into their third pint. So much for cutting down.

'And you lay side by side bathrobes similarly knotted like star-crossed lovers, miss crème a la crème waiting for Mr. Grey Suit to do something?'

'But that's it Gurney, as she lay there and talked increasingly urgently about how she had changed, had become purer, more giving so I began to reciprocate, to understand that a 'no' or a 'not now' could in fact blossom into a very beautiful 'yes...'.

'But *not now*?'

'It was as if the word 'no' had joined us on our road of transformation, our quest to move beyond rejection and acceptance to a state of affirmation, a centre-piece for something nobler we were building together, a bridge, much larger than a mere 'yes', more durable, more sustainable, more us.'

Gurney felt a slight frisson of annoyance, not for Linden or Lucy who were clearly destined for a Moonie wedding in Seoul or wherever they held them, but more for his fellow Men, for the poor benighted souls who spent hours in search of the Holy Grail: empty apartments and the unknotted bathrobes of opportunity. He snorted.

'So, nothing *happened*?'

'If you mean did we set aside our bridge-building for a quick fuck then the answer is no, but if you are asking did we achieve something at a deeper level, then yes something did indeed happen.'

'So, you were right it was 'yes' and 'no'?', said Gurney keen to return to their earlier mateyness. He went on.

'Semantically a *yes* and not an indicator of indecisiveness but rather an accurate description of the spiritually ambiguous. In other words, *no* bonking - yet - but a *yes* to finding a life partner?'

He burped. Linden beamed at his friend's summation, impressed as he always was at the academic's ability to cut to the chase and get to the kernel of the matter.

'Presumably you then fell asleep exhausted by your spiritual intercourse, awakening next morning refreshed and ready for the next step in your journey together?'

Linden nodded happy that his friend - though understandably cynical - could appreciate and celebrate another's good fortune.

'And you Gurney what happened to you?'

Apart from being unable to remember anything that had occurred between breakfast and departure, Linden's story had provided him with no shared reference points, though he felt his account of what had happened to him possessed elements of *yes*, quite a few of *no*, and a significantly number of *maybes*. But without knowledge of what had happened he was adrift in an ocean of nothingness unable to know anything which seemed paltry given his friend's clear recollection of what had happened. He confessed to being stumped for words.

'Come on chum, fair's fair – and oh is Lucy fair! – I've spilt the beans so now it's your turn.'

With nothing much to say Gurney attempted his sage-like smile of munificence, his trusty academic man-of-the-world look - an oxymoron if ever there was one – and fell back upon the academic fall-back position, which is if you haven't a clue about anything that has been said so far start to discuss the theoretical implications of what has just been described.

'Well like you Linden it was not straightforward, was not predictable, but I do think, like yours, my life journey will reach some Brechtian *conclusion.*'

'You think? You're not sure?'

Gurney found he had no problem recounting the aborted journey to Exeter, the diversion to Frome General, the first evening with George and Araminta, and the moment up to spreading homemade jam on his breakfast toast. After that nothing. It was as if his cerebral dongle had been wiped clean; and yet it was clear from what Amy had said later that he had been party to a generally enjoyable *this* and possibly a more specific, ecstatic t*hat*. Perhaps the passion, that passion had robbed him of an ability to remember, an evolutionary development that solved the evolutionary problem of desire by de-linking the reproductive function from the recreational?

Theory: Scientists using scanning techniques to observe men's brains during and after orgasm found that the entire cerebral cortex, the 'thinking' part of the brain, shut down during orgasm. Then two other areas, the cingulated cortex and amygdala, told the rest of the brain to deactivate all sexual desire. This was backed by a surge of soporific brain chemicals such as serotonin and opioids.

'Sounds to me like you should write a very delicate letter to Amy explaining that upon returning from Frome, in a state of euphoria, you stepped unwittingly in front of a bus, and post-concussion have found that you can remember not only little of the accident but all that occurred after you had breakfast with George.'

If fact, implausible as so often is the truth - Gurney agreed, that he would indeed write to Amy omitting all reference to an 'accident' or 'post-concussion' and tell her simply that he did indeed love her and that he looked forward to March when they could do not only *this* but quite a lot of *that*. And he added as a footnote: roll on the Centenary, roll on her visit, and roll on the pronoun!

As they left the Open House the landlord offered them two cheese sandwiches *gratis*.

Chapter Seventeen

Privatisation is a process, which can be defined as the transfer of assets, management, functions or responsibilities [relating to education] previously owned or carried out by the State to private actors - Coomans & de Wolf.

Tuesday morning and he felt fine. Two emails to write; first to George and Araminta thanking them for the weekend; second to Amy declaring undying love and looking forward to seeing her at the Centenary and what would follow. The telephone rang.

'Gurney Sleep? I don't think we've met. My name is Abigail Williams, Professor Williams's wife (he was married?), we're throwing together a surprise party this weekend – it's his big six 0 – and I wondered if you'd be able to make it? Terribly short notice I know but you know how things are (how are these things?) - and he's terribly fond of you (is he?) - but I'd appreciate it enormously if you'd keep mum. Oh, and do of course bring a partner (who?) - The Cedars, 73 Beaconsfield Road, a stone's throw from St Vitus Catholic Church. 7.30 Saturday.'

A partner? Alice. Why not? Assuming she had thrown off her flu she could work the room and dig up the lowdown on Bundy and any centenary fall-out. He rang her mobile. She sounded awful, reduced she said to sitting wrapped in a duvet in front of the TV watching re-runs of *Judge Judy*. But touch wood she'd be fine and up for it. They'd rendezvous at the *Open House* which she informed him was just opposite the church - why had he and Linden never noticed it? Who would have thought it, the randy play-away professor married all the time to an Abigail who sounded like she could easily hold her own?

Saturday came and he found himself marching out towards his rendezvous well-scrubbed up in pressed jeans and a crisp white shirt.

His mood lightened as they approached The Cedars, one of those double-fronted Victorian villas popular in the more well-to-do areas of seaside English towns. As they had walked from the *Open House* she had brought him up to speed on Bundy and what it meant for the Centenary. The Dean was adamant it would go ahead but instead of the university funding most of it, ninety percent would now have to come from corporate sponsorship. And it would have to be more modest in scale, an outcome they agreed was a blessing in disguise. Apparently, Bundy was protesting his innocence whilst awaiting extradition proceedings claiming that he had been duped by a Florida-based venture capitalist into investing a large amount of university income into the establishment of a Cayman Islands publishing house. He was being charged by the authorities in Britain with fraud and embezzlement, and in the Caymans with the abduction and attempted seduction of a minor. It turned out the Islands still considered twenty-one as the age of legal responsibility and so the student was technically a child when she boarded the flight west with the pro-VC (Finance).

The undergraduate was free to go - being an unwitting accessory after the fact - whilst Bundy got to see the inside of a small police cell on Grand Cayman. Her only misdemeanour had been to run off with a man thrice her age and who it was rumoured possessed half her staying power.

An extra-ordinary faculty meeting was scheduled for nine on Monday morning when the new 'centenary schedule' and accompanying responsibilities would be laid out: Williams would remain in overall charge with Gurney and Alice responsible for all the 'heavy lifting'. March was rapidly approaching and a sense of urgency now walked the corridors on the fifth floor.

'But, Gurney, let's leave the Centenary till Monday and enjoy the party', she had said as she took his hand and guided him up the lichen-covered flight of steps to the front door of the professor's home. Instead of a conventional knocker or bell pull there was a small African drum attached to which was a wooden stick and a sign which read, *beats me*. They did so and then discovered the door was unlocked. They went in the direction of a hubbub of conversation accompanied by what sounded like *Tubular Bells* played at twice the normal speed. Entering a room with a pretty girl has three advantages for a man: first you are immediately 'noticed', second you are 'beckoned over', and third you are offered a 'drink?' such as champagne or a cocktail. The beckoner turned out to be Abigail Williams. She was extremely short, coming up to Gurney's shirt pocket but what she lacked in stature she made up for in bonhomie and a kind of English prettiness one associated with Felicity Kendall.

She offered them glasses of buck's fizz.

'We're role reversing tonight: my husband is slaving away in the kitchen telling the two au pairs what to do, and I'm here doing what he normally does which is getting drunk and telling you all what to do.'

Gurney laughed. This woman was formidable but then she'd have to be, wouldn't she? As she engaged him in conversation – each guest allocated a strict five minutes – he watched Alice out of the corner of his eye make her way from group to group talking, laughing, or frowning to match what was being said or implied. Abigail Williams knew the three golden rules of hosting an academic soiree: first treat everyone from Vice-Chancellor to those on temporary contracts equally, second never disagree with anything anyone said - even if the professor of music told you *Rolling in the Deep* was on Adele's second album - and third, keep everyone happy with an endless supplies of good quality wine and beer.

Food, if provided, is an unexpected extra. And if provided should consist of quiche, cold ham, French sticks cut into slices, and various salads and crudités, even if served in the midst of winter. Academics, as a rule, care little for what they eat, and then they tend to prefer it cold, preferably salted in a little bag, and accompanied by copious quantities of cheap lager. Parties of this kind, Alice informed him on return from a useful circuit of the room, rarely went beyond ten thirty, allowing the guests to escape to the nearest Chinese where they could indulge in monosodium glutamated food chased down with more cheap lager.

Gurney looked around the room. It was spacious and tastefully decorated with a water colour of an African Thorn Tree, a green stone chess set in one corner of the room, and an enlarged black and white photograph of an African boy holding a gourd out in front of him, as if a gift to the photographer. The atmosphere was convivial, the murmur of voices around him containing no rancour or dissent. For a moment, Gurney wondered if the professor would emerge from the kitchen. He felt proud to be part of this gathering even if he knew no-one apart from Alice. There was no sign of Linden or Lucy though he recognised one or two folk from the office.

Abigail, it turned out was an accomplished academic in her own right, her doctorate examining theories of knowledge amongst the Andean peoples prior to the conquest by Spain - but with few academic openings in Latin American studies she had made a success in academic publishing, something she told him she enjoyed apart from dealing with her authors who she found were mostly unable to take criticism or understand that most of what they wrote was incomprehensible, 'present company excepted of course.'

One or two people were beginning to leave, the party heading for that tipping point when it seems it is not impolite to leave and the *Peking Duck* remains open.

Alice beckoned him over to the corner where she was sitting with a distinguished older man dressed informally but expensively. He appeared something of a cross between Philip Schofield and Michael Parkinson.

'Gurney, this is Professor Craig Thomas, our new Vice-chancellor, Doctor Gurney Sleep, lecturer in contrastive linguistics, my boss and leader of our fantastic centenary preparations.' The Vice-Chancellor smiled disarmingly at him, gesturing he draw up a chair and join them.

Should he have known about this change at the top? And more importantly would silver fox here support the Centenary?

'I'm not technically in post for another month, Gurney, but Godwin, my predecessor, has been, to use Alice's term, fantastic in the hand-over, giving me ample time to learn the ropes, and importantly meet folks like you and Alice here.'

Clearly not British. American or perhaps Kiwi or Canadian in search of excitement in the old world? So far, he'd said little apart from 'hi' and 'pleased to meet you.'

One of Gurney's few party tricks - his only in fact - was to possess an uncanny ability to narrow down the accent of a speaker from broad continental area, such as Indo-European, to region and then to state and then - if he was lucky – to a specific language community. As a lecturer in contrastive linguistics an opportunity now presented itself - risky to be sure - in which he could demonstrate a competence that would stand him in good stead when his next application for promotion was considered after the successful centenary of course.

'Vice-Chancellor, if I may I'd like to reflect for a moment on where you hail. As a linguist, this is important to me and so I hope you will bear with me for a moment.'

The VC said nothing - but his continued smile in the direction of Alice seemed to indicate assent.

'First, your use of the term *folks* is my first clue that you learnt your English in the New World, the second, your flattening of the vowel in *like*, suggesting the Antipodes, third your employment of the current VC's first name being illustrative perhaps of a more relaxed social environment. This leads me towards the South-east corner of Australia, which allows me to bring to my analysis one or two paralinguistic features, namely that the state of Melbourne possesses two fine universities – one rather more formal and established, the other La Trobe a little like ours in its trajectory and desire for excellence.'

Craig Thomas placed his empty wine glass on the chess table and looked closely at the young man in the white shirt and Levi's.

'If I said *bonza mate* – not that anyone says that anymore – you'd be right. I am indeed a refugee from that fine institute of higher learning who some three weeks back received one of those life changing telephone calls from your Vice-Chancellor, Godwin, informing me that he was stepping down because of some 'little local difficulty' and that what was needed was someone new, a fresh face on the block and – well - here I am.'

He paused and eyed them both.

'But in case either of you should get the wrong idea about us folks from down under let me make one thing clear: I may be informal and a good bloke but I expect you both - and I mean both of you - to deliver on the Centenary of ours, to raise your game, to secure the necessary the funds – and then of course to reap the rewards to be had.'

With that he smiled at them both, picked up his glass and ambled off in the direction of the kitchen. Alice moved her chair closer to his.

'You were brilliant Gurney, brilliant! I didn't know you had it in you. You should go on Britain's Got Talent or start your own Derren Brown type TV programme.'

Before Gurney could contemplate this suggested career move, Professor Williams marched briskly into the room with a tray of chipolatas in his hand. So much for cold quiche. He came directly over to them.

'Fucking awesome Gurney, fucking awesome! Not only is the honourable Ned Kelly bowled over by your hidden talents but he's told me these are just the qualities he's looking for if we're to move this fucking event forwards. Have a sausage.'

The professor warmed to his theme.

'Examine closely, Gurney, the parallel occupations held by cabinet ministers, those charged to decide on our behalf, and you'll find they range from something in the City to the law, perhaps something nebulous but useful in politics concerned with marketing, the rest relying upon family money to beef up the pittance accorded a minister of state these days. None will be an academic. Whereas it is common – as you know - to find a Minister of Finance of an important European state has enjoyed a previous life as an esteemed professor of economics, it would be unheard of for a newly installed prime minister to call upon the services of anyone remotely connected to a university. This is partly a firmly held belief that expertise in politics will cause no end of problems - particularly with the permanent secretaries who prefer their ministers ignorant, and if educated to have expertise in say the Classics which has no practical use whatsoever. If those within academe are to permeate the public sphere (apart from graduation ceremonies when it is important they dress appropriately and look benignly upon those whom they have taught), then it is best the more photogenic populate Sunday night television programmes devoted to why the universe came into existence or perhaps why the dinosaurs died out. And talking of dinosaurs that's what most of the public think we are – dinosaurs living in some ivory tower offering this fucking philistine country – nada.'

Which made the Dean's extra-ordinary meeting the following Monday all he more extraordinary. It would result in a raft of *clear and purposive* decisions.

Five to be precise.

The *first* was brutal; the Centenary would go ahead but rather than be solely funded by the university would now rely upon all its support from private benefactors; *second* that it would now be reduced or compressed into a long weekend; *third* the Centenary would be opened by the new VC who had clearly indicated his support and encouragement; *fourth*, that given the tight financial climate faculty members would be encouraged to open up their homes to visitors, particularly those alumni willing to contribute to the costs of the festivities; and *fifth* that the 3 days would culminate in a dinner dance details of which would be organised by an ad hoc entertainments committee to be led by a newly-convened sub-group.

Back in his office-cum-sanctuary, Gurney consulted his diary and counted the days left. Two weeks of teaching left of the term, one week of assessing anything students might have learnt, and then three weeks of Christmas leave. Then it would be the New Year and downhill all the way to March and the big day. But first he and Alice had to draw up some sort of list of likely donors and what they'd get for their money; and second what preparations were necessary to ensure that Christmas with Mother with Alice would be bearable. Every time he thought of mother and Christmas the thought of Albert and Doris intruded accompanied by an important philosophical question: would drinking vast quantities of Harvey's Bristol Cream make the situation better or worse? He remembered Alice would be there so there was no point in getting 'pissed', or worse 'pissed off'. At the heart of his anxiety was the fact that she would spend a significant amount of time in the proximity of his mother and her two stooges Albert and Doris. This was what economists call an 'opportunity cost' or more accurately a matter of 'cost-benefit'. His mother would have the 'benefit' of telling Alice the stored half-truths about what a little rascal he was and then he would suffer the 'cost' to his reputation, self-esteem, and the 'opportunity' of advancing things with Alice. He groaned. Why was everything so difficult?

He could endure it all if he had some 'hope' that his mother might say something new. Or perhaps something truthful. He groaned again. The telephone rang. It was his mother.

Amontillado, yes and they would buy the turkey, a golfing sweater would be very nice, and an Uzi sub-machine gun would be very handy. Mistletoe. Alice. Very handy too. And yes, after the Queen's Speech a couple of rounds of the popular board game *Deal or No Deal* would be just fine.

Chapter Eighteen

Formal education will make you a living. Self-education will make you a fortune.
- Jim Rohn

Christmas Eve day was as ghastly as Christmas Day eve, the latter more so because it was a repetition of the former. During the Battle of Inkerman – Alice had given him a book of famous land battles – surgeons had relied upon copious amounts of alcohol to induce the required state of mind and body to withstand the intense pain of amputation. Unfortunately for Gurney it would take more than four glasses of amontillado to anaesthetise him to the kind of war-injury inflicted upon him by Albert and Doris during the festive two days.

To be fair it had started well. His mother had clearly tried: clean house, clean sheets on his bed and in the spare room, clean towels. They had arrived late on Christmas Eve in time for what his mother called 'high tea' which comprised boiled eggs and slices of Dundee cake. It was just the three of them at this stage, Albert telling his mother that Doris was having a 'turn' but that they would join them later for Christmas dinner after the church service in the morning. As he contemplated the order in which he should eat the egg and the cake it struck him how quiet the living room was. No hum of a printer or beep of a mobile phone. Even the television was switched off. He decided it was best to fill his mouth with cake and leave the conversation to Alice who had already finished her egg and was clearly enjoying the tea.

Freud said, we are defined by *love and work*. In Gurney's case, it was an abundance of the latter and a yearning for the former that he thought about as he traipsed up to his bedroom to see if he had any emails. He was glad of the dongle as his mother had no intention of connecting to the internet.

He had two messages awaiting his attention: a red Lada had left its lights on in the university car park, and the university was pleased to Announce that *doitnow* was up and running. He logged out and back onto Google to discover that *doitnow* was an expensive new platform that helped organisations such as universities keep track on who was supposed to be doing what – and more importantly - when they were supposed to be doing it. *Be part of the now generation* was the motto of this expensive piece of software. Gurney logged off, worried that *doitnow* might also incorporate satellite tracking and uploading images of his dilapidated bedroom just off the A409.

Downstairs lay the prospect of another glass of sherry and the pulling of a cracker with Alice. *A cracker. Un-pulled.*

*

He went into work on the first day of January: a new month, a time of fresh beginnings, a month of resolution and purpose. With such resolute thoughts in mind, Gurney accelerated forcefully into the space between the red Lada – it wasn't going anywhere – and the university shuttle bus.

The campus was eerily empty, most staff and certainly all students recovering from being defined by an intense period of love and drink. He wrote down the three words that seemed to dog and define him: 'recognition', 'promotion', and 'sex'.

A successful centenary with Alice's help would certainly land him the first and second; the third would also require her help. And then there was Amy who had emailed over the break that she hadn't forgotten about their *lost* Devonian weekend but all was not lost and that she would definitely make March.

He groaned. Nothing else of any interest in his inbox, except one from Lada owner who seemed outraged that no-one had found him and told him about the lights.

He got up and headed out to the half-deserted cafe. Eliot was right, it was possible to 'measure out your life in coffee spoons'. Too late he saw Williams who smiled at the sight of his younger colleague.

'I've resolved to be a bit more fucking sociable, Gurney. Good vac?'

'Yes thanks. And you?'

He collected his double espresso and joined the professor who was perching at the counter bar.

'Abigail and I spent an extraordinary week with her half-demented brother, Alan, his three teenage boys, and her mother Mildred who suffers from wheat, lactose and academics intolerance. But...shame on me.' He spread his hands beatifically, 'peace to all men - Alan included - let us celebrate difference and inequality, let us not judge!'

Gurney wasn't sure if he didn't prefer the old Williams to this passable impersonation of his namesake Rowan.

'Centenary, Gurney, centenary. I feel in my newly awakened sentimental old Welsh heart that we are on to a winner here.' He put down his cup and stood before him, perhaps to incant some kind of Bardic blessing.

'This is our time, Gurney, our time to show these narrow-minded, self-regarding cretins...but forgive me Gurney for prejudging our fellow colleagues who I am sure are doing the very best with the limited intellectual resources at their disposal.'

With that he smiled benevolently and walked away slowly, head erect, eyes firmly fixed on the middle distance. Gurney was rather glad of the double shot of caffeine. Clearly the professor had been at the sherry early or there really was something wrong. His mobile vibrated.

'Linden?'

'Yes, it's me. Nothing wrong? No, I've just met him.'

'Good will, peace be upon you, pray do sit down?'

'Exactly. But more important, does it mean anything? Any plagues of locusts we should know about?'

Linden assured him that nothing had changed, and anyway no university ever took a decision in January. Like a Wednesday afternoon, the first month of the year was regarded as the 'early closing period' in the busy calendar of senior management.

'But having said that Gurney, I hear that they are thinking – and its only thoughts at the moment – that the Centenary will have to be run on some sort of cost-recovery basis.'

Gurney wondered if they might approach Green Flag or the Automobile Association for sponsorship. Or perhaps Alcoholics Anonymous?

'Yes, apparently, the new professor of ethno-mathematics - that Greek guy that no-one can understand - has managed to persuade the VC that all university activities are best played out by the rules of the 'zero sum game', which I think means that all sums must balance profit and loss. And if they don't, then the game's up.'

Gurney wasn't surprised particularly as there'd been no recovery of any of Bundy's losses.

'But fear not Gurney. I 've been sounding out dear Lucy who informs me that they've been spouting this kind of stuff at her place and what it boils down to is finding a few fat cats who'll sponsor you – logos, talk of business meets the varsity, honorary degrees, that kind of thing. And if you do end up with a small profit then you can take all the credit and get, as the new VC said, the recognition and promotion you deserve.'

The line went dead. Forty-three minutes into the new term and he already felt exhausted. But Alice had worked at Boden's and would know a thing or two about business deals, lost leaders, and the like.

He returned to his room and sent Alice an email suggesting a coffee and a chat about lost leaders. 'Perhaps a drink at the *Open House* instead?' She replied immediately – was she sitting there on New Year's Day waiting for his email? – A drink would be 'lovely'. 'Tonight, at eight?' His mood lifted. Delayed gratification. He rang Linden back who agreed to join them for an hour as he had a VC power breakfast to arrange for the following day.

The pub was completely empty and surprisingly clean. Clearly there had been no hordes of drunken revellers seeing in the New Year. After five minutes a barman appeared. Gurney carried his pint over to their table wondering how long he'd have to wait for his administrative assistant and research fellow. Linden arrived first sporting a long purple and green Dr Who type scarf, a present no doubt from Lucy.

'Alice has just called me on her mobile – by the way she says it would help if you'd carry yours – saying she's missed the train and will see you in the morning.'

He felt miffed about the phone – where had he left it? – but more so at the further delay in his gratification at seeing Alice - and missing an opportunity to share the company of his only two friends - at the same time and in the same place.

'Lemonade for me Gurney or I'll be unable to work later. But listen to this, I have a great idea for raising money for the Centenary.'

He extracted a small folded piece of paper from his purse.

'Three names and contact details of three entrepreneurs within a five-mile radius of the university who have a *record of accomplishment* for their support of the Arts, and if pushed, social sciences.'

'Who are they?'

'In order of most-likely-to-cough-up there's 'Creaven Creams. makers of the famous honeycomb biscuit that thinks it's a cake'; the bicycle wheel replacement company, 'Bespoke'; and 'Bottoms Up', who I've never heard of but apparently, they're very big in personalised beer mats.'

'And the plan?'

'First, we work out how much we want - but more importantly how much we'd settle for -. second, we dream up an enticing list of benefits they would get if they jumped on board. And thirdly, we take Alice along to sweeten and schmooze; given that all CEOs are suckers for big blue eyes and big tits, not that Alice has blue eyes from what I remember.'

Gurney laughed. Men behaving badly, and on lemonade too. And Alice with her big blue eyes.

*

Creaven Creams prided itself on its unique selling point: *the biscuit that thought it was a cake*, a half-baked idea dreamt up by the current CEO - and son of the founder - Mister Gerald Creaven, who had also coined the slogan, 'I'm cravin' a Creaven'. Both father and son loved not only the business of biscuits, but what they saw as an important part of British heritage. Think Marmite, land rover and Cadbury's flake – all resolutely British if all now in foreign ownership. But *Creaven Creams* would have none of that. It had been in the Creaven family for two generations and Gerald hoped that one day he'd hand over the reins to Gerald junior.

They were welcomed at the factory gates by Gerald's PA, Miss Anthea Williams who shared her boss's love of the great biscuit.

On the way to Creavens Alice had briefed them on their pitch: 'more than 300 hundred influential people would have the opportunity of listening to some of the brightest stars in the world of linguistics whilst at the same time munching on a Creaven cream. And an opportunity for the chief guest and great benefactor to award the Creaven Prize for the most promising newcomer'.

Anthea informed them that Mister Creaven would be arriving shortly but perhaps they'd like a biscuit and a coffee? They were sitting in the board room which was extremely small, made up of a long oval-shaped table and eight leather backed chairs, the walls adorned with photographs of an older man shaking the hand of mayoral-looking characters, who all had a passing resemblance to Sir Edward Heath. When he arrived Gerald Creaven launched forth,

'No, no, no! Gerald Creaven senior didn't just sell biscuits! Definitively not! No, he did more than that - he produced with *care and passion* - sadly lacking in the youth of today - a confectionary demanded from him by a public who had come to expect more than a biscuit from a biscuit. A cake in fact! But no ordinary cake but one which carried with it social responsibility!'

Clearly Gerald had missed his true vocation – lecturing – and once in full flow was difficult to stop. Pausing for breath, he concluded his welcome address by reminding his three visitors that Creavens would not shirk its civic duties, hence his positive response to the invitation to become a sponsor of the Centenary! As he spoke his words were carefully recorded by Miss Anthea Williams who unbeknown to the three university visitors was the younger and much neglected sister of Professor Nigel Williams.

The deal was a good one, a win-win situation for both parties. Creaven Creams would underwrite three quarters of the Centenary's costs in return for sole rights to appear on all stationery, napkins, welcome banners and would be mentioned in fulsome and glowing terms at appropriate moments throughout the whole festive event. No mention was made of an honorary doctorate of Letters but Gurney was sure that Williams - who sat on the awards committee - would be 'mindful' of such an honour for one so supportive of the University.

When Williams heard the news, he was ecstatic,

'Righto boyo, get down to Finance and tell them to sort out all the contractual stuff before the bugger has a chance to change his mind.'

Gurney wasn't sure exactly where *Finance* was but assumed it would be on the fifth floor of the administrative block close to the centre of power. It turned out that the only finance officer was closeted in a meeting with the external auditor trying to sort out the university's 'little difficulty' involving Bundy and his extradition. An intern was 'holding the fort'. Unfortunately, the intern had no authority regarding contracts but could offer him a cup of tea and a biscuit if he would like to wait. Gurney declined – he'd had enough biscuits for the day – and walked back to the car park where he noticed a yellow ticket had been stuck firmly on to his windscreen.

Chapter Nineteen

Life can only be understood backwards; but it must be lived forwards -
Kierkegaard

When the call came, it was 'nasty, brutish, and short.'
'Mr. Sleep?'
'Well, sort of.'
'I'm calling from the hospital. Your mother. She has a broken hip and mild concussion.'
'She fell?'
'Of course, and we are concerned that she appears to have given up.'
'Given up what?'
'The will to live. When the paramedic team found her, all she could say was *pointless*.'
'Can I ask at what time was she found?'
There was a pause during which a clipboard was no doubt being consulted.
'At 25 minutes past four, why do you ask?'
'*Pointless*. She watched *Pointless* first and then '*Deal or No Deal* on Channel Four plus one.'
There was a longer silence.
'But I will of course leave immediately and I'd be grateful if you would inform my mother that I'm on my way.'
Why is it that he was never delayed on his way *into* work but try and leave early to visit your dying mother and you will find yourself interrupted, stopped, and blocked by a whole series of people - until the only sensible thing to do is to make a run for it. A health care assistant directed him to his mother's room. She was sedated but conscious, lying bolt upright with her eyes open but clearly asleep, a pose that reminded him of his Monday morning second year class.
'Mum, it's me, Gurney, your son.'
'You don't need to shout dear. I can see it's you, and I know you're my son.'
Clearly the fall or concussion had done no harm to her mental state though she looked pale with that translucent pallor much favoured in the elderly wards.
'A lot of fuss about nothing if you ask me. Not that they did, ask me.'
'Ask you what, mum?'
'Whether I wanted to be brought here when all I did...'
'...was break your hip mum, that's why they brought you here.'
He thought it best to avoid mentioning the stroke lest this bring on another one.
'But more to the point, how are you?'
'I'm fine, thank you Gurney, and thank you for coming son. I do appreciate it, what with you being so busy and everything.'

The health care assistant - who was called Dorcas - arrived with two mugs of tea and a plate of digestive biscuits.

'Nobody said you shouldn't eat, so tuck in dears.'

They both ate quietly and in unison.

'They thought you might have given up the ghost, mum.'

He slid his plastic chair a little closer.

'To be honest, I think I have Gurney.'

She looked at him directly, something she hadn't done for as long as he could remember.

'I've had enough Gurney - had enough of living.'

He wondered what to say.

'I thought you were happy mum. At home – with everything you need. And Albert and Doreen, you like them.'

'Doris - her name is Doris - Gurney, and no - I don't like them. If you want to know the truth I find them boring, small-minded even.'

'But you invited them for Christmas, last year too?'

'That was for you dear, to show you that I had friends, that I was OK, that you needn't worry about me.'

Gurney looked at his mother in the threadbare nightdress his father had given her the year before his death which she had worn, he guessed, every night since.

'I haven't been happy since your father died, Gurney. In fact, I've been miserable - lonely even.'

He looked towards the window. The light was fading. The other three empty beds increased the sense of aloneness he felt sitting close to his mother's bed. They had eaten the biscuits. He felt hungry. He wondered what to say to his mother.

'I should have visited you more mum. I'm sorry. Busy with my work, my career, my life.'

'I'm not accusing you son, far from it. If I'm accusing anyone it's myself for letting things slide, letting things go when I should have made more of things, more of the time I've had since dad went.'

'What would you have liked to have done, mum?'

She smiled. Gurney moved his chair closer to the bed.

'Do you remember, mum, when we stayed at that guest house in Devon, and you said you'd have been an explorer in Africa if they'd allowed women?'

She reached out her left hand and took his. His was clammy, hers cool.

'It wasn't Africa I wanted to explore Gurney but ideas - ideas about the world and our place in it - what makes us tick, why we are attracted to people.'

'Psychology, mum, that's what you're talking about, psychology.'

'When I met your father Gurney I knew from the first moment that he was for me. My *ballast*, he would do, he would be the one I could live with.'

'And how did you two meet?'

'Well your father liked to tell people we met on VE day but that was just one of his stories. In fact, we met about six months before the end of the war. We were stationed at the same AA base on the Norfolk coast.'

'AA base?'

Gurney had a disarming image of his parents in brown and yellow uniforms - dad on the motorcycle goggles firmly attached, and mother in the side car saluting members of that illustrious motoring organisation.

'It was an anti-aircraft base Gurney, a training camp perched on the edge of the salt marshes. Lovely place if you like that kind of thing. Wide open skies. Not a bad way to see out the war.'

'What were you both doing on this base?' For some reason, he found it hard to imagine either of his parents wearing military uniform let fighting the enemy.

'Well I was in the WRAC logistics department making sure the boys at Mildenhall sent us all the bits and pieces we needed such as munitions for the guns, spare parts for the whirligig...'

'The whirligig?'

'Yes, it was a strange contraption a hundred yards or so along the coast. Like a maypole, it was cranked round tight and then it propelled a drone high up above the base so that your father and his mates could shoot at it.'

As she spoke she seemed to change, shrugging off the years, her eyes gleaming, her voice firmer, more resolute. Why hadn't he talked to her before about all this? Was he so busy he didn't have the time to hear about his own origins?

'So how did you two meet on this base? Was it a whirligig romance?'

'It was nothing remarkable really. We met like most people did in those days. He picked me up, but in your father's case, literally would you believe.'

She laughed as he imagined she had laughed when she was a lot younger.

'At a dance or a local pub if there was one?'

'No, Nora and I had gone off on our bikes on one of our free Sundays not knowing that your father and his best friend Dickie Egan had decided to follow us which turned out to be fortuitous what with the narrow twisting lanes crowded with speeding Army jeeps and the like. And just before the Cley-next-the-sea windmill there's a sharp left-hand bend.'

'You fell off and he rescued you?'

'It was Dickie who arrived first. He always had to lead but it was your father who dropped his bike and came running over to see if I was all right.'

'What was Nora doing?'

His mother laughed.

'She was checking her lipstick in the mirror of her bike - you wanted to look your best - and what with Dickie taking a fancy it all turned out to be most fortuitous my tumble.'

'Have you ever been back?'

'Just once, Gurney when you were little. Not much has changed, there's a lovely campsite on the base now but it wasn't the same.'

'No army jeeps thundering past knocking you off your bikes?'

'No, it was much the same in what you could see around you - the skies and fields of sugar beet, but it was us who had changed, Gurney. We were not the same people we once were. Wiser perhaps but somehow, we'd lost that spark we had back then. Of course, just getting on a bit, having you had calmed us down a bit but...'

Gurney squeezed his mother's hand.

'Well I'm glad you *did* have me mum because I couldn't have asked for a better mum and dad.'

He surprised himself with his candour - with the ease he found himself talking for once from the heart rather than the head. For a moment neither mother nor son said anything.

'It's not good to look back Gurney. If life has taught me anything it is to live in the moment, in the present. It's what we believed in in those days Gurney. Who knows, one of us might not live to see tomorrow so you had to have some fun whilst you could. Maybe that's where the spark came from?'

Live in the moment. Hadn't he tried that on that weekend in Frome and then he couldn't remember anything of it?

'And you Gurney. Are you living in the moment?'

What could he tell her? That, at the moment, he had one love called Amy promising to make up for a lost weekend, her cousin Alice – equally lovely – but sort of out of bounds – and a recently met East European linguist called Andrea who had shown interest in more than his supervisory skills? That basically he was living in a very *complicated* moment. He decided to be brave.

There is someone special mum - not Alice who came up for Christmas - but Amy her cousin who lives in the States and sells scented candles. I first met her if you remember when I was doing my Master's down in Exeter.'

'And where is she now? This Amy, Gurney? I do remember you mentioning a young woman but we never actually met her, did we?'

'No, you didn't mum. It was all a bit fleeting but like you and dad, I think she is the one. My ballast.'

'So why haven't you made a move Gurney?'

'I didn't then, mum, because I didn't know then that she would be much more important to me in the future if you see what I mean.'

'So, you aren't living life in the present, Gurney? Even now?'

He looked at his mother more closely. She would have made a damn fine psychologist. Perhaps she still had time. A foundation course?

'If this Amy was sitting here now Gurney would you tell her what you have told me, that she is the one, the ballast in your life? The person you want to spend every present and future moment with?'

Once more he was the ten-year-old boy wriggling during an uncomfortable moment, at an uncomfortable truth.

'Or would you hide behind your bookish-self Gurney thinking too much about things instead of actually doing something about it?'

Years ago, as a postgraduate student he would have bridled at his mother's dismissal of his proclivity for inaction over action but he knew she was right, that for all his learning, for all his acquisition of knowledge he knew nothing of life, or what it meant to take a chance. Worst of all he knew nothing of himself. What he had gained was a doctorate in diffidence, a bachelor's in bachelorhood. He had to laugh.

'Share the joke – Gurney – and I'm sorry if my directness has offended you. It's just that I'm worried about you. Worried about you not being happy.'

'I'm not laughing at anything you've said mum, though you'd easily get a first in psychology if you'd had the chance. No, I'm laughing because you know so much more than me which is pretty ironic given all the time and effort I've put into trying to know so much.'

It was her turn to laugh.

'Well who knows Gurney - once I've got out of this place and found a new place to live I might just do that degree.'

'You're moving? Why?'

'Not just to get away from the neighbours but I've been thinking it's time for a change, for me to move on, to try something new.'

She paused to take up the last digestive.

'I've even thought about going to work in some poor country, teach English to the Africans, that kind of thing, if they'll have me, what with my dicky heart. But we're drifting Gurney from you - and this Amy girl - what are you going to do about it?'

He thought about the *Double Locks* and his fantasy weekend. Perhaps a splash of realism might help?

'I guess we could hire a couple of bikes and go for a long cycle amongst those Devon lanes…'

'…You'd have to raise the saddle Gurney but why not? Then you could engineer an appropriate moment - a puncture perhaps - and whilst you are mending the tire could tell her – tell her what you've told me, that she is the one… And then see what she says.'

'And if she says no?'

'Then you'll know won't you that she isn't the one, and then you can focus your attention on someone else, her cousin perhaps who I thought was rather fond of you.'

Gurney remembered something Alice had said as they left his mother's house after Christmas.

'You know I've always been rather fond of you Gurney ever since the interview when you put me at my ease, made me feel as if we had known each other for much longer than we had. Thank you'.

And she had kissed him tenderly on the cheek. He kissed his mother goodbye with a promise he would indeed follow her advice, raise his saddle - if not his game - and who knows, perhaps some whirligig of romance would enter *his* life?

Chapter Twenty

When I give a lecture, I accept that people look at their watches but what I do not tolerate is when they raise it to their ear to find out if it has stopped – Marcel Achad

When he returned to the university the news wasn't good. *Craven Creams* were having a rethink, centenary support was on hold, and the professor's wife had phoned to say that Nigel had had some sort of seizure and was in a private ward at the Royal recovering.

When faced with two conflicting demands upon his attention: telephone Abigail Williams for an immediate update on her husband's condition or call Alice about *Craven Creams* - he did what most academics do - invented a third.

Grand Canyon's webpage had a handy button in the bottom right corner of its webpage, *contact us.* Surprisingly, after a series of automated options he was put through to a human voice. The voice with a reassuring drawl informed him that their ex-Vice President, Sales, was now working for a specialist perfumer called *Scent of Success*, the contact details for which could be found on their 'innernet' page. He jotted down the address and returned to the matter of the professor and his seizure. 'Seizure?' What did that mean? But more to the point, what should he do? What did you do when your Centenary chairman was *seized* by something? He decided that he'd call the professor's wife. She answered immediately. She sounded drunk.

Gurney decided to get to the point.

'Just heard. Terrible. Sorry. Just terrible. What happened?'

There followed a longer silence than seemed necessary followed by a short cough or just an audible sob.

'Sorry, Gurney, just topping up my glass. They say he's had some kind of stroke brought on no doubt by all the shit he's having to deal with, not helped by Gerald Creaven getting cold feet so his dear sister tells me, which considering the time and effort we've given the little creep is a bit rich.'

Gurney agreed wondering in what way it was 'rich'.

'Thank God it hasn't affected his mind, so they say at this stage anyway. He can talk though only through the corner of his mouth which is a bit weird. And yes - he would most certainly welcome a visit particularly if you can deliver some good news.'

He decided to call Linden. He'd fill in the details. He answered immediately. Clearly the professor's sudden illness had put everyone on high alert.

'It was at a Faculty Research Excellence meeting. As you know FREAC never discusses anything important but Nigel suddenly got all het up about zero contracts, workers' rights, that kind of thing. Well Harber-Birder - who chairs it, told him to calm down, but instead of calming down he sort of fell onto the lap of the new pro-VC finance Francis Cox, his words slurring, face going all pale. Luckily Ankie Wanstead the new committee secretary – on a *zero hours'* contract by the way – knew something about first aid or it could have been a lot worse.'

Gurney tried to remember what the professor had told him about Bundy's replacement, Cox.

'Let's hope this Cox is better than the last little prick we had foisted upon us. What I hear is that in his last place he made his name privatising everything that moved - and that included several senior academics who had taken up permanent residence in the senior common room – told them that they could expect redundancy notices by noon.'

He next rang the hospital. He was progressing well and could receive visitors in a day or so. An impending visit meant he had to think of some strategy that would rescue the Centenary from disaster. Alice answered immediately.

Apparently Creaven's cold feet had been brought on by learning that he'd have to share catering responsibilities with final year students from the Department of Tourism, Catering and Hospitality who were being encouraged to try out various products at nominated university functions. It had been decided by the new Pro-VC finance that this was one of them. The Department were also the cheapest supplier of food and beverages in town, freed up from having to pay the dragooned students a penny for their time and effort.

'Cox wants to extend his SSL business model to all university services but has run into trouble from the unions.'

'SSL?'

'*Slave Student Labour* I think he called it at the FREAC meeting forgetting that Annabelle Wilberforce, she of the famous family, and student rep, was in attendance.'

'And do we have any wriggle room?'

She thought they had.

Five minutes later Gerald Creavan was speaking to Alice Hildebrand. He'd rather taken a shine to her. He began by reminding her that, he hadn't gotten to where he was by being 'soft'. No - he might live temporarily in the lily-livered South - but he was 'hard' and 'hard' he remained. Not that he wasn't susceptible to the soft tones of Alice Hildebrand's sweet and persuasive voice. In fact, Mr. Gerald Creaven was a push-over. After about ten minutes of gentle coaxing he agreed that the students could handle the conference snacks and drinks whilst he would concentrate on all the evening food including the final dinner.

'And let's not forget the logo Alice, Craven Creams upon all items from serviettes to conference jute bags.'

The managing director put down the phone pleased at both the bargain struck and the opportunity to listen to ten minutes of intelligent and agreeable conversation. It was important also to keep on the good side of his PA's brother Williams, uncouth bugger he might be. Who said northerners weren't 'hard'?'

Alice lost no time in telling Gurney the good news. Unlike most academics, Gurney liked to congratulate a colleague when they had done well. He called Abigail back who asked if he could step by on his way to the hospital. Pyjamas and the latest issue of the *Times Literary Supplement*. When he arrived at The Cedars she was sitting perched on the far end of a dark brown leather sofa that looked it might have been purchased from *Sofa So Good* - a new local company that offered discounts to university staff.

A bottle of *Jack Daniels* and two glasses lay next to a neatly ironed pair of pyjamas and a crisply folded TLS. She offered him a drink.

'Just a small one thanks. I'm driving.'

He waited for her to say something.

'At first when I rang I thought it must be cerebral malaria what with Nigel's recent travels so I was surprised as the next person when the doctor told me he'd had a seizure – brought on by malaria they thought - but thankfully only a mild one.'

She sipped her scotch. Gurney wondered if she normally drank at five in the afternoon. Must be the shock. He sipped his whiskey in silence. Difficult to know what to say really.

'Cerebral malaria?'

'Yes, prevalent in parts of East Africa resistant to several commonly used prophylaxes.'

'The professor has been in Africa?'

'Yes, but not for work but to support 'our' school. I say 'our' but in fact we only kick started the thing off with money that Nigel got from his Linguistics Reader which is apparently selling like hot cakes.'

'How long have you two been involved in the school?'

He tried to keep a tone of amazement out of his voice which might suggest he didn't believe a word of what she was saying or the possibility that he was being had.

'Oh, ten years or so. Nigel likes to pay a personal visit early February. He calls it the dead time when nothing happens other than piles of marking which he says he polishes off between the first and second drinks on the flight out.'

'Sounds marvellous, Abigail.'

He chose his next words carefully.

'What exactly does he 'do' it for?' He sipped his whiskey hoping he looked earnest and perplexed.

'Because someone must, Gurney. And anyway, isn't that what professors are supposed to do, you know, *do*'.

'Do?'

'Yes, do – do the right thing. Lead. Profess.'

Gurney was taken aback. His mentor and line manager – and now chairman of the Centenary event – was clearly extremely capable of professing – he recalled his campaign to abolish the intelligent lighting in the new building –

but actually *do* something? And something that seemed to result in no personal benefit? Clearly something was up. She topped up their glasses. He went on,

'It's just that Nigel has never struck me - Abigail - as someone easily distracted from what my mother would call 'getting on'. Doesn't Africa sort of get in way with all that?'

She looked hard at him her upper lip curled in what might be taken as a snarl.

'I'm not sure what you're getting at Gurney but let me ask you a question: what is it that you *do* that isn't in your own self-interest. Enlighten me.'

He wanted to tell her about the two days at Christmas with Albert, Doris and his mother, the over-indulgence in Amontillado sherry and having to endure nights sleeping alone in a room next to the one being used by his lovely Centenary assistant. Instead he apologised for being taken aback.

'Don't look so surprised Gurney. You're like so many academics. Just because you don't know about something you assume it doesn't exist.' She took another long pull of whiskey. He covered his glass.

'I'm impressed rather than surprised,' he lied.

'It's just that Nigel has always struck me as so single-minded in his relentless rise to the top which must have left little time for anything else.'

'Like me, you mean?'

He decided it was best not to answer that question. Instead he took refuge in posing another.

'It's easy for me to talk as a bachelor, but I don't think academic success and marriage are good bed partners. Neither are having children. When did you ever hear of a happily married successful academic? And more so, still married to the mother of his children?'

'*The pram in the hall?* But you're right Gurney, academic life has been designed to reward the selfish egoists who cynically convince themselves that what they are doing is for some professed greater good - when in fact it is mostly made up of individuals putting off the evil day when they might have to leave school and go out and get a proper job.'

There was no answer to this.

'But let me reassure you Gurney. When I met Nigel – our then rising young star - he met a suicidal anorexic researcher eager for anything or anyone who would offer her an escape from whatever it was imprisoning her. And you know what? This egotistical power crazy senior lecturer-on-the-make found time and something in him to nurture me, to listen to me, and to take me on.'

She looked like she was about to cry but instead held out the newly pressed pair of pyjamas.

'He's more than he seems, Gurney. Like several of your colleagues.'

Gurney drove slowly to the hospital which was thankfully near.

The Royal had recently been renamed but was little different from the sort of 1950s hospital he remembered from his childhood. The newly privatised

Adam Smith wing was different though: a reception desk that would have graced the Hilton, pot plants everywhere, and newly-painted walls advertising holidays in Mauritius. Even the copies of *Country Life* were current. His professor was in the *Wellcome Suite* on the first floor.

Hospitals are curious institutions rigidly protective of status and hierarchy. Name badges, stethoscopes draped casually around the necks of smiling doctors, pinstripe suits for the consultants, - all signifiers of separation from those unfortunate to be admitted as patients. Any status the sick might have is immediately removed or unnoticed so that the Professor becomes at best 'Nigel' or at worst 'love'. Was it a matter of mind over matter? 'We don't' mind, you don't...'

His thoughts were interrupted by a nurse holding what looked like a large pair of forceps. He asked her where the professor could be found.

'Nigel? He's on the first floor. Cantankerous bastard.'

'And which room might this cantankerous gentleman be residing?'

'1b next to 1a.'

'Oh, and he might be asleep, love.'

He knocked on the door.

'Fuck.'

He waited for the phrasal verb to be completed. When it wasn't, he entered. The professor was sitting bolt upright with several pillows behind him. A laptop was balanced on a tray on his knees which were drawn up. He looked - and sounded like - he was in rude health.

'Oh, it's you. Thought it was that imbecile nurse with another cup of what she calls 'elixir' but we all know is some shit to shut you up and put you out.'

The stroke had done little to reduce the volume though his diction did sound slightly slurred. A little like his wife's.

'And what brings you to this land of the semi-living boyo? Good news I hope? Sit my friend sit and bring me up to speed.'

Gurney sat down on an expensive easy chair next to the bed. He knew the professor well enough now to avoid 'hesitation, repetition, or deviation' if he wanted his attention for more than just a minute. He explained where he thought they were, late February with about three weeks to go.

'Good work, Gurney, good work. You've done well.'

Gurney added,

'Alice helped.'

'No doubt she did boyo if only to keep you on target, diddly-dum.'

Nitrous oxide or the New Year goodwill holding firm No other explanation for this sudden outbreak of benign philanthropy. The professor seemed to read his mind.

'Wondering why I'm not my usual razor-sharp self?' he said a smile playing around the corner of his mouth.

'Takes a near miss to bring home one or two home truths Gurney which, if you will indulge me, lead inevitably to changed behaviour, altered discourse, and a certain re-ordering of priorities.'

Gurney considered for a second raising the point - often made by the professor - that *discourse* was in fact not a distinct entity but a form of behaviour loaded with semiotic meaning. Instead he asked him what they should do next.

'Keynote Gurney keynote! If this is to be a success it all hangs on the opening address, an event that must remain in the memory long after the drunken sods who attend these things have put in their expenses claims forms and wondered why they attended in the first place. It's at the beginning Gurney when we can make our mark! Like fresh lambs to the slaughter they will be sitting awaiting the keynote - anxious, wondering if this will be the one conference to break the mould providing them with something memorable.'

Other than Williams himself, Gurney couldn't think of anyone suitable to open the event.

'Three names come to mind Gurney. Let me run them past you.'
The smile was now playing around both corners of his mouth. He was clearly enjoying this. Gurney retrieved the small black notebook from his inner pocket.

'In no particular order of importance, let's start with big beast number one - distinguished professor Dick-the-Prick Pryke of Duke University who claims to have written the seminal work on the fricative vowel. Wanker of course, but seminal.

'Then there's my old drinking buddy, Doctor Oswald Browne from the University of the frigging north in frigging Finland, whose four-star masterwork was based on his extensive ethnographic fieldwork amongst the alcoholic sub-culture of Tampere. His book will certainly outlive him even if he does gets the liver transplant he so richly deserves.

'Finally, there's Doctor Julian Jack John - who as you know Gurney - is one of those super demi-god types who actually live up to their reputation. And check this out - when asked 'what's your field?' always answers. 'Field? How retro. My field is no field, my discipline is no discipline, my research is no research' - which you have to admit is taking the concept of existential negativity to a new level.'

'But what would he talk about?'

'Ah, this where he is a genius. He will talk about 'everything and nothing', 'words and the silences between them', but more importantly given he's a lazy bugger whatever we tell him to talk about.'

'And if we invite him should we keep the other two as first and second reserve?'

'No chance I'm afraid. Once they found out – and they always do – that they are playing second fiddle to Doctor No, they'll take umbrage like only an academic can, and tell you they've had a better offer elsewhere. But fear not, I am sure JJJ – as he is known - will agree particularly when he hears about the hefty fee we'll be paying him.'

Gurney didn't like to ask where the *hefty fee* was coming from.

'I know what you're thinking Gurney but fear not. When you phone him and fill his over-large jug ears with praise - and promise him that the treats we can offer will including sitting next to fragrant Alice or my lovely Abigail at the Centenary dinner - he'll come like a shot.'

On the way home Gurney, narrowly avoided colliding with a Lidl van. He needed to be more careful lest he found himself in the next bed to the professor. His small house – it was never a home – seemed more drab than usual. He had to move. Go somewhere with more style, somewhere more befitting to a man of his stature. Somewhere larger, somewhere Alice, or Amy, or even Andrea might be willing to visit or better, *stay over.*

Another van - this time with *Ocado* emblazoned on its side - cut him up at the T-junction. He parked in the disabled bay opposite where he lived and then resisted the temptation to call Linden and suggest they have a swift half at the pub. He had some important calls to make in the morning and he'd need his wits about him.

Chapter Twenty-One

By failing to prepare, you are preparing to fail - Benjamin Franklin

Gurney felt surprisingly chipper. Since Christmas it had all gone much better than he had expected, the professor had arranged for him to have a lighter teaching load, and he felt that he might just pull it off: recognition and promotion in one fell swoop! Less than a month to go, until ground zero - the opening keynote. Today he'd work his way down the professor's list of potential keynote speakers. He started with Doctor Julian Jack John, JJJ.

JJJ rather enjoyed being the resident Englishman at a prestigious American university. In fact, he had fashioned an identity along the lines of the *Englishman abroad*: brown corduroys with matching Oxford brogues and a floppy Hugh Grant fringe that suggested a touch of the dandy. His speech was also modelled upon Grant - slightly hesitant - but not enough to indicate dim-wittedness beneath the flop. Early on he realised that most - if not all - of his American colleagues - despite their Protestant heritage and can-do attitude - were more than content to simply 'have a nice day' supported not by their university salary - but daddy's wealth accrued from shrewd investments in real estate. Being a distinguished professor accorded him one luxury, however – a personal gate-keeper who made damned sure no one disturbed the distinguished professor in his distinguished work. His gate-keeper – or personal secretary – was one Agnes Sweinsteiger, a stout dragon of an individual whose gender was effectively disguised within several layers of woollen clothing irrespective of the weather.

What made Agnes remarkable - and useful - was her unfailing loyalty. Out of hours she became another person, the writer of the first - and soon-to-be-published - definitive biography of one of the world's much maligned historical figures, Prince Vlad of Transylvania, who had developed the unnerving habit of impaling the bringers of bad news. It was to this Agnes that Gurney was connected via the university switchboard.

She would indeed ask Professor Jack – all American academics are professors – to call him back. 'Have a nice day.'

He called Alice to suggest she call him back. If it could work on Gerald Creaven it could work on Jack.

'I can try my best flirty voice if you think that would work?'

Gurney agreed that she should, not adding that he wondered if she'd tried out this voice on him over Christmas? They agreed to meet at noon when she was due back from Creaven Creams.

There was a knock on the door. Surely it wasn't Alice, early? A young woman who looked young enough to be a student came in. She smiled and offered her hand - a gesture of politeness that unnerved him slightly.

'My name is Annike Grobbelar, your new intern – and assistant to your assistant, Alice.'

Assistant to an assistant? He detected the aroma of an expensive perfume, Chanel. Did they assist each other with buying perfume?

'Yes, I've been told by Professor Williams that it involves a minimum hourly wage, no employment rights, and brutal hard work but I think he was joking, ya?'

Gurney nodded and thought for a moment

'I'd say you are from your accent that you are from South Africa, the Western Cape, Grahamstown perhaps?'

She smiled an even brighter smile suitably impressed.

'Close - from Port Elizabeth actually - but I did varsity at Rhodes - which is just up the road.'

'Oh, and the professor said you were a soft touch. Another joke, yes?'

'Yes, his humour is legendary.'

He suggested she return at twelve with coffee when she could meet the rest of the team. Team! He was leading a team now! When it was just Alice, Linden, and himself it had seemed more like a bunch of friends, but now it was a *team*, and he was the team-leader of it. He rubbed his hands. He rather looking forward to the strategy meeting. A ping announced he had mail, one from Alice telling him she might be running late from her meeting with Creaven, another from Phoenix to say, 'we must talk. I've got some news to share. Love you, Amy.'

He checked his watch. He couldn't remember if she would be just getting up or just going to bed. Whatever she'd be wearing a soft cotton Victorian nightdress, be bare foot and dreamy.

He pinged a reply.

'Hi, what about now if the time is right for you?' Love you, Gurney.'

What a difference the second personal pronoun *you* can make - especially if following the verb 'Love.'

She pinged back a reply to his reply. Apparently, a new private university to the north of Phoenix had established a small - though growing department of applied linguistics - headed by a Professor Anneliese Langsprechen - who had not only heard of the Centenary but had persuaded her Dean to fund her all-inclusive attendance. She knew Amy from some candle-lit function they had both attended and would travel with her business class.

'So, this is just to confirm, Gurney that I am coming and with a friend, Anneliese, who is very nice, if a bit American if you know what I mean.'

She added that her friend was also very impressed with his last paper on the use of the modal auxiliary verb in non-western language communities, and hoped her university could 'entice' him over to the States. He did indeed know what she meant, German by name, American by nature? Amy and Anneliese had booked adjoining rooms at the Grand – 'double rooms, Gurney' – and with that she signed off with a promise that she would 'touch-base' immediately after she landed. He rang Williams, who had returned from hospital fit and well.

'A lot of fucking fuss about nothing'. Accommodation is now being handled by a new bunch of half-wits buried in Registry headed up by a Gill Krill. It is not enough that our teaching and research might have had some social engagement - or even have led to the making of a bob or two - now we need another fucking unit made up of fucking mediocre graduates fresh out of fucking universities such as ours - telling us how to not only 'engage' but get this - make an 'impact' Whatever that means.'

With that he uttered a half-strangulated cry and rang off.

Time to review where he was, with the Centenary – and more importantly his quest for the holy trinity of 'recognition', 'promotion', and 'sex'.

In terms of the first, he was clearly much more visible amongst his peers than before. Mention 'Centenary' and it was likely someone would say. 'Oh, isn't Sleep running that?' Of course, recognition only worked in the long term if what was recognised was successful. But the omens were good.

Promotion? What had Williams said?

'Handle this in a half-decent manner boyo and your SL is in the bag' - and he should know given he chaired the committee. But he had added somewhat ambiguously,

'not that you don't deserve advancement on your publications so far but as you know none of the pricks on the committee ever read anything, and that includes their own work.'

Adding value - not business as usual - that's what mattered. The Centenary was clearly adding something - and anyway he could hardly wait a hundred years for the next one to come around. And finally, *sex?* He sat up in his chair and tore off a page of yellow paper from his pad. There was surely a short-list of three possibles plus a handful of out-riders.

Amy: The favourite given her familiarity. She was coming to the Centenary and had been suggestive, flirtatious even in the last email – 'double rooms, Gurney' -, and anyway they had history. She had form. *Could* - and if he played his cards right, - a strong *would.*

Then there was *Alice*: clearly coming up fast on the rails, eager and ambitious, a *might,* and possibly a *must,* given their own recent history. And not only likeable but agreeable - a rare trait in the moral landscape of academe.

Finally, *Andrea*: the German dark horse, expert in the popular theoretical field of gender relations though he'd have to watch what he said - and no doubt what he did. But a distinct *could*, possibly a *would.*

And then the out-riders: *Abigail*, the lonely professor's wife or *Annike*, the ''assistant to the assistant' or even the unseen *Anneliese* Langsprechen approaching fast from Arizona who had at least *recognised* him. An abundance of riches: Amy, Alice, Andrea, Abigail, Annike, and Anneliese. Six alpha women to his one gamma male.

He groaned. He could hear the redolent tones of his mentor playing in his head, 'Up your game boyo! Up your fucking game!' It was all right for him - he had climbed up into the heady and confident stratosphere of the modal *must* only to find himself still psychologically rooted in the foothills of *maybe*.

Without knocking Alice entered his office wearing a crisp white blouse, short blue pleated skirt, a pair of matching Birkenstocks, and an enticing dab of Chanel No. 5 behind each ear. And they all dressed better than him. Her assistant followed fast on her heels. Both women were carrying matching small black notebooks. They clearly meant business.

'I thought you might not make it Alice?'

'So, did I. Gerald Creaven can talk the hind legs off a donkey but I told him I'd be back which seemed to shut him up. I think he's taken a fancy to me.'

Gurney arranged the chairs into a semi-circle whilst Annike took an order for coffee and sandwiches. Alice opened proceedings with an update,

'Attendance? Seventy-five externals have booked for the full package – three nights' accommodation, drinks reception, conference dinner and centenary compact disk composed of abstracts, background papers, list of attendees etc. One hindered internals have indicated they will attend some of the events with twenty-five signing up for the reduced-price dinner - and let's not forgot opportunity to purchase a signed copy of JJJ's latest tome – he's agreed to come by the way - but the current total of internals doesn't include us or the VC, the Dean, the new Head of Finance or the newly appointed Head of the University Council, Lord somebody the VC will introduce us to soon.'

All presumably with partners. Gurney rubbed his hands together, happy that things looked under control. His turn to be leaderish, Churchillian.

'Alice, you travel back to Creavens and run a final check with Gerald he is happy about everything; Annike, you confirm rooms with hospitality and technical support for I.T. then I suggest you ask Estates about signage; I'll handle an early piece for the local rag and anything else we've forgotten.'

He stood up. Meeting closed. Team dismissed. Watches not synchronised but they agreed to meet 'same place same time' every other day until the big day.

On his way out to the loo he ran into Linden.

'Put us down on the dinner list Gurney. And try to wangle us next to you for we have some stupendous news to share'.

And with that he was off. He wondered if he and Alice would be seated with the VC, Williams, JJJ, the Dean and Registrar - but he couldn't be certain. Worker bees did not frequent the same level as the queens. Perhaps where he sat - and next to whom - would be the most reliable measure of the amount of recognition he had accrued?

He suddenly thought of his mother. Would she want to come? See her son at his finest hour? Talk to whoever she was seated next to and tell them long stories about how her only son was such a quiet boy and yet look at him now. He crossed her off his list. Anyway, she'd find it very dull. If it was a success he'd tell her afterwards.

Conferences rely upon academics to present their current research in the form of a brief presentation, usually by PowerPoint, supported by a longer paper which is included on a compact disc as part of the proceedings. Nobody ever actually reads these papers during or after the event, the central purpose of the conference being to be recognised, to be able to network, and to be afforded an opportunity to get drunk – and at another university's expense. He had decided long ago that he himself would not submit a paper to the Centenary screening committee. It would be one less thing to worry about, he could channel his energies into making sure nothing went wrong, and anyway since the Oslo symposium he had done no research whatsoever and therefore had little new to say. Not that this would have precluded his paper being accepted for inclusion.

When he returned from the loo an email plus attachment had arrived. From Andrea. In her characteristically brusque manner she informed him that her paper had been accepted - who had read it? Williams? - and that she would arrive in plenty of time to meet up with other members of the women's panel - women's panel? -and that she would be staying in the spare room of the landlord of *The Open House*. And that it was a 'double'. She had highlighted 'double'.

Gurney felt a stirring in his loins which receded fast when he read that she would be presenting, 'Genitive genders: the emergence of *herstory* in one hundred years of linguistics'. Her argument was that, whereas *history* was the unfolding hegemonic story of the dominance of men over woman – think Dale Spender's *Man-Made Language* – *herstory* was an 'alternative narrative foregrounding the hidden matrilineal script that was a natural home for all that really mattered – human rights, natural justice, think the blind-folded female holding the scales of justice, Joan of Arc, nay Angelia Jolie?' This hidden language she termed *femspeak* - and what is more she intended to deliver the final part of her presentation in it.

Gurney was impressed. She had clearly discovered a neat way to smash through the glass ceiling by coining a new term for an old problem, a sure-fire way to gain recognition and promotion.

Femspeak might well become the *leit motif* of the Centenary, which would at least be one in the eye for Dr Julian Jack John.

As he pondered the vagaries of fame Gurney closed his eyes for a moment...He awoke to find himself still in his office. He wrote back to Andrea congratulating her on her paper, ending with the hope that if his busy schedule allowed he would swing by her lodgings. He signed it 'in haste, Gurney'. And added as an afterthought, 'I see you are presenting first on the second day. Fear not about oversleeping, if all else fails I can pop round and knock you up.'

He logged off and went in search of Williams who had fully recovered from whatever he'd had. He liked to work late. He found him with his head down on his desk. Was he asleep? Or dead?

'Come in boyo and close the door behind you. We have a small problem which I'm sure you can solve.'

Gurney sat down.

'It seems that our biscuit baron Gerald - fucking - Creaven has heard about your suggestion of contacting the local rag but has taken it upon himself to alert them – a certain junior hack called Amber Brookes – about his over-inflated role in our fucking event. Jumped our gun, if you get my drift - which is made worse by the fact that this Brookes character is an alumnus of this fucking university - and this fucking university department – so what I suggest is that you hop over to her no doubt grubby office and appraise her of what is actually what.'

With that he resumed his position, head bowed before the altar of his blank computer screen.

Gurney went back to his office and looked up the location of the city's newspaper. One good thing – it was a stone's throw from where he lived, time to change his shirt and pick up something to eat, if he had anything in his fridge.

Chapter Twenty-Two

Bigamy is having one wife too many. Monogamy is the same - Oscar Wilde

Gurney rang the *Gazette*. He was told he could see her later that day when the paper was *put to bed* which would be around nine in the evening. Their offices were a stone's throw from his house which would give him time to change his shirt and pick up something from the nearby convenience store.

A little before nine he walked briskly towards the premises of the town's only, and perhaps last, newspaper, *The Daily Gazette*. Once inside Gurney followed a narrow corridor into the *news room* - a huge open plan space consisting of small cubicles in which a journalist or editor typed feverously away or sat staring blankly at a pin board upon which were faded cuttings of the Gazette's more recent scoops. Gurney had never read the paper and wondered what they wrote about. Somebody once told him that whereas academics know 'more and more about less and less,' with journalists it was the other way around. He stopped and asked a large man with a beard if he could show him to Amber's cubicle.

Amber Brookes was a flame-haired young woman who looked tired and a little dishevelled. He introduced himself.

'Fraid I don't remember much of uni but then who does? Not till you start working in the real world do you realise what a cinch uni was, don't you agree?'

Gurney wasn't sure if he agreed or not.

'Depends on what you mean by *cinch* I suppose.'

'Yeah, but I had a great time y'know and hey probably wouldn't be sitting here now if I hadn't learnt a thing or two about the jolly old modal auxiliary verb.'

She smiled. He returned the smile. Clearly, she had done her homework or had a good memory.

'So, what do I need to know about this centenary of yours? Some bloke called Creaven bent my ear yesterday about the logo and all the dosh he was spending on making it a success but I'd like to hear from you the chief honcho'. She said this with certainty.

'Tell you what, Gurney why don't I interview you? Now if you've got time?'

He glanced at his watch. Wasn't that the point of the meeting? If she could wrap it up in fifty minutes he might still make the pub for a swift half.

'OK, what do you want to know?'

'How about I start with some of those weekend colour mag questions, you know, who you'd invite for dinner, what's your most frightening moment, how often you have sex...'

He laughed, nervously. Clearly it wasn't only the paper that was put to bed at nine o'clock.

'Sorry, I've obviously embarrassed you. Let's start with the Centenary and what's the point of the whole thing.'

She opened her small black notebook and quickly scribbled down everything he said. In just under thirty minutes he summarised the history of the subject over the past one hundred years, how important the Centenary would be for 'town and gown', and who the key note speaker was. He even added a few personal morsels to 'whet the appetite of the general reader', how he was on a difficult personal 'journey' – we are all on journeys these days – but that if all went to plan he felt confident they would hold a similar event next year.

She seemed pleased. For an academic he had been remarkably concise, attractive even. She promised to email him the final copy the next day.

As he left the building he texted Linden to see if he was up for a drink. The *Open House* was empty apart from Linden who was seated at their table reading a copy of the *Gazette*. Perhaps he was checking his lotto numbers? He ordered a pint and two packets of pork scratching.

'You look frazzled Linden, tough day?'

'Yes and no. Yes, in that the meeting was brief, no in the VC's decision – which over-rules FREAC – to, what was his exact phrase - take the bull by the horns – and move fast on the complete reorganisation of the university. The result he says will be a 'leaner, simpler, and saner' organisation. Like most of us Gurney I can buy *leaner* and *simpler,* but *saner*?'

He took a long draught of ale.

'What it boils down to is this - which by the way is top secret at the moment - faculties are to become schools, schools are to become departments, and departments are to become history. In other words, your beloved department of contrastive linguistics will be merged into a school unless they scrap the whole thing and do nothing, but from what I hear of our new VC that's not an option.'

'But the Centenary?'

'I know what you are thinking Gurney, what about linguistics swallowing up a couple of other social science outfits and becoming one of the new Schools? Well it has been decided by those who know better - particularly those with an ear to the mutterings on the fifth floor - that what will determine the status of a new school will not be scholarship or teaching, but *reach and significance,* which as you know is sadly lacking in our department, present company excluded.'

Gurney swallowed some pork scratching.

'Which means, Linden, we're screwed? Which means that our centenary will be our swan-song? But what I don't understand is why go to all the bother of marking over one hundred years of intellectual contribution when the plan all along was to turn out the lights and shut up shop?'

'Because, Gurney - and you're using appropriate metaphors at last - your shop is no longer selling what the punters want. Forget intellectual curiosity or blue-sky thinking - what's at stake here is corporate consumerism. Your only hope is to persuade the powers that be – that contrastive linguistics not only has another hundred years of life in it – but it can align itself in some way with the new corporate identity - which incidentally the VC will unveil at the Centenary dinner.'

'Which is?'

'Well, the word on the street is that the University must be wedded to RI 'reach and impact'. *Reach* meaning what it can produce outputs that will reach the attention of those in the city who have already worked out that our great universities are much cheaper than their R&D division - and *impact* which is interpreted as something making a difference to what really matters, namely profit and loss...'

He was on a rant. Gurney thought it wise to let him finish

'...knowledge, ideas, - speculation if you like - means nothing if it cannot be reduced to 'impact' - and when I use this word - I mean that which can be measured and weighed at the end of the year – which in case you are wondering will be the financial year.'

Gurney listened to his friend speak wondering what economic or social impact his work had had since his arrival at the University.

'...which in strategic terms this means that from now on we will give you some money, you will find out what we need to know, do it within our prescribed period of say three to six months, and then if what you have discovered makes a difference to something – they're not sure what that might be yet - we'll then give you some more money to carry on with what you're doing. It used to be called *market research* - an oxymoron if ever I heard one - but now it will be called *impact research* unless someone in linguistics can dream up a better description. Come to think of it here's an avenue that might just save you – the production of euphemistic terminology for our changing times. I'm sure, the university would fund that.'

Bitterly he sipped his bitter. Gurney had never seen him like this and wondered if Lucy had ditched him - or worse the university had decided to 'let him go'? Gurney ordered another round and whilst at the bar asked the landlord if his room with a double bed, was free during the next couple of months.

'Sorry Gurney, I've got the painters and decorators coming in next week, after which a bird called Andrea, has booked it for your conference thing, but it'll be free after that.'

'Did this Andrea say why she wanted it for a whole week given the Centenary is just three days?'

'Yes, she did actually - something about celebrating an engagement - but she wouldn't elaborate further.'

He tapped a grubby forefinger against his nose.

'Sounds like you could get in there lad and develop a little engagement of your own, hey?'

'Is it really a double?'

'Indeed, it is my friend - and what with its own entrance via the back passage - if you'll excuse my French – and what's more, as it's you I'd give you a deal.'

Gurney told him he'd let him know. When he returned to the bar Linden stood up to leave.

'Sorry about that Gurney, just had to get a few things off my chest, but whatever happens let's go out with a bang, what? And don't forget Lucy and I have that semi-surprise to spring on you at the Centenary dinner. Let's go out as a foursome after just like the good old days. You can bring Alice or what's her name from the States if she's coming.'

They shook hands as always.

'And Gurney remember you and I both have tenure so whatever happens they can't boot us out, can they?'

Gurney paused before his front door expecting his mother to call at the exact moment he withdrew his mobile phone from his pocket. It remained silent. The house was empty just as he had left it, unloved, uncared for, and bereft of a woman's touch. Like him he thought as he trudged through the living room to the small kitchen at the back. He glanced around looking for the bottle of scotch. What *impact* had he had on this place? Or more to the point *it on him*? No, there had been no economic or social engagement on his part, because - if the truth be known - this pile of bricks and mortar had only really been a pit-stop, a refuelling bay, a habitation that was frankly uninhabitable.

On his mat was a long white envelope with his name handwritten on the front. He must have walked over it. It was from the professor's wife.

'Gurney, forgive my intrusion but I must write to you. Nigel arrived home last night and announced that he was leaving me. To cut a long story short it seems his journeys to East Africa were all a sham, he was in fact spending all those days – and nights – not in the deepest bush doing good but rather in the company of one of your colleagues, a certain Miss Alice Hildebrand - who he tells me is about to be promoted to PA to the new head of the School of Informatics and Social Science, a post the VC will award to Nigel, funded by a consortium of mobile phone companies and internet providers.

'He's pleased as punch - has sworn me to secrecy - but - what the hell - given his despicable behaviour, what I think you should know is that they have decided that in the new School contrastive linguistics will be integrated into informatics or abolished. Apparently, he says that tenure means sod all if your department is no longer economically viable.'

Gurney felt slightly sick.

'The new VC says it's about 'thrusting disciplines of a new age. Nigel clearly agrees, which I assume is another reason sweet Alice Hildebrand fits the bill.'

The letter ended with a suggestion, if he was free, he should 'come over' -
if only to discuss the *impact* all this might have on the final prep for the
Centenary.

Though slightly drunk from his three pints, he picked up his mobile and
dialled Abigail's number. If the professor answered he'd belch a response and
hang up, if his wife responded he'd call a cab and scoot straight over. Abigail,
loyal wife of a power-hungry fuckwit of a husband, and a friend who needed
comforting at this time.

She held his hand as they sat together on the sofa - a newly-opened bottle
of single malt between them. Tearfully she recounted the 'awful moment' she had
found out. Apparently - uncharacteristically - he had left his computer logged on
whilst he went down and paid the milk bill during which she had glanced at a
string of emails directed to one - PT - who - when confronted - told her it was his
affectionate name for his 'posh totty', who he said worked at the university – and
who she assumed was Alice.

'Do you think Alice - if it is Alice - is the first?'

'You're right Gurney I'm sure there were others - probably quite a few -
given his jokes about trading me in for 'younger' and 'fresher' models.'

Gurney thought of some of the 'freshers' he'd met at the beginning of the
year. They were certainly looking younger. Alice was certainly young and on the
side of 'freshness' – and what with the pearls she did possess something of the
PT about her but on the other hand he couldn't see her and the professor…

'He told me I could stay here until after the Centenary was done and dusted
but then we'd have to sit down and have a serious discussion about the division
of the spoils.'

At this she began to cry, her hand holding his in a vice-like grip. He wasn't
sure what to say other than to murmur something about 'the evil men do' - and
'what comes around, comes around', though he wasn't exactly sure what he
meant. She cheered up a little when he reminded her that today's *young* were
tomorrow's 'middle-aged.'

It was almost midnight by the time he left The Cedars - his time with her
rewarded by a full-on-mouth to mouth kiss lasting several seconds - and a
promise he'd call again in the next few days. He also had to promise he'd tell no
one of what he knew and most certainly not the professor or Alice. He rang
Linden. He was still up.

'It is just possible Gurney that Alice is just a smokescreen to disguise the
true identity of PT and if so I'd be careful about making false accusations.'

There were two other possibilities. The first was the wife of the VC –
though in that direction professional suicide lay – or a lissom new Australian
professor called Genette someone whose inaugural lecture Williams had attended
and had been 'most impressed' with. Apparently, it was all about Antipodean
queer literature but towards the end the Genette somebody had thrown her
prepared notes down and had announced that she was 'coming out of the closet'

and celebrating her new status as 'metrosexual,' whatever that meant. Rumours were that the professor made sure he was number one on her new list of male friends.

Gurney felt tired and troubled. At tomorrow's centenary strategy meeting he'd try and tease out what exactly, if anything Alice was up to. At all costs, he'd avoid Williams. Let sleeping loins lie.

*

Annike had left him a post-it on his door to say that she'd be late. He arranged a chair next to his and awaited Alice. At the appointed hour, she breezed in sporting a sheer pink almost see-through blouse, distressed blue jeans, and a pair of espadrilles. She smiled, offered him a cup of coffee, and opened her little black book. He thought about what Abigail had said, and the promise he'd made to keep mum.

But needs must, 'are you having an affair with Professor Williams?'

She burst out laughing.

'Are you serious? First, he's just not my kind of guy, second, he's an academic – and no disrespect Gurney – and third, isn't he happily married to what's her name?'

'Abigail. But more to the point where did you hear this rumour if I might ask?'

Gurney blushed.

'From an impeccable source but to give her credit she did acknowledge that all this might be just a case of smoke and mirrors.'

'That I am some sort of decoy or stalking horse so that whoever he is having an affair with can remain hidden from view?'

'Something like that - and sorry for asking - it is just that it's the last thing we need now for a distraction to blow us off course.'

She seemed happy at his explanation but was clearly hurt.

They concluded the meeting agreeing a set of urgent and less urgent tasks in the remaining twenty or so days before the balloon went up. After his team had gone, Gurney considered what was or what might be going on between Williams and Alice. For a start, he believed her. Williams was a master at using and abusing whoever was to hand, but the news of the pending reorganisation and Alice's promotion did have a ring of the truth about it. The subject of *her* promotion could wait until the dust had settled.

His landline rang. It was JJJ from the States confirming he'd be doing the keynote.

'Sorry about Agnes, Gurney but she's one helleva fine PA.'

When talking with fellow Brits Julian Jack John found it amusing to adopt the laconic laid-back style of the East Coast; likewise, when having to discuss anything with his American colleagues he preferred self-deprecating diffidence, just as long as it did not denote any underlying weakness. Code-switching, a most useful component in the arsenal of the upwardly-rising professor.

For the next two weeks, the team met every alternate day, tasks were assigned and then rapidly ticked off as the Centenary celebration gradually took shape. The logo – an open book emblazoned with, *in the beginning was the word* was approved by Williams – he hardly turned up to any of the meetings, deciding that he'd keep his organisational powder dry until the final few days when inevitably something was 'bound to go wrong.'

But it never did. Up to the night before the welcome drinks reception all delegates had been accorded their accommodation of choice, caterers – nominated by Gerald Creaven - at a twenty percent discount – had confirmed menus, the signage was in place, and the students had mostly disappeared to complete assignments due in at the end of the month. His mother called telling Gurney that she and Albert had been selected to be one of the 'pilgrims' on *Deal or No Deal*, with the promise of one week's compulsory attendance rewarded by the chance to sit in the 'hot seat'.

Williams turned up at the final strategy meeting the day before the opening. They were to decide the seating plan for the conference dinner, a top table of twelve raised above the remaining tables of six and eight. It was clear that neither Gurney nor Alice would be on the high table but seated at table two along with Alice, Linden, Lucy, Andrea, and Amy. Amy had written to say that at the last-minute Anneliese had cried off so she'd be coming on her own. Gurney wondered if it was a good idea to have the two cousins sitting at the same table as himself and Andrea but, hey, 'let's live in the present!' He separated Linden from Alice, put Amy on one side of him, he on the other with Andrea and Alice making up the arrangement.

That final evening, with nothing left to do, he and Linden agreed to meet at the *Open House*, just for old times' sake. He ordered a bottle of cava and a couple of rounds of 'sandwiches of the day'. Linden arrived punctually, freshly shaven and sporting a new polyester shirt.

'Present from Lucy. I've got her a solar-powered thesaurus which can translate any word into seven major European languages. Will be handy when we take off for that 'special holiday' at the end of the month'.

At this he winked.

'Cava! Thanks Gurney. What's the occasion?'

'To celebrate your well-known secret Linden plus the fact that in just over three days it'll all be over, I will be deservedly promoted - and more to the point - will be taking a leaf out of your book and enjoying a weekend away with the love of my life.'

Linden laughed.

'And by the way who are we talking about here?'

He sipped his cava.

'Promise me you won't tell even Lucy - but though as you know I'd be happy - whoever it was - if it was Amy - but wouldn't be unhappy if it turned out to be lovely much-misconstrued Alice - or the equally abrasive yet underneath-it-all fair Teutonic maiden Andrea.'

'Glad that's clear. No-one else?'

'Well there are a couple of out-riders but without wanting to paint myself the campus Lothario, let's just say that if push comes to shove, I do have several possibilities tucked up my sleeve. But most important Linden is my decision here - my decision - to turn over a new leaf and strike out boldly. Faint heart never won far lady, and let's face it never again will I have the enviable opportunity to have within my grasp three, possibly six, female friends in the same place at the same time, several whom who have in the past few days shown more than a passing interest in my attentions.'

Linden wondered if this was Gurney's lecturing style. They looked at each other across the table. Men of the world. They drained their glasses, stood up, shoulders back and performed a short ceremonial bow to each other as if they were sumo wrestlers about to participate in an ancient, honourable contest of strength, mental agility, and superhuman courage. Which for Gurney about as accurate as you were going to get.

He slept fitfully before the big day. In one of the dreams he was fleeing down a poorly-lit corridor -the kind you find in an old NHS hospital – chased by a large bearded man wielding a meat cleaver. Running towards him - towards danger - was a young woman wearing a flowing white robe, a necklace of daisies in her hair, her mouth making sounds he could not hear. Though she looked more like Amy she also possessed the features of Alice.

He awoke in a sweat, his fingers gripping the duvet, his pillow thrown across the room in his haste to escape the deranged killer and protect his Lady A with the garland of flowers. Not a particularly auspicious start to the most important day of his life.

He closed his eyes for a second.

Smiling she turned to him, her right arm propped up on the pillow. The small attic bedroom above the Double Locks had just enough room for a double bed, small bedside table – upon which she had placed a few wild daisies in a small bottle – and a chest of drawers into which they had placed their few possessions the night before.

Full English for me!

Just croissant and coffee.

Oh A...!

When he awoke for a second time he found himself lying prone, face pressed firmly into where his pillow had been, buttocks slightly raised.

Chapter Twenty-Three

Sex without love is a meaningless experience, but as far as meaningless experiences go it's damn good — Woody Allen

He staggered out of bed. No cereal, no coffee, no milk. So much for the full English. Black tea. It was surprisingly refreshing. He felt better. The Centenary! He chose his clothes carefully: new dark cord trousers, white shirt, grey jacket he had last worn at his father's funeral. No tie - what academic ever wears a tie except at an interview?

The welcome reception wasn't until the evening but it seemed wise - prudent even - to get in early - be at his desk – ready for all comers. And who knows perhaps Amy or Andrea would drop by? Good to be seen as bright and fresh, the team leader hard at it! Whatever *it* was.

The Department was deserted. He sat at his desk, an aura of calm settling him. It would be all right. He looked across at Williams' office which was unoccupied. He resisted the temptation to log-on and instead withdrew a yellow legal pad of lined paper from the top drawer of his desk. He began to write,

Centenary, day one.

He chewed on the pencil.

The conference. My big moment - my chance to seize the day! To live in the moment!

He had heard that the Appointments & Promotions committee would hold its next meeting three weeks after the Centenary closed. OK so he'd done no research that had any *reach* or *significance* – but the Centenary had to count for something? It would surely reward him with *recognition* and *promotion*, the VC had intimated as much. As for *sex*, well he was surely well-placed now for some success on that front, what with three desirable women showing more than a modicum of interest in him. He thought of his mother and father seizing their moment on that country lane in Norfolk. If only one of those delicious, intriguing sirens would winch him onto the rocky shores of love. He folded up the single piece of yellow paper and put it back into the drawer with the pad.

A stooped figure was moving around in Williams' office. It looked a little like Betty who cleaned the offices. She probably had more knowledge of the world than he had. Knowledge? So, what did he know of the most important thing in his room – himself?

Well, he had an armoury of formal qualifications that was impressive. He had - he looked around – an office - and one he didn't share, yet. He had a loving mother and a small group of friends – he thought of Linden and Alice – and a house – OK so it wasn't perfect but it was a roof over his head. But - and here was the epistemological niggle – what did he *know* of himself, the Gurney Sleep who had washed up in this modern institution of higher learning teaching contrastive linguistics and yet, for all his accumulated knowledge, knowing so little of love? Perhaps he would find an answer to that question sooner than later?

*

'Canapés, lovely word, don't you think Gurney?'

Gurney nodded. For some reason holding a small sausage in one hand and a glass of warm Riesling in the other robbed him of the power of speech. But the reception seemed to be going well. Williams didn't seem to mind chatting to his junior lecturer. Talking to Gurney was rehearsal for the bigger fish he could see circling around a rather pretty waitress who was holding a tray upon which were glasses of fizzy white.

'But Gurney, before I partake of my leaving, I must just say, fucking well done boyo for getting it all fucking well done - on time -, and from I've heard - under fucking budget.'

He drained his glass, swivelled his hips neatly for a man of his size and headed towards the pretty waitress with the tray.

Gurney swallowed the remains of the sausage. He'd find another if he could. The room was gradually filling up with some of his colleagues he vaguely remembered, most of who nodded sagely in his direction. *Recognition.* A few people he didn't know smiled wanly, wondering whom he was and whether he looked important enough to approach.

Academics are not good at small talk - they have bigger things to think about – most preferring to use social opportunities to self-promote a book 'in the pipeline' or, if they are forced, praise the academic achievements of their offspring – Tamsin, Tristan or Tara, a complicated task given that most are on their second or third marriages, and find it increasingly difficult to remember much about their progeny.

At precisely seven o'clock, Professor Craig Thomas, Vice-Chancellor and Chief Executive Officer of the university tapped his wine glass.

Silence.

G'day! Titters and ripples.

'As you know I'm the new bloke here, so apologies if we haven't met yet but the night is yet young...'

Further laughter, mostly from the VC's office.

'...We are all here to celebrate, to mark a milestone in the shining path that has been carved out by Linguistics in this fair university of ours...'

He paused for effect.

'...I have to say that when I landed up in this fair university of yours a few weeks ago I was not convinced of the wisdom of using our resources - time and money - to support what looked to me like one of those backward-looking affairs you Brits are so fond of...'

Louder silence.

'...but I have spoken with those of you involved...'

And here he waved an expansive Antipodean hand towards Gurney.

'...and can say that what you have achieved here in terms of significance and reach is worthwhile...'.

He paused to allow a small round of applause.

'...but we are not a university that rests on its laurels. I am the bringer of *good* and *bad* news...'

Gurney looked directly towards the VC who appeared to wink at him.

'The bad news is that from October 1st, the Department of Linguistics, whose centenary we are celebrating here today, will cease to exist'.

He paused for dramatic effect which he achieved.

'...but the good news is that the during the next one hundred years Linguistics will be part of a future, a glittering future - that will see its place firmly established within an inter-disciplinary family of intellectual areas that will forthwith be called the School of Informatics and Social Science. Within this family will grow a new child, a new centre of special interest, a new COSI that will be Linguistics!'

Those on either side of the Vice-Chancellor applauded loudly.

'So please raise your glasses, colleagues, and friends, to the new head of that School, Professor Nigel Williams! Good on yer mate!'

With that he smiled and moved back to allow Williams to step forward, who uncharacteristically decided to say nothing pointing instead to the waitress with the fizz. The room applauded. Clearly on this occasion saying less was more.

Three glasses of wine, two pork sausages and little chance of anything else to eat. Gurney looked for anyone he recognised. No Andrea or Amy. Alice he had seen very briefly but she seemed to have disappeared along with Williams. No sign of dear old George either, who was the new chair of the University governing body. Perhaps there was a better party going on elsewhere? That's the trouble with academic life - he thought - there's always something better happening somewhere else if only you knew where *else* was. And were invited. Linden came up to him.

'You're looking your usual miserable self, Gurney.'

'And where is the delectable Lucy, dear boy?'

'She's wisely left this one to me Gurney but she did say that I was to drag you kicking and screaming to the *Open House* in fifteen minutes' time. Apparently, there's someone important waiting there to meet you there in person.'

'Amy? Andrea? Alice?'

'Well, if you get a move on you'll find out won't you. And talking of good news you'll be able to celebrate our announcement too.'

Gurney walked slowly behind his good friend, stopping now and then to acknowledge a smile or nod of the head from one or two colleagues. So far, the reception had gone well. With any luck the tomorrow would be well-attended too, and then the highlight of the day, the centenary dinner would wrap everything up equally well. Which was why he felt perplexed at his sense of impending doom. What was it that created this sense of despair? The abolition of his department had been on the cards for some time - and anyway - more than likely he would continue in post, particularly with George at hand to make sure he wasn't given the boot. Perhaps it was the imminent prospect of meeting one of the three sirens – and it had to be one of them - and then being confronted with what - rejection? Or perhaps worse - acceptance?

The pub is empty when he arrives. Standing in one corner, head slightly bowed, hair parted neatly down the middle, she looks up, smiles, and runs into his arms.

But it is Lucy who smiles as he walks in. She looks radiant, her engagement to Linden clearly being the source of that.

'Congratulations, Lucy, well done!'

Linden returns with a round plus a packet of pork scratchings.

'For old time's sake Gurney.'

As he munches his way through the scratchings – thank God for something edible at last – Linden, tells him of their exciting plans to,

'...start a new life together up North.'

Yes, the inevitable had occurred, Lucy was to become assistant registrar at one of the most northerly Russell group of universities, steering a huge expansion in the recruitment of overseas students – leading on the implementation of a redundancy programme for staff who were deemed incapable of rearranging the two words, 'wood' and 'dead' in the correct order.

Gurney laughed

'You're not serious, Lucy?'

'Not completely - but we are launching a huge recruitment drive in Hong Kong and Brunei - and there are plans to offer staff who were judged to be just 'nationally recognised' in the last assessment exercise voluntary redundancy.'

Linden chipped in,

'And if they don't volunteer – Gurney – they'll be moved into shared offices with the insurance team, find themselves teaching double-shift first year undergraduates, and be nominated chair of the departmental sickness fund, assuming Lucy's university allows for sickness.'

'What are you going to be doing Linden?'

'Well, at first, given Lucy's whopping salary I thought I'd take early retirement but, you know me and work, so in the end I have decided to set up my own business - a head-hunting and recruitment company specialising in niche positioning for academics, folk like yourself, eager to move onwards and upwards but with insufficient time or expertise to find the openings, get their cv up to scratch, make themselves presentable, manage an interview – that kind of thing.'

Gurney admitted he didn't know *that kind of thing* but thought perhaps he should be given the possibility that if it all went tits up in the morning he'd be out on his ear, but on the other hand, if it went swimmingly he might need Linden to help him deal with the offers that would come streaming in.

'So, this is it, Gurney I'll be off after the summer. Not sure where we'll live but we'll rent for the immediate future, and take our time…'

He was interrupted by the entrance of Alice clutching a large bottle of champagne.

'Hi, everyone! And Gurney too! Great!'

It was clearly going to be a conversation of exclamation marks. Linden began to open the champagne. She smiled towards Gurney.

'Like the VC Gurney, I'm the harbinger of good and bad news…'

She was running off with Williams? Was relocating up north too? She turned her cornfield blue eyes towards him.

'Unless Anyone can persuade me otherwise, I've decided that this is the moment to leave my post, Gurney - to move on to fresh things - new opportunities - new people…' Up north?

At which point Linden stood up - swigged back his champagne - and with a wink to Gurney - that is two winks in an evening - pulled Lucy to her feet and bade them farewell.

Alice moved closer to Gurney who wasn't sure whether she had just told him the good or bad news.

'…I'm glad they've both gone – and don't get me wrong Gurney I love them to bits – but what I must say now is just for you and no-one else.'

He poured some more champagne into his glass. When was the last time someone had said something for him and no-one else?

'My bad news is that I don't want to work as a research assistant anymore – and the centenary will be over soon – but the good news is that I love you Gurney - realise now that I have always loved you ever since that hilarious interview. I know you hold a candle for my cousin Amy but I think I know you well enough now to know that you do feel something for me, don't you?'

He nodded and wondered if kissing a mouth that had recently been eating pork scratchings was entirely unpleasant. A mouthwash of Sainsbury's best champagne and he was ready to answer. He lent across the corner table, put one hand on each side of her beautiful face and pressed his lips onto the most wonderful mouth imaginable. As he came up for air he felt an unfamiliar a warm feeling flooding over him. He had forgotten what it was like to be kissed, to be recognised, to be loved. She got up to leave.

'Where are you going?'

'I'd love to stay darling but I've got to go. Uncle George has made me promise I'll meet him for dinner in about an hour. I tried to get him to invite you too but apparently, he has something important to say to me alone, to do with money, inheritance, something like that. Amy has already met him. It is why neither of them were at the do tonight - all very mysterious - but I'll let you know more tomorrow - or if it's all too hectic - I'll drop you a note before the end of the conference - and anyway we'll be at the same table won't we at the dinner? There's a proposal I want to put to you...'

With that she kissed him once again on the lips and left.

He remembered little of his walk home or his tumble into bed or his brief telephone conversation with his mother or his shout of 'Yes!' as he entered his house.

*

The conference dinner. At first, he couldn't see her for the fog of academics obscuring his near vision.

'I guess you are looking for me?'

He spun around too quickly almost losing his balance.

'Sorry, I didn't see you and now I'm glad I can.'

He felt the blood rushing to his feet, a result of the over-hasty twirl or the fact – and it surely was a fact – that he was standing before a truly beautiful woman. He noticed she had spilt a tiny drop of red wine on her white blouse just above her left breast. He had spent the whole day thinking about Alice and what she wanted to propose and now he was standing before another vision of loveliness.

'Amy?'

'Gurney?'

He steered her towards an empty space in the corner of the room next to a pair of large French windows. She was first to speak.

'Did you meet up with Alice last night? She seemed very eager to talk with you.'

'Yes, we met but only briefly at the pub but I think we are going to carry on our conversation later, perhaps tomorrow.'

He paused wondering if he sounded at all believable. He put an index finger on to the red spot on her blouse.

'Vanish, should do the trick, though it might not work given I think it is only for certain stains.'

'I'm not asking you to tell me what you two talked about last night Gurney, I love Alice and I think you know how I feel about you...'

'Feel about you'? He had no idea how she felt about him, or come to that how he felt about himself. He put on his I-am-slightly-short-sighted-look and looked hard at her. She was beautiful - he wasn't wrong there – and...'

A bell rang for dinner.

'I'll be quick Gurney, because I don't think we have much time before all the small talk starts, and anyway I don't think, for whatever reason, you are going to say much tonight which is all to the well as after what I am going to propose to you, I want you to sleep on it and promise me you will call me tomorrow after breakfast when I'll be packing for my unexpected return to the States.'

They moved slowly to their table.

'I just wanted to tell you Gurney - in case you are wondering - that I had a call from Alice ten minutes ago, to say she wouldn't be coming to the meal, to pass on her love to you, and to apologise for leaving a seat empty next to you. But this is the deal I want to offer you Gurney. You are clearly on a losing wicket in this place, OK you might hang on for a few years until Williams eventually retires or is kicked out by which time you'll be a desiccated old has-been who frankly has allowed all the good things in life to pass him by. Which would be a shame Gurney as I think there is more to you than meets the eye...'

She paused and lifted a mouthful of the admirable first course into her admirable mouth.

'...so, with the aim of *not* allowing such a thing to happen, I would like to propose that you allow me to book you a ticket on a flight to Phoenix say in a month or so – you would have to serve out your notice – whereupon you join my company in a not insubstantially paid position in our expanding marketing and publicity department. In preparation for this I have had a few quiet words with my senior line manager who is quite a fan of the idea of employing a British linguist, albeit one who is interested in the modal auxiliary verb.'

He looked at his chilled soup.

'...and in case you were wondering an added incentive would be you'd come and share my house, my car till you got your own one, and of course my bed unless you wanted your own one.'

Here she stopped multi-tasking gazpacho and talk to look shyly at him. As he contemplated what the second most beautiful woman in the world had just said to him another – Andrea - had slipped into Alice's vacant seat to his right. Gurney slipped his hand beneath the table cloth and grasped Amy's hand which was as cool as the soup.

'Say nothing now Gurney, sleep on it but promise me you will talk to me tomorrow before I head out to the airport.'

He squeezed her hand to show assent at the same time as Andrea placed a warm Teutonic left hand upon his right thigh.

He sighed out of pleasure and bewilderment. You wait for a bus and three come along.

'Gurney! Wilkommen,' a raspy though not unattractive voice whispered on his right.

He turned away from Amy - who was buttering some toast - to see Andrea resplendent in a white blouse and what looked like a full-length tartan skirt.

'My grand uncle on my mother's side was a McTavish.'

She laughed lightly her hand still resting upon his knee. She continued to squeeze his thigh.

'Gurney, I must talk with you later, tonight before you become asleep, you understand?' What is it about incorrect grammar that is so sexy?

Amy had started a conversation with Linden to her left. As she bent her neck to hear him talk, Gurney noticed a small birth mark just below the hair line. To be kissed. He turned back to Andrea

'All right I can talk tonight. Let's meet in the saloon bar of the *Open House.*'

She removed her hand. Amy had long since removed her fingers, leaving him strangely bereft but free to sit and consider what exactly was happening to him.

Chapter Twenty-four

We are our choices – Jean-Paul Satre

The dinner finished early but on a high note. Julian Jack John and all agreed that the centenary had been a roaring success. *JJJ* had also managed to pull off a masterly after-dinner speech which effectively balanced the need to praise all present whilst at the same time insulting all absent - but in the guise of gentle rib-pulling academics are so fond of. Williams suggested they all 'repaired' – his word of the week – to a local hostelry which Gurney was sure would not be the *Open House*, given the well-healed look of most of the participants.

Alice had left a smiley face text message with three kisses; Amy, a similar message but with the reminder that they talk after breakfast; and he saw another from Annike asking if he would see her tomorrow, to discuss 'something important'. He groaned, telling her he'd be tied up all week but perhaps Tuesday if - and it was a big if - he was free.

He felt bewildered and perplexed at the place he now found himself in - much desired by more women than even in his wildest dreams - but worried that in trying to please all of them he'd end up with pleasing none.

At least with Andrea he could be firm and resolute. Germans would understand that. As he entered the pub he saw her sitting alone with her head down writing intently on a large card, with what looked like an expensive fountain pen. She was wearing her crisp blouse and tartan skirt. She looked 'seriously nice.'

'Thank you for coming Gurney, I hope I haven't embarrassed you. I know how important it is for the male identity not to be made to feel uncomfortable by the advances of a woman, ja?'

Gurney matched her seriousness with directness.

'I think it depends on the intention of whoever is causing the embarrassment - which in our case seems to be mutual?'

'You are right, I have underestimated you Gurney, and I think to talk honestly and frankly have underestimated the respect and feelings I have for you.'

As she spoke he felt the mobile phone vibrate in his trouser pocket.

'Sorry but this might be important.'

It was a PPI company asking him if he'd been miss-sold a product.

'As you know Gurney I am not only a feminist but a woman as well.'

There was no answer to this.

'And you are a *beautiful* woman too.'

'Well a woman needs to look good when she intends to propose, yes?'

'Propose?'

'Yes, I have before you arrived here drawn up a list of the pros and cons of being with you – and despite my over-rational self - I have concluded that you have more in the agreeable than the disagreeable column - and so I would like - my kind Englishman - to ask if you will marry me?'

He did what every self-respecting gentleman would do in that situation - he bought a few precious minutes by offering to buy a round of drinks. And then he did what no self-respecting gentleman should do in that situation, he avoided giving a direct answer by proposing in return that he 'respect the enormity of the offer' and sleep on it until morning by which time he would be able to respond, 'honestly and generously' to the said proposition.

Andrea smiled at this, clearly not surprised at the answer.

'Thank you, Gurney, I am happy and now I will go -if you please - up to my room. It has been a long, tiring but ultimately thrilling day and think I need to close my eyes and dream of what I am sure will be a lovely future for us in Baden-Württemberg.'

With that she left leaving behind a hardly touched pint of lager top. He sat unsure about what he thought - and like every good academic - he decided to write. She was right about one thing - the pros and cons of deciding to live with another human being for the rest of your life was something that was *seriously nice*.

He took out the moleskin notebook he had bought recently from the remaining bookshop in town.

Chronologically in order of arrival:

Alice – a known category who was clearly the kind of beauty capable of gracing a Boden calendar, if there was such a thing. Kind, helpful and loyal – which might be important if he needed Uncle George's help in keeping his job – she clearly was all pros and no cons, but unlike the other two perhaps she knew him a little too well?

And then there was *Amy*: the 'love of his life' - his Phoenix rising - offering him not only a shared bed but a source of income, 'recognition', and a fresh start. The memories of skimming stones, Exeter, and the *Nobody Inn*? And there would be George too...

Finally, there was *Andrea*: the outsider - the rousing feminist who would not allow him to wallow in his lazy assumptions - who would no doubt be as fierce a lover as she was an advocate. And let's not forget the tartan skirt, clearly a winner for most men over a certain age.

And *Annike* and the 'important thing I must tell you tomorrow?' And what about *Abigail,* the spurned wife, who had sent him a text during the centenary closing speeches telling him that 'perhaps the best thing that has come out of this sorry business is that we've met each other.'

He downed the remains of the lager top and made his way home. Tomorrow was another day. Not only that, but the 'first day of the rest of his life.'

*

Exeter. The *Double Locks Inn*. Three years from now.

Professor Gurney Sleep enters the public bar, smiles in his practised distracted way, and orders his usual pint of Boddingtons. Behind the bar is a new employee, one of the many university students unable to even think of completing a degree without the support of such work, however poorly remunerated. She pulls his pint and tells him she will bring it over to him. He wanders outside to enjoy the unusually hot May sunshine. A swan is gliding serenely towards him.

Whilst he awaits his beer he casts his mind back to those chaotic days, an earlier life almost. How lady fortune has smiled on him! Since his rapid promotion to professor three years ago, he has acquired the habit of benignly chuckling to himself, particularly at moments of reflection or in recollection of the good fortune that has come his way.

Life at the top he realises is much more about *might* and *could* and *maybe* rather than *must, ought* and *will*. He looks at the two swans gliding towards the Inn. Paddling furiously beneath the surface yet appearing so calm above. How appropriate a metaphor for his previous life.

He thinks about the days immediately following the centenary.

Sitting alone in the bar after Andrea had gone upstairs, he was right to reject the proposal of Alice – ah beautiful Alice! – as well as the German from Baden Wurttemberg. He chuckles and shudders at the *schadenfreude* of it all. Alice - who had seemed relieved when she thought about it more seriously - had quite rightly rejected offers from Williams to indeed be his new PA – and instead had returned to the retail sector- where last he heard - she was doing very nicely, thank you, - and had renewed her acquiesce with Gilbert, who was also on the way up. They'd shared a drink the day after the centenary closed during which she thanked him for all he had done, how he had given her more confidence in managing people like Williams but that she knew - in her heart of hearts – they would only make each other unhappy. She'd kissed him gently on the cheek.

'You're a sweet man, Gurney, and I shall always have a soft spot for you. You must come and visit us in the Village. I know mummy and daddy are very fond of you.'

Andrea? At first, she had refused to say anything to him. Clearly the English had no taste for the good things in life. Last, he had heard she had completed her doctorate in two years at a university in the far north and was happy in a serious relationship with a professor of Middle English.

And Amy – the love of his life? She had returned home – initially hurt at his rejection but soon happily betrothed – what a lovely word – to Kyle, an insurance executive she'd met on the *red eye*. George and Araminta had sent him a nice card – and seemed to hold no grudge against his rejection of their daughter and niece. As George, had written, 'take your time Gurney, take your time.'

Funny how things work out well when you least expect them. The closure of the department, the sudden resignation of Nigel Williams – Annike's appointment being based less on merit and more on her availability - and then the icing on the cake: the offer of a chair in linguistics at the University of Exeter, his alma mater. The nearest swan glides closer to the professor sitting alone at the table.

It was then that the Exeter Professor of Linguistics had an original thought, an insight linked to something his mother had said to him at her bedside. She had been partly right when she had told him to stop living in the past, to seize the day, and live not *in* - but *for* the moment. But there was something else. Not only had he lived 'a life backwards' but it was a life lived in the head, in his imagination, in his thoughts. Alice, Amy, and Andrea were not real individuals - with qualities and faults of their own - but idealised lovers he could really only enjoy at a distance. Bring them close and they might upset his ordered, academic, if lonely, life. And an academic obsessed with words, representations of reality, such as names, he had allowed the name of the thing to become more important than the thing itself.

He sighed, realising that if he really did wish to share his life he would need to be less of the academic and more of the man. Being *purely academic* was not enough.

He looked around him. Quite an appropriate place to contemplate such things. 'Philosophers have sought to interpret the world, what matters is to change it'. And what better place to start than with himself?

The barmaid came out of the bar with his pint. He allowed himself another chuckle. Life! She put the beer down and turned to face him.

'Professor Sleep - sorry to interrupt you - but can I just say that I attended your inaugural and it was fantastic. So much help to me.'

'Thank you. What are you studying?'

'My PhD was on Hardy - a discourse analysis of 'Madding Crowd'. I've been at it five years but I've just finished. Successful viva – and now work here to pay off my debts!' This time it was her turn to chuckle.

'I'm glad I could help.'

He looks at her more closely. Dark brown hair parted in the middle. Nice shoes, possibly Boden - green eyes - a few worry lines around them - but a nice face -beautiful even.

He takes a sip of his beer.

'If I can help some more just let me know.'

She thanks him. She holds out her hand.

'Thank you', and turns to go.

He looks up. The swan has been joined by its mate.

'It's...?'

She smiles and holds out her hand.

'Doctor Arkwright, Angela Arkwright. Pleased to meet you.'

***

Acknowledgements

This is a work of fiction. None of the characters or events described in this novel relate in any way to real individuals or events, though the climate of neo-liberalism is real enough. Some of the settings are drawn from universities I have been fortunate enough to work in during my long professional life as an academic.

There are a one or two people I'd like to thank. A few years ago, I was the fortunate recipient of a university teaching award, and used the prize money to attend an Arvon Foundation writing course. I'd like to thank the two course tutors, Naomi Alderman and Helen Oyeyemi, who encouraged me to persevere with this novel.

I'd also like to thank friends and family for their help and encouragement, particularly my daughter Anna, who made a number of useful suggestions concerning the ending.

My thanks to A. My muse.

Finally, greatest thanks - and love - to a wife and friend, Claire - whose name does not begin with the letter 'A'.

***